DEFIANCE

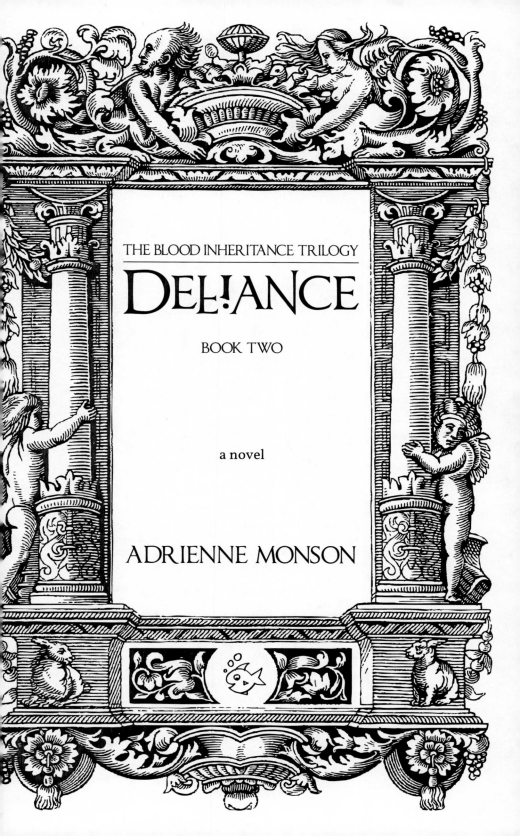

THE BLOOD INHERITANCE TRILOGY

DEF!ANCE

BOOK TWO

a novel

ADRIENNE MONSON

DEF!ANCE

Copyright © 2015 by Adrienne Monson

First Paperback Edition: February 2015

For information on subsidiary rights, please contact the publisher at rights@jollyfishpress.com. For information, please visit our website at www.jollyfishpress.com, or write us at PO Box 1773, Provo, UT 84603-1773.
Printed in the United States of America

THIS TITLE IS ALSO AVAILABLE AS AN EBOOK.

Library of Congress Control Number: 2015930146
ISBN 978-1-631630-06-4

10 9 8 7 6 5 4 3 2 1

To Adam. I love you more than words can express.

DEFIANCE

JOLLY
FISH
PRESS
Provo, Utah

CHAPTER 1

January 9th

The street was deserted. It was getting late, and anyone who knew this end of town stayed away when it got dark. Walking down the darkling sidewalk, Leisha was the perfect victim. Her head was down, her long hair hiding the sides of her face. Her clothes were loose, but clean. Any predator out was bound to target her.

That's how she liked it. It was amusing to know the men who would attack her believed that they were in control. They had no idea.

A scuffling sound caught her ear, and Leisha knew she was not alone. The person nearby wasn't any ordinary human predator. This one actually posed a threat to her.

She didn't bother to look around. This stalker wouldn't be seen in the muggy night, not yet. She walked into a vacant parking lot with plenty of space to maneuver in case it came to a fight. Turning to face her pursuer, she reached over her shoulder and pulled a machete from its spine sheath. There was a chance she wouldn't need it, but she couldn't take any chances when an immortal was near.

As the man entered the lot, she caught a hint of dark hair and light skin. She suppressed the flutter of disappointment; it was not Tafari. It had been six months since she'd almost killed him—ironically while trying to save his life. Maybe he was holding that against her.

This was an immortal named Sean. He stopped a few feet away from her with a sword already held loosely in his right hand.

"Hello Sean," Leisha said with pleasant sarcasm. "It's been a long time. Care to explain why you decided to drop by so suddenly?"

He sneered. "There was nothin' sudden 'bout it. I've been trackin' you down fer months," he said in his Scottish brogue. "It took a while ta find you, but I finally did. As fer my reason," he smiled wickedly, "why, that would be good ol' fashioned revenge." He pointed his sword at her. "It's your fault that half of our council was slaughtered, and Tafari just ain't himself no more. You and that twit of a girl turned my world into a hellish nightmare." He crouched into a fighting stance. "And now, yer gonna pay!"

Leisha matched his fighting stance. She was not surprised at being blamed for what the vampires did to the council. She hadn't been in league with them at that time, but she had certainly made it possible for them to infiltrate the immortals' lair, even if it had not been her intention.

She raised her machete. "I don't want to fight you, Sean. Out of respect for Tafari, I'll walk away without a backward glance, but you have to promise not to track me down again."

Snorting loudly, the immortal took two steps closer. "Nothin' is gunna stop me from killin' you this night. I'm gunna cut off yer head and put it on a pike fer all immortals ta see!"

The scenario was incredibly similar to the last time they'd

fought. Leisha had tried to reason with him then, too. She could see in Sean's eyes that he wouldn't be swayed. Clamping down her regret, she gave her best haughty attitude. "I can tell you won't be talked out of this. So instead," she shrugged, "I'll simply have to kill you. On the up side, it will be good to drink an immortal's blood again. I need to feed anyway, and your blood will sustain me for some time." She winked at him. "You just saved me the trouble of killing a human tonight."

Sean growled and raised his sword as he lunged forward. Leisha deftly blocked his blow and pounced, swinging her machete in a powerful counter strike. He jumped away before her blade struck the skin, but a piece of fabric from his shirt drifted to the filthy pavement.

The immortal saw the tear gaping open above his navel and his sage-green eyes glared at her through the darkness. Once again, he came forward, his sword missed her head and jarred into her raised machete. He aimed blow after blow at her while Leisha held him off.

The old highlander was aggressive at his blows, but Leisha defended herself deftly, thanks to her honed reflexes. After a few repeats of the same attack and defense, Leisha suddenly went on the attack, dropping into a spinning kick that smashed him to the ground.

She pounced again, landing on his stomach. She seized his wrist, and twisted it. Sean dropped his sword with a grunt of pain, but lashed out with his other hand, punching her in the jaw. The blow snapped her head to the side, but she stayed astride him.

It was enough of a distraction to chop at the wrist holding her machete. She held her weapon, however, and smacked him with her free hand.

Sean snarled, his frustration peaking. Glaring up at her, he spat in her face.

With a grunt of disgust, Leisha wiped her face on her left

shoulder. Quick as snake, Sean twisted his weight, and suddenly he was atop her. His body pinned her down, his lips contorting with fury, his eyes raging like a mad man's.

Gaining control, he seized her throat with both hands before she could react. Sean smirked as her windpipe threatened to crush under the pressure.

Suddenly, Leisha felt a tremor rush through her body. It felt like electrocution, but without the shock of electricity. The sensation vanished as quickly as it had come, and Leisha realized Sean's grip had loosened a little. His attention seemed to turn inward for an instant. Taking advantage of the moment, she swung her machete as hard as she could, sinking it deep into his shoulder.

Grunting, Sean let go of her throat, and Leisha rolled atop him again. Sean snarled and scratched at her face, leaving deep gouges in her cheek.

Sucking in her breath to keep from crying out, Leisha swung her machete down into Sean's neck. Despite the blow, tendons and muscle tissue still connected most of his neck. She hadn't even cut into his spine. But the wound wasn't healing. She saw the life drain out of his eyes. Wasting no time, she bent down to drink the sweet nectar of his blood.

As she moved toward his neck, she remembered drinking Tafari's blood. It had instilled her with unbelievable power. She remembered what it had felt like having that energy humming through her body. She licked her lips in anticipation.

She pulled her machete out of his throat and began to gulp down the blood.

Leisha had already taken two large swallows, when she choked, jerking away and coughing uncontrollably until she vomited on the pavement. The blood tasted like normal human blood, not like an immortal's. But human blood should not have made her sick!

The combined scent of vomit and blood caused Leisha's

stomach to convulse. She stood after a few moments of dry heaving. Her hands trembled slightly and she still felt a little queasy. Shocked and confused, she stared down at Sean's lifeless body. What had he done to his blood to make it undrinkable? Even the smell repulsed her.

She shook her head and began walking back toward her car, just a few blocks away. Sheathing the machete as she walked, she pondered the disturbing events of the night.

If Sean had found her, that meant that Samantha's father, Mason Campbell, could find them as well. This meant they had to move again, and fast. Leisha sighed at the inconvenience, but there was no help for it. She really didn't want to tell Samantha about this, but they had agreed to keep no secrets from each other. She would keep her word.

Leisha smiled to herself, despite her roiling stomach. These past months living with the teenager had been nothing if not enlightening. Samantha had been telling Leisha almost too much, just to be certain that she wasn't keeping anything from the vampire. Leisha understood, of course, that Samantha was trying to make amends; after all, it was her deception that had led to the deaths of half the immortals' council.

Leisha had explained time and again that Samantha was too young and could not be held entirely responsible for her actions. After all, Ptah and Annette had used extremely frightening tactics on the poor child to get her to cooperate. But that didn't appear to ease Samantha's conscience.

Leisha spotted her beat up Toyota Camry parked on the side of the street. She had taken the car tonight because she would be in the crime-saturated downtown part of Cincinnati. She didn't want to deal with a stolen vehicle while she was trying to find a suitable victim. She grimaced, irritated at the reminder her appetite had not been sated. Then Leisha realized... she was not experiencing any hunger pangs.

Shrugging it off, she decided to worry about that later. At

the moment, she wanted to go home and think. She had to figure out how Sean found her and what he meant about Tafari and the other immortals. Was it really that chaotic right now? She wondered if Tafari thought of her as much as she thought of him. Sighing, she scolded herself for being so sentimental.

Just before she reached her vehicle, a man stepped out of the shadows of the nearest building. Leisha jumped. She hadn't heard his heart beating—*still* couldn't hear his heart beating. In fact, she couldn't detect any other distant sounds, which she usually ignored as white noise.

He chuckled. "She looks like some fun, eh?" He spoke in a Spanish accent.

Feeling a hand on her back, Leisha whipped around to see a tall man in a wife-beater tank. He held strands of her hair between his fingers and raised them to his nose. After a deep sniff, he licked her locks. "I get her first."

A new voice called out from the side. "It's my turn to go first!"

Leisha counted eight men altogether. Half of them were quite muscular and could hold their own. The others looked like they were probably on the low end of the gang's hierarchy. The closer they came, the more she could smell a combination of liquor and unwashed body, scents that should have hit her nostrils from a hundred feet away.

Pushing away the curiosity at her inhibited abilities, Leisha decided to give the men a chance to walk away. And if they didn't, she certainly wouldn't want anyone else to have to deal with this gang tonight.

She pulled her hair away from the tall one. "Gentlemen," she said calmly. "I'm really not looking for a fight here, so why don't you look for your 'fun' elsewhere?"

They all snickered and continued to move in. Leisha shrugged. "Fine, but remember, you asked for it."

With that, she smashed the heel of her hand into the nose

of the guy with the hair fetish. While her blow landed with perfect precision, it lacked her usual strength. The bone and cartilage should have shot into his brain, killing him instantly. Instead, only a little blood spurted over his mouth, and his face twisted in rage.

After staring in shock for a moment, Leisha shook herself and tried to kick the man at her side. Impossibly, he caught her foot and twisted it, sending jolts of searing, stabbing pain shooting through her ankle.

An unfamiliar sensation of panic stole her breath. She reached for her machete and pulled it out, only to have it yanked away before she could use it. Hands closed in over her stomach, more snaked over her shoulders, and then even more over her hips and legs, like an endless mass of tentacles creeping over every inch of her body.

Leisha struggled in earnest now, punching and kicking where she could. Her arms and feet were bound by the live shackles until one of the men pushed her. As she fell to the pavement, a scream of genuine terror wrenched itself from her lungs.

CHAPTER 2

"Math sucks," grumbled Samantha. She glanced at the clock to see that it was past ten.

Hearing laughter from the right, she turned to send a good-natured glare at Spencer, one of her classmates. He raised his dark eyebrows at her to say, "What?"

"You have no compassion." She grabbed his empty glass and went to the sink to get him more water. He always commented on how clean her house was when he came over. She supposed that, since Spencer had three siblings, it was harder to avoid clutter.

"Come on, Sandy. It's really not that hard. You're just complicating things."

Trying not to react to the sound of her new name, Samantha wondered if she'd ever get used to it. She didn't think of Leisha as Angela, and definitely couldn't think of herself as a Sandy.

When she didn't respond, Spencer ran a hand through his brown hair. "Look, you've got most of the answers right. It's only these last four that have you stumped."

She sat back at the oak table and picked up her pencil. Her

fingers brushed his in the process, and he turned his brown eyes to her. Samantha felt a spark between them and couldn't bring herself to look away. Spencer began to lean his head closer, his eyes on her lips. Samantha froze for a second, tremors cascading down her belly, but she turned away before he could kiss her.

She didn't look at him as he sighed. "I don't get you, Sandy. You act like you want me around, but whenever I want to . . . you know . . . take it up a notch, you turn into an ice queen." He put his hand on her shoulder. "Do you want me to leave you alone?" Samantha shook her head and watched him frown before he said, "Why does this have to be platonic?"

Well, for one thing, you don't even know my name. "Spencer, I don't want a boyfriend in high school. It's as simple as that. You're a great friend, but that's all I want right now."

A picture of Nik came into her mind, with his vivid hazel eyes and sandy hair. She couldn't remember him smiling much during her stay with the vampires, but he always had an amused crinkle at the corners of his eyes. Samantha brushed the memory away. Though they emailed back and forth whenever possible, they had not spent any time together in more than six months. There was no reason for her to think of him whenever Spencer tried to make a move.

Spencer looked like he was about to argue when the doorbell rang. Happy for an excuse to end the conversation, Samantha sprang into the front room and answered the door. The frigid, wintry air hit her before she could even see who had rung the bell.

Two policemen stood on the porch, both looking grim. The one on the left spoke. "Are you Sandra Templeton?"

"Yes," she answered, eyeing them warily.

"And your sister is Angela Templeton?"

She nodded, still unsure what to think.

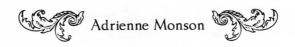

"I'm afraid your sister was attacked earlier this evening. She's been taken to Memorial Hospital."

"Oh no!" Samantha gasped. She imagined doctors discovering Leisha's secret, poking and prodding her while they called the government. That would lead to her father and all kinds of horrible experiments. When she got Leisha out of the compound last time, the vampire's arms had been crushed by a sledge hammer. They'd done that to see how much pain she could withstand before blacking out.

"Would you like us to drive you there?" the second officer asked.

"I have my own car, thanks." The officer gave her the information to find Leisha at the hospital, and then they left. Samantha turned, only to run into Spencer. His arms came around her and held tight.

"Don't worry, Sandy. I'm sure she'll be ok."

Samantha wormed out of his embrace and forced a smile up at him. "I know she is. But I have to go now." She went to the closet and slipped on her sandals. "Thanks for your help, Spencer. I'll see you tomorrow."

His brow furrowed for a moment, and then he seemed to mentally shrug. "Call me if you need me, no matter how late."

"Thanks." She squeezed his hand as they walked out the door of her two-story home, then ran to the driveway and hopped into her old Yugo. Leisha still wouldn't let her drive any of the nicer cars. The vampire claimed she lacked experience since she'd just gotten her driver's license a few months ago.

Samantha arrived at the hospital forty-five minutes later. The fermented odors of cleansers and medicines wafted around Samantha as she walked the halls. It took little time to find the correct floor and a nurse to direct her to the doctor overseeing Leisha's care.

"I'm Angela Templeton's sister, Sandy," she asked the doctor. "Where can I find her?"

The doctor's lips thinned into a grim line. "She's unconscious right now. It may be a while before she wakes up."

"Unconscious?" Samantha blinked a few times, and then shook her head. "Are you sure we're talking about Angela Templeton? Blond hair down to her waist, emerald colored eyes, about this tall?" She held her hand right above her shoulder.

The doctor nodded. "Yes, we're talking about the same person. Do you know the details of your sister's ordeal?"

"Only that she was attacked."

He put a hand on her shoulder. "Yes, by a gang of eight men." When Samantha showed no reaction, he hesitated before continuing. "She's sustained some very serious injuries. Concussion, cracked ribs, broken arm, three lacerations on her head. She's lucky a patrol car spotted them before they were able to do anything . . . worse. On a slightly better note, there are no signs of rape or internal injuries. She's very lucky. This might have been a much worse scenario, and your sister could easily have died."

At this information, fear started to seep through Samantha's confusion. "She can't be that badly hurt." The doctor shot her a funny look, and Samantha bit her lip and tried to feign more concern. "I mean, I can't believe this is really happening. I can't imagine her in so much pain. Please, just let me see her."

The doctor nodded. "It's fine, but don't try to wake her."

"Alright."

The doctor called the nurse over to show Samantha to Leisha's room. As soon as they entered, Samantha stopped. The woman on the bed was Leisha. But Samantha had never seen her vampire friend like this. She had seen Leisha bloody and battered plenty of times, but she always healed so quickly. The vampire that lay unconscious before her looked . . . broken.

"How could this happen?" she whispered to herself. The nurse gave her a sympathetic look and quietly left the room.

Samantha forced her feet forward and sat in the chair next

to Leisha's bed. She took her friend's limp hand and gently patted it. "Can you hear me?" she asked softly. No response. She leaned in closer. "Leisha."

The vampire's eyelids fluttered but stayed closed. "Wrong," Leisha mumbled. "Something's wrong."

"What's wrong Leisha? What happened tonight?"

No response.

After a few more promptings, Samantha gave up. She knew she wouldn't get anything else out of her friend tonight. *Why can't my visions cover things like this?* she thought to herself. *If only I could choose what they were about, then I would know more!* She sat back and tried to push away any thoughts of what had made Leisha so vulnerable.

Without intending to, Samantha fell asleep in the chair. She woke to realize there was drool on her chin, her neck was cramped, and her butt was asleep. She slowly sat up and arched her back. After rolling her head a few times, she looked over at the bed. Leisha was sitting up and watching her, a smirk on her face.

"You look like you're ready for the next Miss Ohio pageant," Leisha quipped, her voice raspy.

Samantha groaned and finger-combed her hair as best she could. Suddenly she remembered where they were, and her attention snapped back to Leisha.

Her friend was awake and making sarcastic remarks, but she did not look at all like herself. Her left eye was swollen and purple. Her skin was pale instead of its usual healthy glow, and there were scabs lining her knuckles.

"I could say the same about you." Samantha cleared her throat. "Leisha, what happened last night? Do you have some sort of . . . vamp illness that weakens you or something?"

Leisha shook her head. "I'm not sure." She told Samantha about her run-in with Sean. "Maybe he put a spell on his blood

that affected me when I tried to drink it. That's the only thing I can think of that makes sense."

"Do the immortals practice a lot of magic? I don't remember seeing anything like that when we stayed with them."

Leisha shook her head, then stopped, wincing, and put a hand to her temple. "As far as I know, they don't practice very much Voodoo. Just enough to create more immortals. Since that battle between them and the vampires, the oldest immortal among them is Tafari. He may have learned the ways of a shaman, but I have no idea how much of it he's retained after two thousand years."

Chewing on her lip, Samantha contemplated before responding. "So it's possible that Sean cursed his own blood, but not likely. But, since you're in this hospital, I'm betting he must have done something." Glancing at the I.V. on Leisha's arm, another thought occurred to her. "For all intents and purposes, you're like a human, right? At least for the time being?"

"I wouldn't go that far."

Samantha gestured to the EKG machine. "I'm no expert, but no one seems to think your heart beat is off. To me, that machine is showing the normal rhythm of a human heart."

Eyes wide, Leisha glanced at the equipment, then placed a trembling hand over her chest. "What did Sean do to me?" she murmured.

"Did you end up feeding at all last night?"

Leisha shook her head.

"And do you feel The Hunger in your mind?"

Leisha blinked a few times, then shook her head again. "I don't, but I do feel something." As if summoned, her stomach growled. Leisha jumped and looked down at her midsection with what could only be described as horror.

Samantha burst out laughing, but covered it up as best she could.

"Sorry." She said, trying to be contrite when Leisha frowned at her. "It's just the look on your face. You're *never* rattled." Clearing her throat, she forced herself to sober. "You're hungry for, you know . . . food, I think."

"How can this be possible?" Leisha's eyebrows drew together.

Samantha didn't have a clue, but she could at least take care of Leisha's immediate problem. She reached over and pushed the button for the nurse. When the nurse saw Leisha awake, she said she needed to get the doctor. Samantha asked her to bring Leisha some food, and the nurse pointed to a menu on the table next to her and walked out of the room.

"Guess nurses don't get much congeniality training in school." Samantha looked at the breakfast section of the menu, and then followed the instructions to place the order over the phone.

A few minutes later, the doctor came in, though not the one she'd met last night. He did a thorough examination and looked impressed. "Well, besides some nasty bruises, you seem to be alright. Your file says you broke a couple of ribs, but that's not how they feel to me. They're definitely bruised, and maybe cracked, though I'd need to confirm that with some x-rays. Take it easy, and as long as your x-rays look good, I think we can get you released today." Nodding to the cast on her arm, he continued. "You'll need to make an appointment with your primary care physician in about a week so we can check on how the bone is healing."

"And there's nothing else that you can see that's odd about her?" Samantha glanced at the heart monitor Leisha was hooked up to. Her EKG really was looking normal...*human?*

The doctor shook his head. "I'll make sure the nurse comes to check on you in a little bit."

As soon as he left, Leisha grabbed Samantha's hand in a tight grip. "This doesn't make sense. I'm healing faster than

humans do, but not nearly fast enough for a vampire. But besides that, everyone is treating me like a human. None of them are even showing me a curious glance. Under normal circumstances, my vitals would have them completely stupefied."

Samantha shrugged. "I don't know what to tell you."

The food arrived. It was placed on a tray over Leisha's bed, and she didn't waste any time diving in. As soon as the omelet entered her mouth, Leisha made a face.

"What?" asked Samantha.

"This food is so bland."

Samantha leaned over, took Leisha's fork, and sampled some of the breakfast. "Actually, this is pretty good." She threw Leisha a strange look. "Try something else."

Leisha cut a piece of French toast smothered in syrup and took a bite. Looking over at Samantha, she shook her head. "Same," she said around her food. "I can taste a little sweetness from the syrup, but that's about it."

Samantha took the fork from her friend and tried a bite herself. "Are you kidding? It tastes amazing! I think they may have put nutmeg in the batter or something." Her eyes got wide. "Maybe Sean's spell did something to your senses so they're not working properly."

Green eyes squinting in thought, Leisha shook her head. "Actually, I think my senses might simply be at a human level." Nodding her head, she continued. "It makes sense when you think about it. After all, I've had heightened senses for a couple of millennia, and now . . . Everything is just dull."

Taking another bite, she grimaced while chewing. "This is going to take some getting used to," Leisha grumbled.

It wasn't too long before someone brought paperwork for Leisha to fill out. Luckily, they had insurance. A couple of police officers also came to get Leisha's statement about her attack.

After hearing it would be a few more hours before Leisha's release, Samantha went home to shower and change. She also got herself breakfast, since Leisha had been too hungry to share her "bland hospital food". As an afterthought, she grabbed some clothes for Leisha.

Once she was back at the hospital, the doctor met with them to inform Leisha that her x-rays looked fine and she could leave. It took little time to check out "her sister" and head back home.

"Do you need help up the stairs?" Samantha asked as Leisha headed straight toward them.

"I'll manage. Don't worry about me."

The girl watched as her vampire—or non-vampire—friend leaned heavily on the banister and made her way up to her room for a nap. It was almost surreal to see Leisha look so vulnerable. Samantha hoped nothing bad would happen while Leisha was in this condition. If her father found them, there would be no escaping this time.

On a sudden impulse, Samantha sat on the couch as she scrolled through her phone. There, she found a number that was only supposed to be used in emergencies. "Hope this qualifies as one," she muttered as she pressed the call button.

CHAPTER 3

Since all vampire senses were heightened, Leisha knew pain better than any human could imagine. Over the last two thousand years, she had experienced all kinds of pain. She had been tortured, poisoned, shot, and stabbed—just to name a few. But Leisha was very unaccustomed to her current physical state. She wasn't in an immense amount of pain, but her body ached all over. Her head pounded, her muscles were sore, and she was so tired that she could barely think straight.

Moaning through the discomfort, she rolled over to look at the clock. She couldn't believe it, but she had slept through the evening and into the next day. Leisha couldn't think of a time when she had slept for sixteen hours. Deciding she had spent enough time in bed, she forced herself to get up and dress.

Once downstairs, she found Samantha in the kitchen eating oatmeal. Easing herself into a chair, she asked, "Aren't you supposed to be at school?"

Samantha shrugged. "The principal heard you were attacked; and since we don't have any other family, he thought it was acceptable that I stay home to take care of you."

Leisha grunted in reply.

Samantha went to the cupboard and got some pills out of a bottle and brought them to her with a glass of water. "Tylenol and Advil for your aches. Are you in a lot of pain?"

"I'm managing, but thanks." She swallowed all four pills at once, then took her glass to the sink and toasted herself a bagel. After she'd spread cream cheese on it, she took a bite. Although she could enjoy the thick, yeasty texture, there was hardly any flavor. How did normal people live like this?

Samantha glanced at the clock on the wall and sat down across from Leisha. "I think I should tell you that we're going to have some visitors soon."

Leisha stopped chewing and raised a quizzical eyebrow.

Samantha averted her eyes. "I made a call last night to see if I could figure out what happened to you. You know, to see how long it might last and whatnot." She shifted in her seat.

Before Leisha could prompt Samantha to continue, the doorbell rang. She started in her chair. Usually, she would hear people approaching before they ever got to the door. Since she couldn't use her senses to detect who was there, Leisha hesitated. Her stomach churned with unease as she eased out of her chair and walked to the vent by the entryway. Removing the screen, she palmed the gun hidden within. She may be weakened with human limitations, but it didn't mean she'd lost all of her combat skills. Of course, if it were any of her enemies, they wouldn't politely ring the doorbell and she'd probably be dead already.

With the gun hidden behind her back, she opened the door, took one look at her visitors, then slammed it shut. Her sense of foreboding lifted, but was instantly replaced with confusion. "Sam!"

Samantha came into the entryway with a knowing look. "Sorry I didn't tell you sooner, but I thought you needed your rest."

"Why are they here?" she whispered. "I don't want them to see me like this!"

Samantha rolled her eyes. "They only want to talk to us about what happened to you. He wouldn't give me any info over the phone." With that, she strode to the door and opened it. "Sorry guys, I guess you caught Leisha off guard." She stood aside as Tafari and Rinwa stepped inside, each holding a medium-sized suitcase.

Leisha instantly straightened up and combed fingers through her hair while trying to look casual. Tafari stopped in front of her, his eyes wandering all over, lingering on the bruises that marred her face and the cast on her arm.

Heat rushed through her blood. Though it was more subdued with her human senses, she could still smell his aftershave and that natural musky scent that belonged to him alone. She knew his face so well, and yet was still mesmerized by the silvery blue of his eyes, contrasting brilliantly with his dark skin. His broad shoulders and muscular torso were encased in a simple gray t-shirt. She could feel the warmth of his body and clenched her hand to stop herself from touching him.

Realizing she'd been staring at him too long, she looked to the side.

He cleared his throat. "I am glad to hear you are alright, Leisha."

Suddenly, her mouth felt too dry and she gave a nod instead of replying.

Rinwa stood beside Tafari, smirking. As usual, she wore sunglasses; this pair had sparkly skulls dotting the sides. "It's so nice to see you with bruises, *mother*."

Her estranged daughter looked as beautiful as ever. Her long blonde hair matched Leisha's perfectly, and she flaunted an athletic figure that made her stand several inches taller than her mother. The only time Leisha had seen the woman was six months ago, when they fought each other, before she knew that Rinwa was really Adanne—her daughter.

The memory suddenly came flooding back to Leisha in vivid detail.

LEISHA TURNED TO FINISH THE fight, but a sudden rush of realization made her freeze mid-swing. Shocked, she dropped her weapon. She felt weak as she looked into Rinwa's silvery blue eyes. The exact same eyes Tafari had. Adanne's eyes.

"No," she choked out through her crushed windpipe.

Rinwa gave a grisly smile. Her teeth appeared stark white against the blood that poured down from her nose. "What's the matter, Leisha? Didn't think I was still around?" She stood and walked over to pick up her own machete. "I assure you that nothing was ever going to keep me from living out this moment."

Leisha crumpled to her knees, tears pooling in her eyes. She tried to speak, but it came out as nonsense against her broken throat.

Rinwa stalked slowly back toward Leisha. "Now," she growled out. "You will finally pay for what you did to me and Tafari all those years ago!"

Leisha made no move to defend herself. Rinwa raised the blade for a killing blow. She could not deny her own daughter what she deserved. She wished she could explain, tell her the truth, but it was no use.

So, instead, she stayed on her knees and watched Rinwa with a convoluted sense of pride. She was so beautiful, and she moved with such grace. She met Rinwa's fierce gaze and tried to convey all the love she felt for her in her eyes. Leisha was going to die and go to hell, but she didn't care anymore.

She only wished she could say, "I love you," before Rinwa killed her.

A low, baritone roar reverberated through the air. Leisha and Rinwa both looked as Tafari slowly came forward, leaning on Samantha for support.

"You will leave her be, Rinwa," he whispered hoarsely. "For your own sake as well as hers, drop the machete."

WITH MILD AMUSEMENT AND WARINESS, Leisha wondered if Rinwa would take advantage of Leisha's sudden weakness and kill her off like she had wanted for thousands of years.

Tafari pulled Rinwa through the front room and whispered in her ear. Once again, Leisha was surprised that she couldn't eavesdrop.

Samantha grabbed her uninjured arm. "Why don't we all sit in the living room and talk about things?"

Tafari and Rinwa sat on the large sofa. Leisha was all too aware of her estranged husband's gaze on her as she placed her gun on the coffee table and slowly lowered her stiff self onto the love seat, Samantha next to her.

"You do not need to protect yourself from us, Leisha." Tafari's eyes narrowed on the gun lying between them.

Clearing her throat, Leisha tried not to sound defensive as she explained. "Sean found me last night, and since I'm practically human, I thought it best to be cautious."

Rinwa waved her hand. "You can relax on that score. Sean's been *incommunicado* for weeks. None of the other immortals know where you are."

Leisha raised a brow. "I'm surprised you didn't report my whereabouts the moment Samantha gave you our location."

Her daughter forced a sweet smile. "But I don't need all of them when I'll be killing you with my bare hands."

Tafari grunted a warning and Rinwa flattened her lips into a thin line.

Samantha glanced wide eyed at Leisha while her forehead wrinkled. Reading her friend's pleading expression, Leisha changed the subject. "So how are you two doing?" she asked as pleasantly as she could.

Rinwa exchanged a grim glance with Tafari. After a few seconds, they looked back at Leisha. "We're human, too," Rinwa stated.

Leisha blinked a few times, uncertain if she'd heard correctly.

"What?" Samantha's eyes looked like they were struggling to get free of their sockets.

Rinwa grimaced and nodded.

"From what Samantha told us last night," Tafari said, "the immortals made the metamorphosis about the same time Leisha did."

"Which means the rest of the vampires are probably human as well." Leisha felt almost numb with the news. "That makes me feel a little better. I thought I was the only one."

Samantha pulled out her phone. "I'll email Nik right now for confirmation."

Taking a breath, Leisha asked, "Does anyone know why we've become mortal again? Or if it's permanent?"

Tafari answered. "We are looking into all the prophecies that have been recorded throughout our history. So far, there are no answers."

Nodding, Leisha glanced from father to daughter. "I hope you don't mind me asking, but you could have told Samantha this over the phone. Why did you two fly all the way here from wherever you were?"

Rinwa took off her sunglasses, then rolled her stunning blue eyes. "Tafari wanted to make sure you were OK."

Stiffening, Tafari added, "I also thought it would be a good time to meet, since neither of us have our powers."

"So our lack of powers puts us on neutral ground." Leisha finished for him. She forced herself not to be offended by the idea.

"Exactly." He gave a hesitant smile but Leisha didn't return it.

"So before our turning human, you weren't planning to at least email me?" She tried to hide her anger beneath sarcasm. "Because after everything we've been through together I was simply lying in wait to destroy you."

Frowning, Tafari shook his head. It looked like he was barely keeping his frustration in check. "I was going to contact you, but we have been busy trying to keep the immortals under control."

Leisha's eyebrows went up a notch. "And I suppose with the little surprise of turning human last night, things are looking quite dandy for the immortals now."

"No, things are crazy. But…" Tafari seemed to be searching for the right words. "But the new council members are handling it, so Rinwa and I were able to sneak out here."

Still upset, Leisha opened her mouth to argue further, but Rinwa interrupted her. "Really, Leisha? You're getting your panties in a twist because Tafari didn't call you? Stop throwing your little tantrum, and let's focus on the important stuff." The ex-immortal ignored her father's glare and stared at her mother.

Blushing, Leisha clamped her mouth shut before she said something rude to her daughter.

Just then, Samantha's phone buzzed, and she looked at the small screen. "Nik already replied. He says that all the vamps there are human, too. He also advises us to stay away until things have calmed down." She looked up, concern on her face. "I guess things are pretty tense over there right now."

"I'll bet Annette has already 'accidentally' killed a few of the others," Leisha muttered.

Rinwa made a sound with the back of her throat. "Saves me the trouble."

No one else responded, and the silence became

uncomfortable. Leisha shifted in her seat. Tafari and Rinwa glanced at each other as if they were having a silent conversation.

Finally, Samantha spoke. "So did you guys end up staying in England, or did the immortals uproot?"

"Sorry, but you know we cannot discuss that," Tafari answered.

Leisha and Samantha nodded their understanding, and then it grew silent again. After a couple of minutes, Samantha stood. "Why don't I show you two to your rooms?"

They followed her out of the living room, leaving Leisha to ponder things. And to let her temper grow. By the time Samantha returned, Leisha was ready to pounce.

"What the hell were you thinking?" she hissed.

The teenager crossed her arms. "Actually, I thought you might be glad to see them. I know I am."

"Did you not see how awkward it was in here?" She took a calming breath. "How long are they staying, anyway?"

Samantha shrugged. "They didn't say. I know it's a little weird right now, but think about it. You can spend time with them. I know you've been pining for Tafari-"

"I haven't been *pining*."

"And you have a chance to get to know your daughter."

"Who would like to see me dead, preferably by her own hand."

Samantha threw her a sardonic look. "All families have their issues. Look what I have for a father!"

Leisha snorted derisively. "Yeah, but I don't see you dropping everything to go visit him."

"Well, excuse me for being scared of the man who kidnapped and tortured you!"

Sighing, Leisha sank back into the sofa. "Forget it. This is getting us nowhere, and they're already here... for who knows how long."

Samantha sat next to her and patted her knee. "It'll be fine."

Leisha grimaced. "I don't know how to act around him. He's always hated me, so I was always… defensive. He doesn't seem to hate me anymore, but he doesn't like me either."

"So why not give me a chance to learn what I think about you?" queried a deep, male voice behind them.

Both the girls started.

"I hate not having my hearing anymore," Leisha mumbled.

He grinned, showing off white teeth. Leisha's heart sped up and she could feel her blood heating in lust. The effect of Tafari's smile on her reminded Leisha why she fell in love with him in the first place.

"Rinwa has decided to nap, but I am not tired." He shrugged as if to apologize.

"Then maybe you and Samantha can go to the store." She brushed her hair behind her shoulder. "I know you have a refined palate, and I don't think we have anything to accommodate it."

Tafari gave her a hard stare. "Simply because I enjoy wines instead of beer does not make me a picky eater."

"Oh?" Leisha countered. "How about you look through the cupboards and fridge before you decline the offer?" She pressed her lips together to hide the smile threatening.

Tafari shrugged and went to the kitchen. After a few minutes of rummaging around, he returned and asked Samantha to take him to the nearest grocery store.

Leisha couldn't hold back the small chuckle, and Tafari's lips twitched, his eyes warm.

Escorting them to the door, she thought it might be fun to have her husband around after all.

CHAPTER 4

After watching Tafari and Samantha drive away on the icy road, Leisha felt the pain meds kick in and decided to shower. The hot spray relaxed her sore muscles. The only inconvenience was holding her cast-covered arm out of the shower. She felt almost normal as she dried off and eased into her clothes.

However, when she raised her arm to do her hair, something in her right shoulder pulled. She sucked in her breath and held her shoulder for a few minutes as she waited for the ache to pass.

"Please. Are you such a wimp that you can't even do your own hair?"

Leisha turned to see Rinwa leaning against the doorjamb.

"You're used to healing faster than me." Leisha said. "I'm sure you'd be surprised at what it feels like to wait for the body to recover on its own."

Rinwa scoffed, tossing her hair. "I think I'm perfectly capable of handling a little pain." She pinned Leisha with a look. "After all, I got my first whipping when I was only four."

Stomach clenching, Leisha's initial reaction was to accept the guilt, but then decided she had allowed those emotions to rule her for too long now. She met her daughter's gaze. "If not for me, it would have been a lot worse than one lash."

Rinwa raised an eyebrow. "So you say." She turned to leave.

Anger and hurt boiled inside. She had defended herself time and again, but no one believed her story of what happened the night she became a vampire. With her human exhaustion and aches, Leisha found that it was difficult to contain her emotions. Before she could think, she stepped forward and punched Rinwa in the shoulder with her good fist as hard as she could.

"Ow!" Her daughter clutched her arm and glared. "What did you do that for?"

Uncertain herself, Leisha waved her hand unrepentantly. "You said you could handle pain. I guess it'll be no big deal to have a bruise for the next few days."

"You gave me a dead arm!"

"I'm sure you'll make do, Adanne."

Rinwa froze and looked up. "My name is Rinwa."

Leisha bit her lip, wishing her daughter could understand the devastation she felt from being separated all those years ago. "You'll always be my Adanne. Nothing will change that."

It was very quiet, with only the hiss of the heater to pour over them. Her daughter pursed her full lips to the side, as if she were about to say something. After a moment, however, she shook her head and disappeared through the door.

Leisha forced herself not to follow Rinwa. *I can't talk to her when she's not ready to hear me.* Instead, she turned back to the counter to brush through her wet tangles. . She was ready when Samantha and Tafari got back, stomping the snow off their shoes before closing the door. They plopped nearly a dozen plastic grocery bags down onto the kitchen counters.

Leisha went into the kitchen to help put the food away, but

as she reached into one of the bags, Tafari placed his hand over hers. "You should be resting. We can take care of this, and I will cook dinner tonight."

Trying to ignore the heat of his hand, she cleared her throat. "When did you learn to cook?" Leisha asked.

Removing his fingers from hers, Tafari shrugged. "We have been alive a long time, Leisha. I have learned many new things over the years."

Rinwa came in then. "You mean when we weren't out slaughtering her kind," she sniped.

Samantha threw her a warning scowl and Leisha rolled her eyes and retreated to the den. She could hear Rinwa and Samantha setting the table while the sounds of Tafari cooking drifted out from the kitchen. Leisha plopped down on the couch, flipping through channels with the remote. It sounded as if Rinwa and Samantha were talking to each other like close friends. It was difficult for Leisha to not feel jealous, especially because she wasn't entirely sure which one to be jealous of. Rinwa obviously liked Samantha, even after everything that had happened. It seemed that Rinwa could forgive well enough, as long as it wasn't her mother. She wished she could kill Ptah again. The bastard had tortured her daughter until she agreed to become a vampire, and then had sent her home before she knew what The Hunger was. It had taken over and she'd come so close to devouring her father, the shaman, and daughter that night. Fortunately, she'd been able to tear herself away at the last minute, but she'd killed someone else in their place.

Pushing away that thought, she went into the dining room when the food was ready.

Tafari was removing an apron as Leisha sat. She couldn't help smirking, seeing him look so domestic.

They ate mostly in silence. By the way Tafari sent surreptitious glances in her direction, Leisha knew he expected a

comment about his cooking, but she still couldn't taste or smell the way she used to. It was like when a human spent so much time in the bright sunlight that everything was dark when they went inside. Except the darkness extended to all of her senses, and even though it had been more than a day, they still hadn't adjusted yet. So she mentioned how he had cooked the chicken and veggies to perfection.

Her estranged husband smiled at the compliment. The grin softened his hard features, exactly the same way it did in her memories from so many centuries before.

After dinner, everyone was tired enough to turn in early. When saying goodnight, Tafari reached his hand toward Leisha. She thought he wanted to hug her or maybe pat her on the back, but he hesitated, then lowered his arm and walked up the stairs to his room.

She wasn't sure what she would have done if he hadn't retreated.

THROUGHOUT THE NEXT TWO DAYS, tensions slowly began to ease. Leisha forced Samantha to go back to school. The girl only gave a half-hearted protest before giving in.

She and Tafari were becoming a little more comfortable with each other, but they could only make small talk. Whenever the conversation turned toward them or what might happen between them, one or the other would find a reason to leave. Leisha noticed that Tafari also found excuses to touch her throughout the day. Just little brushes of their shoulders, or grabbing some lint from her hair. Leisha realized she was looking forward to what he would do next and what the explanation would be. Maybe it would get creative.

Rinwa continued to make jabs at Leisha anytime she could, but Leisha began to suspect her aggressive attitude was likely a defense mechanism. It was to prevent people, especially Leisha, from getting close to her. So she tried to take the insults in stride. Besides, although Rinwa worked to push her buttons, she'd taken much worse abuse from Ptah, so it wasn't too hard to brush off.

On the third day of their visit, they were sitting together at dinner. Samantha's cell rang and she answered it.

"Sorry, Spencer," Samantha was saying. "Remember how I told you some of Angela's friends are staying with us? Well, they're still here and I've got to stick around." The girl waved a hand even though Spencer couldn't see her. "You know, the whole hostess kind of gig."

Apparently the boy said something amusing because Samantha listened, then grinned. "Sounds good. I'll see you tomorrow."

Leisha and Samantha continued to eat. It took both of them a moment to realize that the immortals were staring at Samantha.

"What?" she asked around a mouthful of potatoes.

Tafari swallowed some water before asking his own question. "How close are you and this Spencer?"

Giving a half shrug, Samantha answered honestly. "He wants there to be more between us. I'm sure you guys can imagine why I don't really want to date, though. It's hard enough keeping up this front with regular friends. And if I had a boyfriend, it would feel like a whole new level of deception."

Rinwa and Tafari nodded. "You have wisdom beyond your years," Tafari said with a soft smile. "I am not saying that you should not have friends and date. But you are right to realize that getting close to regular humans does put you at risk."

Leisha could see from the way Samantha twirled her fingers through her hair that the discussion was making her uncomfortable. Leisha cleared her throat. "Sam, why don't you tell Rinwa and Tafari what we've been doing to find the prophecy child?"

The younger woman straightened in her seat, looking relieved at the change of subject. "Well, as you know, the prophecies about the child are pretty vague. So I've been searching online about stories of pregnancies that might spark something in my mind or trigger another vision, but nothing has grabbed my attention." She shrugged. "Leisha studied all the prophecies about him, but nothing hints at where we can find the parents or predict where he'll be born." Samantha concluded, "It looks like all our efforts are leading us nowhere."

Tafari bit into the grilled asparagus. "I thought in your vision you were there to witness his birth."

"That's true, which is why we haven't given up hope yet."

Rinwa wiped her mouth with a napkin. "So what's your big plan? You put in all this effort to find him. Then what?"

Leisha shrugged. "We're not too positive ourselves. We do want to protect him and the mother from the vampires. They're working to hunt him down and slaughter him."

"You could bring him to us," Tafari said casually. "We are more than equipped to deal with the vampires."

Spine stiffening, Leisha narrowed her eyes. "And what would you do with him?"

"We'd use him to defeat the vampires," Rinwa said, as if it were obvious.

Leisha and Samantha exchanged glances.

"Wouldn't that be exploiting him?" Samantha asked softly.

Rinwa gave a half shrug. "That's what his purpose is."

Leisha could feel her expression turn grim. "How would you know that?"

Tafari looked directly at her, his demeanor also becoming serious. "Obviously, we do not know for certain. But the prophecies give the impression that he will change the course of both of our species. The vampires cannot have him, so we will take him and use him to purge the world of evil."

Leisha watched Tafari's eyes for any flicker of emotion as

he talked. Disappointment fluttered in her chest when she could see none. "And what of the mother?"

Shrugging, he answered, "She will be welcome to come with us. If she supports us, we may even turn her into an immortal."

"What if she doesn't, Tafari?" Leisha asked, frustration lacing her words. "What if she doesn't want to go with you at all?"

Tafari looked at her calmly, but didn't answer.

"If she doesn't want to let him go or come with us, we'll have no choice," said Rinwa. "We must have the baby. Besides, he's better off with us than with the vampires."

Too upset to sit still, Leisha slowly stood, her muscles protesting only a little. "There could be a third option."

"What, you mean you two?" Rinwa pointed at Leisha and Samantha with her fork. "You're gonna be able to convince the mom that you are the good guys, huh? And what about when the vampires and immortals hunt you down? You think you can elude us for long?"

Samantha piped up. "At least we would be giving them a chance to live the way they want to. We won't imprison them and we won't kill them."

Glancing between Leisha and Samantha, Tafari also stood. "But you will prevent him from performing his duty, the very reason he will be born in the first place."

Unable to endure the conversation anymore, Leisha walked to the doorway. "None of the prophecies have been that specific. No one knows what his purpose is. But you'd take him as a baby and raise him to be your secret weapon, and kill his mother in order to do it. You guys are as bad as the vampires." She turned to leave, but felt a large hand grab her arm.

"*You* are a vampire, too," Tafari spat. "Why do you pretend that you are better than them?"

Leisha could feel her cheeks grow hot. "I don't claim to be better than anyone. However, I actually value human life."

"This coming from the woman who kills people on a regular basis!"

Suddenly Samantha and Rinwa squeezed past, both avoiding looking directly at them. "We're going to see a movie," Samantha called from the front door. "Don't kill each other."

"I'd totally stay if that were going down, but that's not really the vibe I'm getting from them," Rinwa murmured as the door swung closed.

Ignoring them, Leisha continued her argument with Tafari, her blood quickly igniting with temper. "I only kill when I have to!"

"You are still taking lives."

Leisha pulled her arm free and headed for the stairs. "And I only kill those who deserve it."

"Who are you to play God?"

She whirled around, Tafari stopping only a few inches from her. "We've had this conversation before. You've seen what happens when I don't feed! Would you rather I waited until The Hunger takes over and chooses anyone from off the street?"

"And you think this qualifies you to be the child's protector."

"If not me, then who?"

He backed her into the wall. "I was the one who took care of our daughter when you left, yet you think you can snatch someone else's child and raise him?"

Leisha pushed against his chest with her unbroken arm, but he didn't budge. "I did what I had to in order to keep her safe!"

"Well she certainly is grateful to you, is she not?"

The slap against his cheek was deafening. It surprised Leisha as much as it did him. Tafari grabbed her wrist and slammed it above her head, his chest touching hers. His other hand held her shoulder back, avoiding her cast completely. Both were breathing hard.

Suddenly, she was very aware of their close proximity, their bodies almost fully together. Leisha couldn't stop staring into his fierce eyes. There was some emotion dancing within them that she couldn't decipher.

She wondered if he could feel the thunderous beat of her heart the way she could feel his pulsing against her. His breath brushed over her face, and she unconsciously tilted her lips toward his. Tafari was more intoxicating than blood, she realized. Even when she hated him, her body craved him. His hot touch and warm mouth beckoned her more powerfully than The Hunger.

The next thing she knew, Tafari's mouth was over hers, hard and urgent. Heat washed through her as she kissed him back.

He released her wrist, and she wrapped her arms around his neck, letting her injured one hang behind his back. His hands roved under her shirt, leaving hot trails along her spine.

Leisha pulled her head back to gasp for breath, but then Tafari was kissing her again. His scent filled her nostrils, his tongue worked magic on her. Blood rushed through her veins, and her body felt aflame.

She knew she would have to stop this before it went too far. They still had much to discuss and sex would only complicate things.

But when Tafari grabbed the outside of her thighs with his large hands and pulled her up, she couldn't stop herself from wrapping her legs around him, cradling him to her core. He started up the stairs while trailing a line of kisses under her jaw and over her neck. He gently bit her collar bone and she melted further into his arms. Clinging to his body, she savored the sensations he evoked.

Soon, Leisha thought while she nibbled on his neck, *I'll have to be the one to stop this.*

But it was already too late.

CHAPTER 5

Samantha could hardly concentrate on the movie. Her mind was still on the volatile conversation they'd had at dinner. When Leisha and Tafari had begun their fight, she could tell from the scowl and stiff posture Leisha exhibited that nothing would calm them, so she'd suggested that they leave and Rinwa had reluctantly agreed.

Samantha hoped that they could come to a sort of compromise or . . . something. She hated the idea of trying to find the child before either the vampires or immortals did, but the thought of keeping it from Tafari and Rinwa was even worse.

"This movie is lame," Rinwa whispered in her ear. "Let's go. If Tafari and Leisha haven't killed each other by now, then they're probably sulking and waiting for us to get back anyway."

Smirking at her, Samantha nodded. They got up as one and moved to the exit. "I take it you're not much of a romantic," Samantha motioned behind them at the movie.

After going through the exit, Rinwa slipped on her sunglasses and looked at Samantha. "Do I look like a romantic to you?"

Samantha chuckled. She'd forgotten how much fun Rinwa was. Their time together at the immortals' compound had been strained, but they had begun a hesitant friendship then. Samantha was glad that, even with her part in getting the immortal council killed, Rinwa didn't hold it against her. In fact, it felt like they were fast becoming as close as sisters.

That thought led her back to Rinwa's sarcastic comment about romance. Growing sober, she voiced her thoughts. "I can't believe that you're so old and yet you still let your parents' issues affect your relationships."

Rinwa stared at her. "I don't know what you're talking about."

They walked outside to the parking lot, leaving behind the overwhelming scent of buttered popcorn.

"Don't you?" she countered. "What about Willem?"

She could see the immortal's face turn hard. "What about him?"

Swallowing, Samantha explained. "When I was staying with you guys, I could tell he was into you and asked him about it. When he hinted that there was an obvious reason you two weren't together, I thought it was because you were Tafari's girlfriend."

"You thought what?!"

Samantha shrugged. "My bad, I know. Anyway, now that I know you're Tafari's daughter, I can't figure out what Willem meant. So I figure you've been pushing him off because of your, you know… mommy issues."

She got into the car and started it. Rinwa hadn't climbed in yet and after a minute, Samantha wasn't sure if she was going to. Finally, her friend got in, but didn't look at her. Samantha sighed, and pulled out of the parking space.

They'd only driven a few blocks, but the silence was too obvious to ignore. Samantha spoke up. "Look, I didn't mean to speak so harshly. Leisha and I have one of those friendships

where you say whatever you're thinking, and I guess now I don't know how to filter my mouth anymore."

Rinwa popped her knuckles one by one, looking uncharacteristically vulnerable. "I don't discuss my relationships or my connection to Leisha with anyone. Do you understand what the times were like when I was turned? We hadn't even entered the first century yet."

Cocking her head, Samantha asked, "You mean the immortals discriminated against you because you were a woman? Didn't Tafari intervene?"

"That was part of the problem. They thought I was turned because Tafari didn't want to lose his daughter. I've had to work harder than all the other immortals to prove myself—that just because I was a woman and my mother happened to be one of those monsters, it didn't mean I would show mercy to the vampires."

Glancing at her, Samantha spoke softly. "That sounds like it was pretty hard for you."

Rinwa huffed. "I don't regret it. It's made me who I am today. I'm trying to explain why I don't appreciate you pulling my personal history into the conversation."

"Well, too bad. Don't get me wrong, Rinwa—I like you. But I love Leisha like a sister," Samantha said firmly. "Did Tafari tell you Leisha's side of what happened when you were a child?"

"Yes, he told me. Ptah threatened to torture me if she didn't agree to become a vampire, etcetera, etcetera."

Samantha raised her eyebrows as she shifted gears. "And? Does that make you feel differently? I mean, it has to."

Looking out the window, Rinwa shrugged. "I don't know. I've spent two thousand years hating the woman for leaving me and Tafari to join with that monster. Suddenly she wants us to believe that Ptah had a strange obsession with her, tried to seduce her, and when she said no he tortured me until she agreed to be turned? It's a little hard to swallow."

"But that *is* what happened! She never would have become a vampire if she didn't love you so much."

"Really?" Countered Rinwa. "Did you hear about the part where she almost ate my grandfather in front of me? I was only four, but I still remember it perfectly."

Sighing, Samantha chose her words carefully. "I think 'almost' is a key word in that sentence. Yes, she told me that part too. Ptah pretended like he was doing Leisha a favor by letting her take you home to her father. But he knew that The Hunger would kick in. Leisha wouldn't know how to control it, and that she would kill you guys without even thinking." She slowed to a stop at a red light. "She was able to get away from you and your village while she was struggling with The Hunger for the very first time. That says a lot."

When Rinwa didn't reply, Samantha paused, deciding to try a different avenue. "Can't you at least try to rein in the hostility a bit? Get to know the kind of woman she is?"

"That's a pretty tall order." Rinwa sighed. "Don't tell her I said this, but I can see that she has an altruistic side that simply doesn't exist in other vampires. But I don't know how to act around her if I'm supposed to be... nice." She wrinkled her nose at the last word.

Samantha bit her lip to keep from mentioning that Nik was also exceptionally nice for a vampire. One thing at a time. "Well, I'm sure she'll appreciate you making an effort." The light changed and she gunned the engine as she accelerated.

Fiddling with the radio, Rinwa picked a punk station. "I'm done with this topic. What's the deal with you and that Spencer guy?"

Taken aback at the question, Samantha cleared her throat before answering. "I thought we covered that at dinner."

"Barely. You never really said if you wanted to date the guy or not."

Samantha lifted a shoulder. "It's a moot point. After all,

if I did want to date him, and we got really close, what would happen next? It's not like I can confide all these otherworldly secrets I'm keeping." She tapped the steering wheel for emphasis. "Even if we ended up getting married, I wouldn't be able to tell him. It would be like living a double life, and I can't do that."

Exaggerating a pouty face, Rinwa teased her. "Aw, is the secret agent with the double identity getting frustrated? Poor baby."

Samantha went to smack her leg, but Rinwa still had good reflexes, even if she was human now. The ex-immortal grabbed her wrist before Samantha's hand could make contact.

Samantha gasped at the sudden pain, swerving dangerously into the other lane. Rinwa immediately let go.

"Sorry," Rinwa said with all sincerity. "I didn't mean to grab you so hard."

Shaking her hand out, Samantha tossed her a wary glance. "Don't worry about it."

The rest of the ride home went by quickly. By the time they walked into the house, Rinwa was making her laugh with her sarcastic antics regarding romance movies.

"And kissing scenes." She made a face. "Don't get me wrong, kissing is great, but it's not meant to be watched. Most people look like they're trying to eat each other when they're onscreen."

"Now we know why vampires are seen as such sex symbols!" They both chuckled, their laughter echoing through the dark entryway. Samantha suddenly realized the house was very quiet.

"I guess they *did* kill each other," Rinwa quipped.

Samantha glared. "I'll bet Leisha's in her room." *Sulking*, she added silently. They climbed the stairs together. At the top, Samantha turned to the right toward Leisha's space, and Rinwa to the left in the direction of Tafari's bedroom. Samantha was surprised to find Leisha's room empty, but wasn't worried. She figured Leisha went for a drive or something.

She heard Rinwa's intake of breath down the hall, then an astounded, "Shit!"

Samantha hurried over to where Rinwa was standing, in the threshold of Tafari's room. The girl was beet red and looked like she was going to hyperventilate. Peering through the doorway, she saw what had set the ex-immortal off.

Tafari was in bed, and he wasn't alone. Leisha was sitting next to him, hugging the covers to her chest, but unable to hide her nudity. Both had color flushing their cheeks, staring at their daughter with wide eyes and looking mightily embarrassed.

And bare assed to boot, Samantha laughed at her own pun. All three glanced at her like she'd grown a second head. "What?" she shrugged. "I've wanted you two to get back together ever since I met you." She clasped her hands. "And now my wish has come true." She grinned.

Leisha shook her head. "Don't jump to conclusions just yet, Samantha."

"Right," Rinwa spoke up. Her sunglasses were off and her eyes bore daggers at Leisha. "We should assume that you guys fought hard enough to tear each other's clothes off and then were so tired that you fell into bed from exhaustion."

If it were possible, it looked like Leisha's face turned an even deeper shade of red. "I meant about us getting back together."

Tafari's expression suddenly went blank.

Samantha frowned. "But if you're not getting back together, what do you call this?" she gestured toward them.

"It's called sex, Samantha. I'll give you the little talk about it later." Though Rinwa was teasing, she looked like she was barely containing herself.

Ignoring Rinwa, Leisha peeked at Samantha and whispered, "A complication."

Tafari's spine snapped tight. "Girls, if you do not want to see me naked, you had better leave. And shut the door behind you," he all but growled.

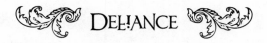

Both Rinwa and Samantha were out the door, down the stairs, and in the kitchen within seconds.

Rinwa grabbed some beef jerky from the cupboard and turned to Samantha. "Our deal is off. There is no way I can bring myself to be nice to that woman."

Samantha pursed her lips. She too, was a little vexed toward Leisha. She had seen the flash of hurt in Tafari's eyes.

CHAPTER 6

Leisha couldn't bring herself to take her eyes off the delicious view when Tafari got up and yanked his pants on. He had been amazing; so tender with her sore body while ravenous at the same time. Leisha truly had planned to stop things before they went too far, only Tafari's skilled hands and mouth and tongue had made her forget herself and she had given in to the strong temptation. And then, the second time, she figured that the damage had been done already.

Leisha rubbed the back of her neck and forced the recent memory away. It was a mistake and now they were going to have to pay the consequences.

Not bothering with modesty, Leisha got out of the bed and tried to find her clothes, strewn every which way. She could feel Tafari's gaze bore into her as she sorted through her clothing, but didn't peek at him until she was fully dressed and had finger-combed her hair.

When she did look up, she saw the usual, cold demeanor on his face. "So, you think that," he glanced at the rumpled sheets, "was a mistake?"

She closed her eyes and realized that her comment had hit him deeply. "Not in the way that you think, Tafari."

He raised a brow. "Go ahead and enlighten me."

She sat, feeling sore in places that hadn't felt that way in decades. "It's not that it was a mistake necessarily, it was merely the timing." She met his stare. "We haven't resolved anything between us."

His silvery blue eyes narrowed on her. "Can we resolve the things that drove us apart?"

"I'd like to think so."

His weight made the bed dip as he sat next to her. His scent was like an aphrodisiac, making her want to pull him down into the sheets again.

"As far as the past goes, I believe that I am getting over it. Your story has the ring of truth to it, and I have already told you how sorry I was to so easily think that you could leave us for Ptah."

Leisha felt something in her chest lighten and her eyes misted. "It's nice to hear it a second time anyway."

He leaned over and gave her a chaste kiss, but she could still taste his essence. "So now we can move forward."

She smiled up at him. Forward sounded good, especially considering how long they'd dwelled on the past. But not everything was cleared away. "What about the prophecy child?"

She scooted away to put a little more distance between them. "We may have resolved the past, but we haven't done anything about the present."

Tafari's eyes focused on the wall as he thought. "You mean the future. Because in the present, we are human and may not even need to worry about the prophecy child anymore."

Brows knitting together, Leisha reflected on his comment. "You mean, you want to leave that argument for another day?"

"Or possibly leave it altogether. After all, why try to settle something that may not affect us anymore?"

While Leisha didn't feel like ignoring the issue was any way to reconcile things, she understood what he was trying to say. *After everything that's happened, things couldn't get resolved this easily, could they?* Ignoring the voice in her head, she forced a wide smile and nodded.

He sat back and stroked the fingers that protruded from her cast. "Now that we have that matter cleared up, I believe we should get a snack and then you should stay here with me tonight." His grin was so warm and carefree that she felt herself melting.

Looking back at his bed, she shook her head. "Tafari, I can't stay in here."

Disappointment flicked over his face before he masked it.

Liesha grinned. "My bed's much more comfortable." She leaned in as if to divulge a secret. "Plus it's bigger. More room to maneuver."

With a deep chuckle reverberating from his chest, he helped Leisha to her feet, and they went downstairs together.

THEIR REUNITED HONEYMOON PERIOD LASTED three days before reality came crashing down.

Leisha was alone in her bedroom when her cell rang. The number was European. Her fingers trembled as she answered.

"Leisha," Victor's tenor voice sounded on the other end.

"How are things, Victor?" she asked with forced pleasantness, glancing out her window. She detected no movement outside, but human sight didn't capture anything hidden in the shadows. "How did you get this number?"

"As you well know, these are strange times. As for tracking you down, I didn't become the leader of our race for nothing." He cleared his throat. "You're needed here with your fellow vampires."

"Should we be calling ourselves vampires anymore?"

His voice turned frigid. "You can either call yourself a vampire or my servant. I don't care which."

Leisha shook her head, even though he couldn't see her. "No, I told you the last time that I want to be left alone. As I remember it, you readily agreed."

"Circumstances have changed, Leisha. We're in the middle of a political crisis and everyone, including you, is being called home. Effective immediately." His voice grew lower. "You haven't been around to see my reign. I can be much harsher than Ptah ever was, if need be. I don't think you want to find out what kind of punishment I've dreamed up."

Sweat sprung on her upper lip as she remembered what Ptah had done to her over the years. What was worse this time, she had no doubt Victor would torture Samantha to get back at her for disobeying him. Leisha paced her bedroom as she thought it through, Victor quietly awaiting her reply. Leaving now when things were going so well with Tafari was discouraging. But if she didn't comply, she knew Victor would make it blow up in her face.

Biting back a sigh of defeat, she finally responded. "I reserve the right to leave if and when I feel like it."

"You must stay for a week at least. After that, I may decide to excuse you."

"For appearances' sake, I assume."

"I don't recall you being so snarky with Ptah."

Leisha grunted. "That's because I always reserved it for private moments, like this. I'll treat you the same as I did him. Respectful in front of others, but I won't censure myself in private."

"Don't push your luck. I've solidified my power by punishing insubordination *very* severely." When Leisha didn't respond, Victor said, "Send me your flight information so I can have a car ready to pick you up."

Sighing, Leisha gave in. "Fine. Where are you holed up these days?"

"At the hotel in Palmona."

"I'll see you in a few days." With that, she hung up. The thought of going back to the vampires' lair was not pleasant. But if she didn't, Victor would make her pay. He'd already found her. If she ran, he'd find her again. Though her mind worked furiously at a different course of action, she knew the only option was to comply. At least for now. Maybe after she'd scoped out the vampires and how they functioned under Victor's rule, she could figure out a way out of this situation. She only hoped Tafari would understand that. Chewing her lip, she went downstairs to deliver the news. Samantha, Rinwa, and Tafari were in the den, watching a movie.

"I've been summoned to see Victor," she announced.

There was an unhappy silence before anyone responded.

"But now that you're human, you don't have to answer to him, right?" asked Samantha.

"I don't exactly want to go, but I think it's best to obey." She glanced at Tafari. "For now."

"Care to enlighten us, oh rational one?" Rinwa didn't even glance away from the TV. Tafari just looked at Leisha, his expression grim.

Hoping he would understand, she met his gaze. "We don't know if we'll be human permanently, but if we are, I would like some answers. They could provide them."

"So can the immortals," Tafari offered.

Leisha raised her eyebrows. "They'd be willing to work with me again?"

He turned his head away.

"Look," she came further into the room. "Since I've been human, I haven't been able to read minds. It stands to reason that they won't have their powers, either. So I'll be relatively safe there. And I'll be able to leave any time I want to."

"Victor agreed to that?" Tafari asked.

"Only after a week, but if I want to leave before that, I won't let anything stop me."

Samantha nodded her head. "It's true." She turned to Rinwa. "You must get your stubborn determination from her."

Rinwa glared and lightly punched Samantha. "See what I mean?" She rubbed her arm and looked back at Leisha. "So when do we leave?"

Leisha hesitated. "Actually, Samantha, I was going to see if you could go back with Tafari and Rinwa."

Before the girl could protest, Tafari spoke up. "I am afraid that we cannot do that."

"Why not?" Leisha and Samantha asked in unison.

"No offense, Sam, but you're kind of hated amongst the immortals after the incident." Rinwa shrugged as if to say, what did you expect?

"It wasn't her fault," Leisha said. "She was being threatened, blackmailed to help Ptah."

Rinwa patted Samantha's knee. "Look, you know Tafari and I don't hold any grudges against Samantha. But it's not the same for everyone among our people. I mean, you were the key to helping the vampires infiltrate our base and slaughter half the council."

"It is true," Tafari confirmed, regret in his eyes. "She would not be safe with us."

Leisha knew she couldn't leave Samantha alone. The fact was, she didn't know what Samantha's father would do if he found her. She couldn't really see any other way around it.

She looked at Samantha. "We'll be leaving in two days." Her gaze met Tafari's. "I'm sorry. I'll try to be in touch when I learn more."

Lips pressed in a thin line, Tafari nodded his understanding.

EVERYTHING WAS PACKED AND READY to go. Tafari and Rinwa were leaving in a few minutes, Leisha and Samantha would be going in a little over an hour. Leisha and Tafari were snuggling on the couch. It had been an amazing week, and Leisha was loth to part. A part of her screamed that their absence would make him forget that he didn't hate her anymore.

She hadn't seen much of him the day before, since he and Rinwa had been packing while she'd tried to find a doctor to take her cast off—there was no way she was going to join the other vampires looking so weak; she'd rather walk naked into the immortals' stronghold. Her arm wasn't complaining much, as long as she didn't lift heavy things or move it too quickly.

"When can we see each other again?" Leisha lightly scratched her nails over his hands.

His arm tightened around her shoulders. "If we are to remain human, then I want to start a new life. Together." His voice was husky, and his words made her heart quaver.

"What if we don't stay human?" She dreaded his answer, but needed to know.

Tafari shifted. "Then I must be true to my oaths. I will do everything I can to find the prophecy child and bring him to the council."

Leisha let go of his hand and turned so she was facing him. "Would he be safe with the immortals? Would he be well taken care of?"

Tafari swallowed and glanced away. "I cannot say."

It was answer enough.

"You would hand over an innocent child to them. Even though they would mistreat him?"

He slid a hand over his short hair. "The immortal council is not evil, Leisha."

"No, but it can be misguided." She locked gazes with him. "They have begun to care as little for human life as the vampires. You've seen this!"

"It is all in the name of the greater good."

Standing, Leisha walked across the room. "I think 'greater good' takes exception to its name being so abused."

The sofa creaked as he stood. "This coming from a blood sucker."

Her spine snapped straight and she spun to look at him. "I thought we moved past this."

"I simply mean that you cannot judge the immortals after having seen what the vampires do. What you have done."

Leisha turned away. "You said we were going to move on from the past," she whispered.

She heard him sigh and faced him again. "Leisha, you say that you are apart from the rest of those vamps, but what are you doing now? Victor called and you obey."

"I'm going to get some answers. But I won't stay with them, even if we turn back into vampires. I do not serve Victor, and I sure as hell wouldn't deliver up a helpless child to him!"

Frustration was evident in his voice. "Why should you care so much about a child that is not even yours?"

She raised an eyebrow. "Samantha isn't your child. Would you like to take her back to the immortals so they can judge her? Why don't you tell them about her visions? That she can lead them to the prophecy child?"

His eyes slid to the floor. Leisha pressed her advantage

"I may not have ever met this so-called prophecy child, but I'm invested in him. I know what his bleak future would be if the vampires or immortals get their hands on him, and I can't allow that."

He raised his eyes to hers. "Your protectiveness of him could be his doom . Maybe you should think about that while we are separated."

Leisha blinked a few times. "Am I supposed to know what that means?"

"What if doing what you think will protect him will actually hamstring him? You could prevent this child from being able to do what he came here to do. It is part of the reason the immortals want to separate him from his mother as soon as possible."

"No, I would help his mother raise him and encourage whatever growth he may need."

"Leisha, you were only a mother for four years. How do you think you can be in tune with those motherly instincts?"

There was a beat of silence.

"Have a safe trip," she forced out through a stiff jaw, and walked away, leaving behind the stinging remark. And her husband.

Tafari didn't call after her.

CHAPTER 7

January 21st

The flight was long and dull. Almost as dull as the food Leisha had forced herself to eat for the past week, though processed sugars were starting to taste better to her muted palate. Samantha had brought Boston Cream Rolls and Frosted Fudge Cakes in her carry on, and Leisha was embarrassed to admit she had eaten more of them than Samantha.

"I'll bet it's probably comfort food. You know, since you and Tafari fought. Again." Samantha rolled her eyes at the last word.

Grimacing, Leisha agreed. "This is the best I can do for now, comfort-food-wise."

"And Tafari-wise?"

She shrugged and forced herself to appear nonchalant. This was something she wasn't ready to discuss. "We don't exactly hate each other anymore."

"I should hope not," the girl muttered.

Heat crept up Leisha's cheeks, but she didn't need memories of their bed play distracting her right now. "But we can't seem to agree on the matter of the prophecy child." She shook her head. "He's almost fanatically loyal to the immortals, and it's blinding him to what seems obvious to me."

"What's Rinwa's take on it?"

Leisha raised her brows. "You would know better than me." Though Leisha thought maybe Rinwa was warming up to her. As they said goodbye that morning, Rinwa had patted Leisha's shoulder. It wasn't a hug, but physical—and non-violent—contact from her daughter was new.

Her parting words, however, were typical Rinwa. "Try not to be such a bitch next time." Still, they hadn't seemed so cold. Leisha could almost convince herself it was said with affection. Almost.

Samantha chewed on her bottom lip. "I think that she'll support Tafari, whatever he decides."

"And since he doesn't seem so keen on changing his mind, we know where they both stand."

Looking disappointed, Samantha rummaged in her bag for another Boston Cream Roll. "It would be nice if we could work together on this point."

Patting her knee, Leisha tried to console her. "Maybe we'll stay human and won't have to worry about this prophecy child anymore."

Samantha's blue eyes bored into hers. "Once I have a vision, it *does* happen. I'll be a witness at his birth."

"Have you had any other visions lately?"

She shook her head. "I had one about Spencer last month, but that's it."

That piqued Leisha's interest. "You didn't tell me. What was it about?"

Samantha waved a hand. "Nothing big. I saw him on the field at school, looking lost. It was like he had the weight of

the world on his shoulders, or maybe he was grieving. Then a man walked up to him, but I didn't see what he looked like." She shrugged. "It was after that vision I became closer to Spencer. I felt like I needed to give him some sort of comfort."

"Are you sad that we're leaving?"

Her brow furrowed. "I'm not sure. Being with Spencer was pretty confusing. Besides, we might go back."

"That depends on what we learn anything about this human thing."

Samantha smiled. "Well, don't worry about me. With everyone human, I don't really feel scared to go to the vampires. Plus, I kind of miss Nik. It will be nice to see him again."

Leisha was about to respond when her stomach lurched a little. She frowned and covered her belly. It lurched again.

"Leisha? You okay? You're looking pretty pale."

"It's my stomach." She realized that she couldn't bring herself to swallow. It was incredibly unpleasant. Suddenly, the plane's recycled air felt stale and dry.

Concern on her face, Samantha touched her forehead. "It looks like you're about to throw up."

Eyes widening, Leisha knew the girl was right. There wasn't enough time to get to the bathroom, so she searched through the pouch in front of her and retrieved one of the airline-provided barf bags. Holding it at her mouth, she waited. Her stomach was rolling again. Leaning forward, her body suddenly heaved, and a sonorous belch escaped her lips, but nothing else.

The taste in her mouth was a combination of bile and sugar. Leisha wished she actually had thrown up. But at least her stomach wasn't hurting as much.

She glanced at her companion. "I'm never touching another Fudge Cake again."

Samantha's face was red from laughing so hard. "I think

it's just that you had too many. What did you think was going to happen?" Samantha squeezed her hand. "You're going to have to get used to a human metabolism again."

Leisha sighed. "Those were the only things that seemed to have flavor. Of course I went a little overboard."

The rest of the flight was uneventful. Leisha couldn't bring herself to eat anything else and hoped that the other vampires had figured out a way to make food tasty. By the time they landed in Spain , Leisha was dying to get off the plane, but they had to wait for half the passengers to shuffle out before they could exit.

Outside the airport, Darshan was waiting for them in the crisp evening air. Leisha didn't know him well, though she was glad that he looked much improved from when she had seen him last. Eight months ago, he had been punished by Ptah over a triviality. Darshan had shown ambition in tracking an immortal, to the point that he disregarded an order from Ptah to kill the immortal. When Leisha had seen him, the vampire had been starved for a month, which makes a vampire decompose and rot. After that point, he'd been sentenced to beg the cruel vampires for sustenance for weeks.

His long, dark hair was pulled back into a ponytail, and he wore a crisp Armani suit. He smiled when they approached. He looked fantastic compared to the starved and decaying vampire from before.

"Good to see you, Leisha. I trust your flight was smooth." He took their luggage and put it in the trunk, then opened the back door for them to slide in. The leather seats were comfortable and the car smelled new.

Once he was behind the wheel and they were on their way, Leisha spoke up. "How have things been lately?"

She could see the corners of his dark eyes tighten in the rear view mirror. "They have calmed down. A lot of them wanted to desert when we became human. They said that Victor wasn't

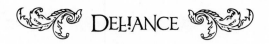

a ruler over them anymore and that their oaths were void. He didn't waste any time in punishing them and putting the fear of God into the rest of us."

"How many were killed?"

He shrugged. "Fifty or so."

Samantha's eyes widened, but Leisha wasn't surprised. Human or not, Victor had a cruel streak.

"The strange thing is that we still can't be in the sun for too long. We can venture out for maybe an hour before we start to burn. And the burns take a long time to heal." He glanced at Leisha in the mirror. "You have always been able to withstand the sunlight, haven't you?"

She nodded in the affirmative.

"Wonder why that is," he muttered.

"I stopped trying to figure it out a long time ago."

The atmosphere in the car went into a comfortable silence. Samantha was looking out the window, as if trying to see as much of the Spanish countryside as she could in the dark.

The drive from the airport took a while, and Leisha was stiff by the time they climbed out of the vehicle. Sore muscles were one thing she'd never get used to. She'd had them when she worked in her village in Africa but two thousand years made it easy to forget things like that.

"Why are we staying at a hotel? I thought we would be meeting the other vamps right away," asked Samantha, surveying the large building before them.

Leisha shook her head, and Darshan answered, "This hotel is your destination. Victor and his people reside here."

Samantha looked impressed but didn't say anything. Leisha supposed that after seeing their last vampire lair— beneath a tiny old Catholic church in India where parishioners continued to worship while vampires did unspeakable things directly below—nothing would surprise her anymore. Memories of the last time Leisha was here made her fingers feel cold. It had been over four hundred years ago and she'd been grabbing victims in the daylight to bring to Ptah and Ellery, Ptah's mate. Thinking of all the wrongs she'd committed made her want to vomit. *I'm not that person anymore. Victor can try, but I won't let him push me around.*

She and Samantha walked into the hotel's spacious lobby while Darshan and a bellboy carried their luggage in for them. The ceilings stretched high overhead and had beautiful paintings lining them. Samantha stared at the large chandelier hanging over their heads with wide eyes. It was plated in gold and held hundreds of light-refracting crystals. Beneath their feet, a marble floor led the way toward the reception area. At the front desk, Leisha recognized a human servant who belonged to a vampire named Ruth.

The woman looked up and smiled as they approached. "Hello, Samantha. I didn't think I'd see you again."

Samantha smiled in return. "Well, I'm glad I got to see you Vanessa. You were my favorite fellow servant."

Vanessa waved a hand. "Only because you didn't stay long enough to meet the others." She handed them an envelope. "Here are your key cards. Victor gave you a suite to share on the fifteenth floor. Danny and Darshan should have already put your luggage there."

Leisha took the envelope and expressed her thanks. As she turned to leave, Vanessa stopped them.

"Since you're arriving so late, Victor is giving you the day to rest. There will be a banquet tomorrow at midnight in the ballroom."

"He's keeping everyone on night hours?"

She nodded. "He says you're still vampires and that you should all act as such."

"Even the blood drinking part?" Samantha quipped.

Vanessa smiled. "It seems as long as everyone gets enough iron, they're fine on that score."

They exchanged nervous chuckles. Nodding goodbye, Leisha and Samantha went to the elevators. As they entered the first car available, Leisha wondered why she hadn't needed extra iron in her diet.

"What floor do you think Nik is staying on?" Samantha asked.

Leisha shrugged. "Your guess is as good as mine."

"Do you know how many floors there are total?"

"Twenty. We're being honored by getting a suite, by the way. But I'm not sure if Victor is trying to show me respect or if he wants something."

Samantha tossed her a look, as if to say, "What can you do?"

Once on the fifteenth floor, they only had to walk a short distance before they found their suite. It was pretty standard for a vampire's taste. Kitchenette, front room, and two bedrooms. Each room with its own gas fireplace and flat screen televisions.

"Is this what first class is like?" Samantha asked, walking around and staring at the architecture around her.

Leisha nodded. "It's pretty nice, though I'll bet the penthouse suites are much better."

Samantha walked into each bedroom on either side of the front room. "I'll take this one," she said from the bedroom on the right.

Leisha picked up her luggage and headed to the bedroom on the left. She wanted to unpack, shower, and then sleep. She hadn't realized how hard traveling was on a human body.

She closed her door on Samantha, who was picking through chocolate covered nuts from the kitchen counter. The chocolate tempted her for a minute, but then she remembered nearly throwing up all the sugar she'd eaten on the plane.

Putting her suitcase down, Leisha sat down on the bed. She'd intended to unpack and take a shower, but fatigue overwhelmed her. She decided to lie down for a minute, and before she realized it, she fell into a deep sleep.

CHAPTER 8

Samantha woke up in darkness. The combination of fresh-smelling linens and thick down cushioning her body made her burrow into bed a little longer. After a few moments of basking in luxury, she glanced at the clock on the nightstand and saw that it was midday. Yawning and stretching her fingers above her head, she got up and stumbled over to the window. It took a moment of fiddling with the blinds, but she figured out how to open them. Sunshine blinded her.

She was impressed with how thoroughly the coverings blocked out the sun. Of course, this hotel catered to vampires, so she didn't know why she should be surprised.

Making her way to the bathroom, she decided to take a long bath. The huge tub fit her five-foot-eight-inch frame wonderfully. She drizzled the hotel-provided shampoo into her fingers and sniffed the light flowery fragrance before rubbing it into her hair. The conditioner was a sweeter scent, more fruity, and made her hair feel like silk running through her fingers. The liquid soap made her skin feel smoother than ever.

"I could get used to this," she mumbled to herself. She felt

something by her hip. It was a button and, out of curiosity, she pushed it. Jets shot water around her body and she groaned in pleasure. "I could *really* get used to this."

When she was finally too pruned to stay in the water, she got out and readied herself for the day. Coming into the main room, she saw that Leisha's door was still closed. She went over and quietly eased it open. The room was pitch black and she could hear Leisha's even breathing. Still asleep.

Knowing it wasn't a good idea to venture out by herself, she sighed and went into the small kitchen. After a brief inventory of the food, she grabbed two candy bars from the counter for her breakfast. She was on a vacation, of sorts, after all. She'd discovered last night that chocolate from Spain was definitely worth having. She wasn't sure if she could go back to eating American chocolate after this trip.

Glancing at the hotel phone on the counter, she wished she knew which room Nik was staying in. Reaching for the phone, she hesitated. She knew if she called down to the front desk, they could direct her call to him, but wasn't sure if it would look suspicious. After all, Nik had to play vampire politics here. She remembered how it had been when Leisha had played those very games. Every move made, no matter how small, could affect the situation. Samantha couldn't wait to see him again, but reconciled herself to hang out until Leisha woke.

Candy in hand, she sat on the couch and was just reaching for the remote when her vision blurred . . .

SHE WAS IN SOME KIND of tunnel. It was dark and hard to see.

"Why can't you just leave me alone?"

She turned to see . . . herself. The Samantha in her vision was against a curved wall, crying and staring at her father across the way.

"We're family, girl. That means I'll never leave you alone."

"You did a first-rate job of it for ten years."

"Things are different! You're with vampires. How can I ignore that? And look at what they've done to you!" Mason pushed a hand through his hair. "But don't worry, Samantha. I think I can fix it. You need to come with me."

"She's not going anywhere with you."

Samantha turned to see Nik blocking the tunnel, looking as if he'd barely arrived. His normally passive demeanor was replaced by something intense, almost feral. There was an emotion in his eyes that she couldn't read. He started walking toward them.

Before Samantha could look back at her father, she heard her vision-self scream out a warning. The next thing she knew, a look of surprise spread across Nik's face and a hideous bloodstain was blossoming around his chest.

COMING OUT OF HER VISION with a gasp, Samantha's heart pounded in her chest. Sweat cooled on the back of her neck as she breathed deeply for a few minutes. Going into the kitchen, she swigged some water. She sat again and let her heart rate go down. Once calmed, she reviewed the details of the vision.

Now she knew that her father would track her down eventually. What had he meant when he said the vampires had done something to her and that he could fix it? She couldn't think of what it would be. Then there was Nik. Had becoming human again made him more emotional? She had seen his barriers come down once, but even then he hadn't shown a lot of expression in his face. The more frightening question of all was making her fingers twitch. Was he still human in that vision? If that was the case, then she had just witnessed his death.

SAMANTHA BLEW OUT A BREATH as Leisha tugged her hair into a chignon. Her ex-vampire friend could pull harder than was necessary at times. However, Leisha was an expert at fashion and knew how to turn a casual teenager into a breathtaking

beauty. While the chignon was simple, Leisha perked it up by putting shining gems throughout the smooth sections. They matched her sapphire jewelry, which made a pretty complement to her light blue dress.

Leisha, as usual, looked stunning in a gold gown that hugged her curves and had many straps that artistically curved over her open back. Her hair was up in a loose fishtail braid that ended in an equally loose bun. Victor had arranged for the gowns to already be waiting for them in their closets before they'd arrived – perfectly sized to each woman.

The cloying scent of hairspray permeated the room as Leisha covered every little flyaway.

Leisha glanced at the clock in the bedroom, visible through the doorway. "It's almost time to go." She shook her head. "I still can't believe I slept so long. If you hadn't woken me, we'd have been late tonight."

"Yeah, you slept over twenty hours straight. That's not normal, even for a human."

Leisha raised a brow, as if she'd been challenged. "Who knows what I am these days. Besides, I feel totally refreshed and we'll be up all night. I'll bet you'll be exhausted before we're halfway through this thing."

"Is it going to be like it was before? Where I serve you, then go with the other human servants to eat?"

Leisha shrugged. "If they don't follow Ptah's tradition, then I think it best if you stay by my side."

Samantha got up from the chair and put on her strappy high heels. She knew it wasn't practical to dress like this all the time, but she did enjoy it. The added height from her shoes probably put her at six feet tall. She hoped Nik would be there so he could see her looking her best.

She turned to Leisha. "Well, shall we?" Her friend nodded and they left.

Once downstairs, they moved toward the back left part of the hotel. The ballroom was large, and housed the thousand people comfortably. The soft lighting created a romantic ambience even though it was completely crowded. Classical music played from overhead speakers while people milled about, some getting drinks at the bars scattered along the walls, and others sampling hors d'oeuvres from trays carried by roving waiters. Leisha grabbed a few spinach balls from a passing tray and handed one to Samantha. They looked good and Samantha was ready for something besides the snack food she'd had all day.

Biting into it, she quickly revised how hungry she was. She searched for a place to spit it out before the salt and heavy spices burned away her taste buds.

"Mmm." Leisha closed her eyes as she chewed. "Finally! Something with flavor."

Samantha stared at her. "You mean this is what food tastes like when you're a vampire?"

Taking the uneaten portion of the spinach ball from Samantha, she answered, "Not exactly. When you're a vampire, you're aware of everything. Like the flavor, and the texture, and even the temperature." She popped the food in her mouth and spoke around it. "These aren't the best, but at least it tastes like *something*."

Samantha smirked. "I think you've convinced me to never become a vampire. I like my palate the way it is, thank you very much."

Leisha's green eyes warmed with her smile.

Right then, the lights flickered a few times. Everyone started moving toward the stage at the far end of the ballroom. Leisha gestured with her head and they followed suit.

Samantha saw Victor, flanked by Annette and another woman on the stage. They were sitting in decorative chairs, Victor seated in front of the women. The three of them were

dressed elegantly in modern formal attire, Victor's tux crisp and tailored to fit his massive frame perfectly. His brown hair shined in the stage lights, and his dark eyes seemed to twinkle.

Samantha swallowed at seeing Annette, looking like a perfect rendition of Snow White—or maybe her evil stepmother. She reminded herself that the woman couldn't hurt her tonight. Forcing back memories of the brunette beauty torturing her, she tried to focus on her surroundings.

Leisha faltered a step when she looked at the stage. Her face was pale.

Placing a hand on her companion's arm, Samantha leaned down. "Leisha, are you all right?" she murmured in her ear.

The vampire closed her eyes, then opened them again. After taking a breath she smiled at Samantha. "Fine. I simply had a little surprise, that's all."

Samantha looked back at the stage and saw Victor watching them with a smile of amusement, and maybe smugness. Knowing it wasn't the time to press her for more information, she followed behind her friend.

Victor waited for a minute before standing and walking over to a microphone. Samantha was struck by how different things were now compared to when Ptah had been running the show. The girl remembered the master vampire's voice clearly. It had been smooth as silk with a hardness hiding under the surface. When Ptah spoke, he didn't need a microphone since his voice resonated with everyone in the room. Of course, Victor was forced to utilize modern technology since they didn't have vampire hearing anymore.

"Welcome, my faithful servants," Victor started. While his tenor voice was smooth, it was not as mesmerizing as Ptah's had been. "I am holding this banquet in honor of the loyal service of those who remained by my side. And also in honor of the vampires who were away and have finally found their way home." His eyes sought Leisha. "While some things have certainly changed recently, many things are very much the same. We have had long lives, and I know that many of you appreciate the consistency that I have provided for you."

He pointed to someone off stage. "Tonight we will be celebrating by executing the leader of those so-called rebels. They have been tortured and killed for their crimes." A burly man escorted a woman to stand on the stage next to Victor. She wore only the heavy chains around her wrists, which did nothing to cover her injuries. Samantha could see that one of her arms was hanging at an awkward angle. Her right eye was sunken. It took a second of staring to realize that her eyeball was gone. Samantha forced her mouth shut when she realized what the blood dribbling down the woman's inner thighs meant.

When Victor looked at the lady, her gaze immediately went to the floor. "I'm assuming you've had time to consider your crimes, Leighanna," he said. "After watching your comrades suffer and die, and experiencing your own torment, I expect you have something to say to me."

Samantha could see Leighanna trembling, and sweat was making her nose shine in the lights. "I'm sorry," the woman whispered.

Shaking his head, Victor nodded at Annette. "What a weak fool you are. You thought you could defy me? Now you know you are nothing without me. A weakling!"

Annette walked toward the two of them with a small knife in her hand.

"I will let you die. No longer will you entertain us as you have this past week." He grabbed her chin and forced her to meet his eyes. "What say you?"

Tears streamed down her cheeks as she answered with a breathless, "Thank you."

Samantha couldn't believe it, but Leighanna actually looked like she meant it. She forced herself not to think about what the woman must have endured.

Annette was on the other side of Leighanna now. Victor turned the woman to face Annette. The ex-vampire smiled benignly as she plunged the knife into the rebel's chest. Leighanna screamed, but did nothing to defend herself.

Samantha started when she felt a hand on her shoulder. Leisha kept her eyes on the stage while she whispered, "You should turn around. I don't think you can handle what they're about to do."

Samantha had seen enough already, so she looked away and tried not to hear the screaming. Leisha pulled Samantha into her arms and patted her back. Samantha heard Leighanna's screams become shriller before suddenly stopping. It seemed like an eternity before Leisha turned her around again.

The man who had escorted the rebel to the stage grabbed an ankle and started to drag the corpse away. Blood pooled around Annette and she licked it off her fingers. Somehow, that was even creepier to Samantha, knowing Annette was now human.

Victor gestured to food laid out on tables to their left. "Now, my servants, go. Enjoy yourselves and celebrate your loyalty to me."

His audience bowed low, both Samantha and Leisha a beat behind the others. Then they all walked toward the food and began dishing up. The music came on the speakers again.

"Are you hungry?" Leisha asked her.

After what they had just witnessed, Samantha couldn't believe Leisha would even ask. Samantha shook her head, her jaw clenched.

Leisha nodded. "I'll eat after I figure out what's going on." With that vague statement, she headed for the stairs that led to the stage. Samantha hesitated, looked around at the people noticing her, and then trailed behind.

After ascending, Samantha slowed. Leisha was paying her respects to Victor, but Annette was looking at Samantha with a predatory smile. Simply being in her presence brought the taint into Samantha's mind again. She remembered feeling the smut of Annette's essence ooze through her brain like oily slime, leaving a trace of filth everywhere. She shivered and once again forced the memory away. Seeing red splattered all over Annette certainly didn't make Samantha feel any better.

Annette caught the shiver and her smile widened, but her arctic blue eyes remained cold.

Leisha loudly cleared her throat and Samantha looked over. Leisha's eyes veered between Samantha and Victor, then tilted her head. Samantha's eyebrows drew together.

After a second, Leisha asked, "Samantha, would you like to pay your respects to our new leader?"

"Oh." Samantha hurried to them, a flush creeping across her cheeks. She knelt before Victor and touched her forehead to the floor, as Leisha had taught her the last time. The pool of blood was less than an inch away from her fingers. The coppery scent filled her nostrils, and she clenched her jaw to keep herself from gagging.

"Rise, servant," Victor said.

She rose and stood next to Leisha. Samantha trying not to look at Annette, or at the gore marking the floor.

Leisha gestured to the woman on the other side of Victor. "You haven't met Ellery. This is Samantha, my human servant."

Samantha sent a sharp glance at Leisha, and her friend gave a slight nod. So that was why she was acting strangely. Leisha had told Samantha about Ellery a while ago. She had been a good friend to Leisha, but had died a couple hundred years ago. Burned as a witch, if Samantha remembered it correctly. Leisha had spoken of Ellery with compassion, saying the woman's friendship was the thing that pulled Leisha from her century-long depression.

Ellery stood, her black gown flowing around her curvy figure. She had chestnut hair, brown eyes, and a fair complexion. There was nothing necessarily striking about her looks, but she

had something that was alluring. Samantha could see why Ptah had taken her as a lover. She was pretty and had a sparkle in her eyes, as if she knew something the rest of the world didn't.

She extended a hand to Samantha. "Nice to meet you, Samantha. You must be something special. After all, you're Leisha's first human servant."

"Leisha and I get along well." She shook Ellery's hand, the other woman lingering longer than normal.

Ellery smiled and looked Samantha over from the top down. Then she grinned at Leisha. "My dear friend. How have you been all these years?" She leaned in and kissed Leisha on both cheeks.

"I'm fine. What I would like to know is how *you* have been all these years." Leisha's gaze bore into Ellery's. "After all, you look amazing for being dead."

Ellery chuckled. "I daresay I do, even by a vampire's standards."

"Care to explain what the hell happened?"

Sighing, Ellery shook her head. "You've become more crass, my dear."

Leisha shrugged. "I've become more myself."

That brought a smirk to the other woman's lips.

"All right," Ellery said. "I'll tell you my little story. Can you remember how I wasn't blessed with any extra gifts? I couldn't lure, couldn't see into the future, or anything else."

"I remember. We thought that you simply needed more time to develop one."

"Well it was a lie. I had developed a psychic gift—possibly a unique one." Ellery walked back to her chair and sat, crossing her legs. "I can feel people's emotions."

"You mean that you're an empath?" Samantha asked. Everyone glanced at her as though they'd forgotten she was there.

"Yes," Ellery confirmed. "At first, it wasn't so bad." She gave

75

an impish smile. "I used it to gauge Ptah's moods so I could better... play with him." She slid a glance to Leisha. "It helped me to understand your depression, my dear. I was able to say the right things to cheer you up." She smoothed out her already flawless dress. "But after a while, it was overwhelming. I couldn't figure out a way to filter it. I was constantly bombarded by others' feelings." She grimaced. "It was rather unpleasant. Taking on a human servant helped me focus a little better, but then I had her emotions to deal with as well."

Ellery shrugged as if she were ambivalent to her own story. "So I faked my death. I moved to a very remote place where there was only one small village nearby to serve my needs."

"But there were witnesses that watched you burn," Leisha protested. "Your human servant died the instant you did. How could you have faked that?"

Ellery smiled, her eyes lighting up. "It was rather clever, wasn't it? I went to this town in France, played the witch— rather brilliantly, if I do say so myself—and set Ida up to take the blame."

"And was Ida so willing to sacrifice herself for you?" Leisha asked dryly.

Ellery waved a hand. "She was my human servant. Her entire purpose in life was to help me, and that's what she did. So, once she was burned as a witch, I collapsed and played dead. Then, they buried me and I had to wait until the next night to dig myself out." She gave a look of distaste. "An experience I would not recommend to anyone."

"Been there." Leisha didn't look happy to admit it.

Ellery's eyes widened. "How did you get buried?"

Victor came into the conversation. "Some silly human had the idea to marry her for her money while she entered society to scope out new recruits for our race. When she refused him, he forged their wedding documents, then poisoned her and

buried her alive." He chuckled. "We like to give her a hard time for that mishap."

Rolling her eyes, Leisha confirmed it. "Yes, everyone loves to retell the story to my face as if I hadn't been there."

"When was that?" asked Samantha.

"When we were in England, sometime during the nine-teenth century."

"What did he poison you with?" Ellery asked. "It had to have really been something for you to let him bury you."

"Ground glass," answered Leisha. "It's extremely painful. Ptah actually adopted it as a form of punishment."

Ellery looked impressed. "Interesting."

"So where was it you lived?" Leisha asked, changing the subject.

"A cave in New Zealand." She smiled. "It was a great place for a retreat. After a few years, the local villagers started bringing me virgin sacrifices to keep me from terrorizing the village."

Samantha swallowed. "Virgin sacrifices."

Ellery nodded. "Yes, usually girls who were too outspoken or didn't fit in. But don't you worry." She winked at Samantha. "They didn't die virgins." When Samantha balked, Ellery blinked. "I thought it was rather nice of me. Most of them were able to experience some pleasure while they died."

CHAPTER 9

"I don't think I'll ever get used to this," Leisha said as she rubbed her feet. They were sore from walking and dancing in high heels all night.

Samantha rolled her eyes. "Yeah, you've been saying that ever since you've become human. It's like your daily mantra." Though her face was still pale from the scene in the ballroom, she gave Leisha a pointed look. "Or should I say hourly."

Leisha couldn't respond to that because it was true. She had said it a lot lately, but refrained from commenting that she'd been thinking it even more frequently. "I guess now I can appreciate what you and all other humans have to constantly go through."

Putting a hand over her mouth while she yawned, Samantha asked, "Don't you remember this kind of stuff from when you were human?"

"Well, I guess I assumed that since humans are so cosseted these days, they didn't have so many discomforts." She pushed on a tender spot below her toes. "Guess you simply traded one hardship for another."

Shrugging, Samantha stood and went to her bedroom door. She stopped and looked at Leisha through bleary eyes. "Do you want to talk about anything before I turn in?"

Leisha gave a sardonic look. "You mean about a dear friend faking her death and returning from the grave?"

"Yep. That's pretty much it." She leaned against the doorjamb, waiting.

After careful consideration, Leisha answered. "As much of a shock as it was, I can objectively say that I'm alright." Grimacing, she added, "Well, maybe a little hurt that Ellery didn't spare my feelings, but I can understand why. If she'd told anyone, Ptah could have found out. Besides, after having a real friendship," she smiled at Samantha, "I can see that Ellery wasn't a true friend. She was just the closest thing I could find when I was in a very dark place, both figuratively and literally."

Samantha smiled back. "I'm glad to hear it." She paused. "I have a bad feeling about her."

Frowning, she studied the girl's tired face. "What do you mean?"

"I'm not sure. I mean, she clearly felt nothing about killing those girls, but that's not all." She shrugged when it appeared she couldn't come up with the right words. "I just don't have a good feeling about her."

Leisha stored the information away. Samantha had good instincts about people, and Leisha decided she would trust them over a strange friendship two hundred years extinct. "Good night Samantha."

The girl yawned again before she smirked. "I think you mean good morning." Then she went into her room and closed the door.

Leisha went to the kitchen and made herself some tea. She felt a bit too wound up to go straight to bed and hoped the tea would soothe her and help her think. As the steam from her cup rose up and tickled her chin, she savored the heated mug warming her fingers. Mulling over the evening, Leisha knew the fact that Victor was allowing Ellery to sit with him and Annette was telling enough. Then, with Samantha's vague impression, Leisha was certain that Ellery would be more foe than friend this time around. Sipping her tea slowly, she decided that trust was something too valuable to waste on a wild card like Ellery.

THE POUNDING WAS MAKING HER grumpy. Leisha pulled the extra pillow over her head, but it did no good at muffling the noise.

"Leisha, wake up! I'm starving. Get that lazy butt out of bed." Samantha knocked on the door again.

Groaning, Leisha forced her heavy eyelids open and practically fell out of bed. It felt like her mind was running on sludge. After opening the door and glaring at Samantha, she went into the adjoining bathroom and splashed cold water over her face.

"I think that your human self is not a morning person," Samantha quipped from the doorway.

"Yeah, well, I'm learning a lot about what my human side is like." She grabbed a towel and dried her face. "If it weren't for having to drink blood, I would choose to be a vampire any day."

Samantha gave her a half smile. "I guess everything has its price." She followed Leisha back to the bedroom where she pulled out some clothes as Samantha continued. "But you have to admit, it's nice being human so you and Tafari can be together again."

A warm sensation flitted through her bones at the mention of his name. "Well, we still can't seem to agree or compromise, so I guess it doesn't make a difference at this point."

Samantha let it drop. "Hurry and change so we can get some food." As she walked out of the room she muttered, "Hopefully some *normal* food."

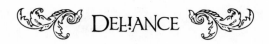

It didn't take long for Leisha to get ready, and they were down in the lobby in no time. Once in the cafeteria, Leisha could see that there were two different lines for food. "It looks like there are only human servants in that line." She pointed to the left. Samantha made a beeline for it while Leisha went in the other direction. By the smell alone, she knew she was in the correct place. Heavy spices of every variety wafted from the steamy kitchen and into the dining hall. Her stomach was growling and she decided to have crepes, a hamburger, steamed vegetables, and chocolate cake.

Samantha's eyes widened when she rejoined Leisha at a table, but didn't bother to comment. Leisha ate half of everything and decided she wouldn't need to eat again until the next day. While finally satisfying her hunger as well as her palate, the food now felt like a bowling ball, weighing her down. She wondered if she should complete the cliché and undo the top button of her pants. Out of the corner of her eye, she spotted a vampire heading her way. He was probably the only one out of the entire race that she might consider a friend, so long as he wasn't ordered to kill her.

Nikita approached and sat next to Samantha, kitty-corner to Leisha.

Samantha's face paled slightly, then she gave a broad smile. "Nik!" Samantha exclaimed and pulled him into a sideways hug. Leisha hid her smile when she saw Nikita's cheeks turn a very subtle pink, contrasting with his light brown hair.

"Hello Nikita." She nodded her head in his direction. "We missed you last night."

He shrugged, affecting his usual nonchalance. "The banquet was only for Victor's most loyal subjects."

"And you're not one of them?" Samantha asked with a touch of edginess.

He patted the girl's hand. "I am neither here nor there.

While I did not join in the recent rebellion, I wasn't too eager to slaughter them either."

Samantha smiled warmly. "That sounds rather profound coming from a hit man."

Leisha and Nikita shared a look before he responded. "Don't make a hero out of me, Samantha. I think you will be disappointed."

A strange emotion flitted through Samantha's eyes. "I wouldn't be so sure of that."

After a brief silence, Leisha changed the subject. "Will you be staying for a while, or does Victor have you out on an assignment soon?"

"I'm supposed to leave in a few days. There is a lead on the prophecy child that Victor and Annette have asked me to look into."

Leisha cocked her head. "And you're not leaving right away?"

At the same time Samantha asked, "They're still following leads, even now?"

"The assassins I'm training need another day of practice." Nikita turned to Samantha. "There's a rumor going around that if we find this prophecy child first, our vampire abilities will be restored to us."

Leisha pursed her lips in thought for a moment.

"You disagree with the theory, don't you?" Nikita observed.

"I do." Leisha shrugged. "I have no clue why we're all human now, but that theory sounds like an ordinary superstition someone made up."

Samantha was nodding. "I agree. I think this child will do something greater."

They chatted for a few minutes more before being interrupted by Jonathon, Victor's human servant. "Victor requests

your presence in his chambers," he told Leisha. When Samantha stood with her, he shook his head. "This is an exclusive invitation for Leisha." He smirked and gave the teenager a once over. "I'd be happy to keep you company while she's occupied." He leaned toward Samantha and sniffed. "I'll bet anything you're still a virgin."

Samantha's face turned scarlet.

Nikita pulled out a dagger and started cleaning his nails. "I won't be leaving her side for the rest of the night." He looked up at Jonathon without expression, but there was suddenly a deadly glint in his hazel eyes.

Jonathon swallowed, glanced at Samantha with a hint of bitterness, then left.

Leisha looked over at Nikita.

"We'll be waiting in your suite," he said in answer to her unspoken question.

She nodded and left. It took a while for the elevator to reach the penthouse and Leisha used that time to mentally prepare herself. Being summoned to the master vampire's personal chambers brought back memories of when she had to deal with Ptah. If a vampire showed much emotion, they revealed their vulnerabilities. Unfortunately, even when Leisha was stoic, Ptah still knew her weaknesses. But since Victor was in charge now, she was hoping she could play her cards a little better with him.

The elevator doors opened to show a suite filled with extravagant furniture, some of it new and others antique. Leisha spotted some original paintings by Botticelli and sculptures by Da Vinci. Victor was definitely enjoying his reign as master. Incense was burning from somewhere, making the front room smell sickly sweet. Under the scent, Leisha could detect a hint of sweat and body odor.

Ellery was lying on a sofa close to the fireplace, wearing a slinky nightgown. She gave a languid smile when Leisha approached.

"Too bad you didn't get here sooner. You could have joined in the fun."

Pretending interest, Leisha asked, "And what fun would that be?"

The bedroom door opened and Annette came out wearing only a robe and a look of extreme satisfaction.

That kind of fun. Leisha shrugged, exhibiting an indifferent air and sat in a large chair.

Ellery sat up and looked over at her. "So, you've finally gotten a human servant. What made you change your mind?"

"Guess I simply had to meet the right person."

"But you haven't marked her yet."

"I wanted her to at least finish high school before making it official."

A predatory look came into Ellery's eyes. "You may not want to wait too long. Someone could snatch her up from under your nose."

Leisha picked imaginary lint from her blouse. "Since we're not vampires at the moment and can't make human servants, I hardly think it will be a problem for me."

Annette became animated, sitting on the opposite side of the couch from Ellery. "That is the question, *oui*? Whether we'll change back." She waved a hand. "But that should not affect us either way. We'll always be a secret society. Victor and I will ensure that our traditions don't die out."

Leisha raised her brows. "Traditions? We don't drink blood anymore. What other traditions did we have?"

Annette threw her a contemptible glare. "We've always been much more than just blood suckers, Leisha. You were too self-involved to see it."

"And that will come to an end this instant." The last was spoken by Victor. He was stepping out of the bedroom with Derek Rose silk pajama pants hanging low on his hips, showcasing the lean and sculpted muscles over his torso. He did not seem pleased, despite his recent amorous activities. "That is why you have been summoned here tonight. You must be chastised for your behavior and attitude."

Leisha hung on to her cool demeanor. "What exactly are you referring to?"

He walked into the kitchen as he spoke. "It became abundantly clear to me after our phone conversation." He opened a drawer and pulled out a large, black leather bag. "You've been spoiled, Leisha, thinking that you can contend with me whenever you like. You think you can do whatever the hell you please and leave the other vampires behind."

She looked between Victor and Annette's accusing stares. "But you agreed to let me be independent."

He walked back over to them. "I've changed my mind. I thought it would be alright, but after doing damage control with this bothersome rebellion, I need to make it clear to everyone that only the most loyal will be rewarded." From the bag, he pulled out a muzzle and a whip and then reached in for more.

Leisha swallowed. "Don't you think you're sending mixed signals, Victor? After all, I was one of the honored guests at last nights' banquet."

He smiled congenially. "This is a private punishment. Think of it as a warning. You'll not get the special treatment that Ptah allowed you."

Leisha almost retorted that she really didn't enjoy Ptah's special treatment, but thought it best to remain silent. Her greatest dilemma at that moment was whether she should take the punishment or fight back. While she had a chance of throwing the three of them off her, she wouldn't be able to get to Samantha and escape. Leisha gritted her teeth. Since there really wasn't much of a choice, she would have to endure it for now.

Ellery licked her lips. "Do I get to participate or just watch?"

Annette snickered. "I thought you two were dear friends."

"We are." Ellery smiled at Leisha. "But even the best of friends should watch out for each other. I'd hate it if you two thought I was enabling her behavior."

Flexing her jaw to keep it from dropping, Leisha wondered how she could have ever thought this person was a close friend.

Victor patted her head as if Ellery were a pet. "I know where your loyalties lie." He turned to Leisha. "Put your arms up, please."

Rolling her eyes at the please, she complied. Annette was suddenly beside her, pulling her shirt by the hem and taking it off. Then Victor walked over and strapped the muzzle on her. It had a tongue compressor and small metal spikes around the mouth, so if Leisha did try to scream, she'd pierce her lips. It wasn't new to her. Ptah had used the same instrument if he wasn't in the mood to listen to his victims howling.

Following Victor's gesture, Leisha lay on her stomach on the plush carpet. Annette grabbed her arms and stretched them over her head while Ellery sat on her legs. Once at that point, Leisha's heart began to pound vigorously. She closed her eyes and tried to prepare herself for the pain that was to come. She had been beaten plenty of times and knew she would get through this just fine.

When nothing happened, she opened her eyes and saw Victor standing over her, watching in what seemed to be amusement. She raised her brow in question and he smiled. "Wanted to play with you a bit, first. Mind games can make the anticipation more intense." With that he raised the whip

and slashed down. Leisha flinched. This whip was the one with sharp metal tips. It came down again and she tried not to groan.

She felt the weight on her legs come off and twisted her head to see Ellery picking up a metal kitchen mallet from Victor's feet. "May I use this once you've finished with the whipping?" she asked politely.

Victor shrugged before he struck Leisha's back yet again. "I don't mind."

Looking down at Leisha, Ellery gave a satisfied smirk.

It was going to be a long night.

CHAPTER 10

Samantha and Nik were sitting on the couch, watching a movie. The teenager felt as if her nerves would smother her. As soon as she'd seen Nik, the vision of him bloody and dying came back to her. She'd almost blurted it to him, but couldn't seem to form the words in her mouth.

It wasn't merely her vision that made her feel on edge. When Nik had been sitting next to her in the cafeteria, her breathing had shallowed and she'd had to keep herself from touching him. It wasn't the same sensation as when he'd used his luring power over her before, but it was similar. She couldn't figure out when she'd become so attracted to him. Maybe she always had been and had simply blamed it on the luring. Thinking of Nik's power brought back the time when he had saved her with it. The night Annette had used her psychic power on Samantha...

"I CAN MAKE IT GO away Samantha. All you have to do is open your eyes and the muck will be gone," said Nik.

He must have been insane. This scum was cemented to her memory. It was more than just the residue from the first time Annette raped her mind.

Annette had ruthlessly possessed Samantha's mind at any excuse the vampire could think of. Samantha was forced to memorize five cell phone numbers, three fax numbers, and ten email addresses—memorizing them wouldn't't be a problem for her if she were given an hour. Instead, Annette had quizzed her immediately after Samantha was able to glance at the list only once.

Each time she got something wrong, Annette would fill her mind with the smut that only someone as evil as she could create. And each time that happened, Samantha found it harder to memorize the information. She had no idea how long the session had lasted; it seemed like it had been at least a week, possibly longer.

If she already had a week's worth of slime coursing through her mind, how could Nik possibly think that she could be rid of it just by opening her eyes?

In answer to her thoughts, he said, "You must trust me in this. You have nothing to lose by simply opening your eyes, do you?"

Unable to fight with his logic, Samantha opened her eyes. All she saw were Nik's hazel irises. Then, suddenly, the muck was gone. Nik was all that existed in that moment. She felt the compulsion to touch him, to be with him, encircled by his arms. She needed him more than she needed anything else in her life, and he needed her as well. She was his; she would give herself over to him completely. Nik was—

Samantha felt a tremor of loss surge through her whole body. Her vision blurred. She blinked in confusion for thirty seconds before she was able to see where she was...

SAMANTHA DIDN'T THINK SHE COULD ever express the gratitude she felt for what Nik had done. The vampire had tried to brush it off by reminding her that he was a hired killer, but Samantha had seen then, as she did now, the softer side to the man.

When they'd first entered her hotel room, Nik seemed to know she was high strung. He steered the conversation toward light subjects. She hadn't needed to talk a lot about her life since they had been emailing each other regularly for the past six months. After a few uncomfortable silences, he suggested that they watch a movie. He'd given her plenty of space. Nik had set up the English subtitles so she could follow it. The atmosphere was decidedly awkward.

When the show ended, they sat in the dim lighting for a few minutes until Nik turned toward her. "What's the matter, Samantha?"

For a split second, she thought about telling him of her vision, but for some reason it felt wrong. Maybe he wouldn't be able to handle it.

"I'm just worried about Leisha. She's been gone a while. What do you think they could be doing?"

"I could think of a few things," he muttered.

"What does that mean?"

He shook his head. "Forget about it. I'm sure Leisha is fine. It would be impractical for Victor to fly her out here just to kill her."

Samantha's brow drew down. "Actually, it does sound like something he'd do."

Patting her on the knee, Nik shook his head. "If Victor wanted her dead, he would have just sent me."

It came out so easily, like going out to buy milk. Samantha blinked at him. "And would you do that, if you were ordered to? After everything we've been through together?"

The ex-vampire sighed. "I've been ordered to do it before ."

"And you did? You went out and killed a fellow vampire?"

Nik looked at her. "Of course. I told you I was a hired killer. Did you think that drinking blood would turn me into a saint?"

It was Samantha's turn to sigh. "Look, Nik, I know what you are and what you've done." She chewed her lip for a second. "I can't condone it. Taking innocent lives is against everything I believe in."

Nik nodded as if he were expecting to hear this.

Without thinking, Samantha took his hand and squeezed it. "But I can't help feeling that there's more to you than killing. You have depth, Nik. I've seen your compassion and consider you a dear friend." It was probably because of her vision, but Samantha felt her eyes tearing up when she spoke. Embarrassed, she turned away only to feel his arms on her shoulders, pulling her into his body.

They embraced for several minutes. Samantha cuddled into his warmth, and breathed in his natural scent. She had the urge to explore the hard contours of his chest, but refrained, not wanting to overstep boundaries. He stroked her hair. After a few minutes, she pulled her head back and softly smiled at him.

His usual passive expression had been replaced with tenderness. She couldn't break his gaze, and couldn't blame it on his luring ability this time. His hands moved to lightly caress her cheeks. Unconsciously, she leaned into him. His warm breath on her lips, an intoxicating smell of brandy and chocolate, he moved toward her mouth.

The door opened without warning, and Samantha and Nik sprang apart. *It's like there was a fire between us,* she thought to herself. *An apt description.* She licked her lips and breathed deep to collect herself before glancing in Leisha's direction.

When she did look, she knew something was wrong. Leisha was pale and shaking. Since there were no visible marks on her, Samantha thought that Annette had raped her mind. But then she remembered that none of the vampires had their abilities at the moment.

Samantha went to Leisha, who was leaning on her side against the kitchen counter. "What's the matter?"

Leisha gave a wan smile. "Nothing I haven't dealt with before." She straightened and winced. "Although the healing process won't be nearly as rapid this time."

"Healing process? What did they do?" Samantha placed her hand on Leisha's back to steer her to the couch. When Leisha flinched, she immediately retracted it.

"Did they whip you?" asked Nik with all casualness.

"Among other things," she answered wryly.

Gasping, Samantha's chest swelled with concern. Glancing between her two comrades, dumbfounded that they both acted like this situation was so ordinary.

"Why on earth did they do that? You haven't been here long enough to piss Victor off!"

Nik approached Leisha and gently pulled her shirt off for her. Samantha grimaced at the intricate pattern of large red welts crisscrossing Leisha's entire back.

"At least he only broke the skin in a few places," commented Nik.

"It was a private punishment." She looked at Samantha. "A warning to behave and not run off on my own again."

"Did he use the steel tipped one?"

Leisha nodded at Nik's question. "Pretty amazing that he left mostly welts, huh?"

Nik nodded, indeed looking impressed.

His expression caused Samantha to erupt. She pushed his chest as if trying to pick a fight. "How can you be so cold?" Her voice was shaking in rage.

With a soft look in his eyes, he stated, "I have the utmost sympathy for Leisha. But you cannot fault me for noticing a colleague's work."

Quickly clamping her mouth shut at his words, Samantha stormed into her bathroom for hand towels. When she came back into the main room, Nik was lightly touching Leisha's ribs on her right side. "They're definitely bruised, but I don't think he broke them. They could be cracked a little."

Samantha could see a strange pattern of broken blood vessels on her friend's side. "That wasn't from the whip, was it?"

Nik answered for the invalid. "A kitchen mallet."

Her mouth fell open. "Did I hear that right?"

Nik nodded. "It doles out a lot of pain while not inflicting too much damage if the user knows how to wield it properly."

Licking her lips, Samantha forced herself not to show her outrage.

Leisha rolled her eyes. "The ribs on my other side just barely finished healing, and now this."

Walking out into the hall, Samantha found the ice machine. Filling her ice bucket, she returned to their room. Now Nik was helping Leisha lower herself onto her stomach on the couch.

"I know you guys are vampires and have lived with torture for centuries, but I still don't get how you can accept this." Samantha handed Nik the ice bucket. He took it without remark and filled the towels with ice, placing them one by one on Leisha's back.

"Well, since I'm human now, the pain wasn't nearly as intense as usual." Leisha sucked in a breath when he touched the homemade ice pack to her injuries. "Don't get mad at Nikita for his behavior, Samantha. It's how we survive this place. If we became affronted every time something like this happened, we'd go crazy."

"And would probably be killed for our insubordination," Nik added.

Samantha put her hands in her pockets, feeling somewhat contrite while still upset. "You're right Leisha." She turned to Nik. "I'm sorry I got mad at you."

He gave a half smile that made her want to capture it in a picture. "You were worried for your friend. No need to apologize."

She nodded, not quite sure what to say. She regarded Leisha. "Is there anything I can get you?"

"Did you happen to pack any pain killers?"

She nodded and retrieved two pill bottles from her

bathroom kit. She got a bottle of water along with six pills and handed them over to Leisha. "Four Ibuprofen and two Tylenol. That's the strongest you can take without overdosing."

Leisha raised her brows.

Shrugging, Samantha murmured, "My mom taught me."

"Thanks." With assistance she sat up so she could swallow the drugs, then was lowered back onto the couch.

They kept her company for over an hour. Samantha watched while Nik periodically switched the ice around on Leisha's back. After a while, Samantha was having a hard time keeping her eyes open and began to yawn frequently.

Nik smiled. "Go on to sleep, Samantha. There's not much more we can do anyway. I'll help Leisha to bed."

Leisha groaned. "I think I'll conk out right here. I really don't want to move right now."

Samantha nodded and walked Nik to the door. "Thanks for your help," she told him. "You're actually quite sweet." Waving her hand, she made her tone more teasing. "For an assassin, that is."

Hazel eyes twinkling, Nik leaned in. "Well, how about we keep that between us." He winked.

Samantha's lips curved up and she nodded. Reaching out, she squeezed his arm before she let go. "Goodnight, Nik."

"Sleep well, Samantha."

She closed the door behind him. She saw that Leisha was already breathing deeply. The night had been intense, but Samantha was too exhausted to reflect on it. Hoping that sleep would help her to think things through better tomorrow, Samantha went into her room to get some rest.

CHAPTER 11

L eisha opened her eyes to see Samantha's light blue ones inches from her face.

"How are you feeling?" her friend asked.

Leisha breathed in deeply only to feel tight pressure over her lungs. Taking a mental inventory, she was slow to respond. "Better than last night." She shifted and pain shot from her ribs, the skin on her back pulsing. "Achy, and very sore, but I'll live." Gritting her teeth, she pushed herself up and gingerly stretched. "Do you have any more of those painkillers? I think they helped."

Samantha nodded. "I'll start some coffee too. My mom said that the caffeine helps speed up the pills."

Leisha smiled wanly in appreciation and went into her bathroom. After taking care of business and splashing her face with cold water, she stepped into the main area. The aroma of fresh coffee greeted her.

Samantha insisted that Leisha had to have food with the pain killers, so she forced herself to eat a candy bar that she could hardly taste. Leisha's shower was a bit awkward, but the hot spray soothed the bruises on her front. By the time she was dressed and drying her long hair, she felt a lot better—still sore, but it wasn't anything she couldn't handle.

Samantha was dressed and sitting on the couch, flipping through channels on the television.

"Let's head down to the cafeteria for some real food."

The girl glanced over at her in surprise. "Are you sure you're up for it?"

Leisha nodded. "I need something more substantial, and I need to show Victor that his so-called discipline didn't affect me."

"Won't he see that as a sign of defiance?"

Leisha pursed her lips. "Actually, I think he'll respect my strength. He has always been more of a warrior than a politician."

"Okay." She went to the phone. "I'll call Nik's room and have him meet us down there."

Phone call completed, they headed out. Once in the cafeteria, they got their food and found a place to eat. It was hard to hear Samantha talking over the sound of most of the other vampires chatting and eating. The crowded room was warm from body heat and the connecting kitchens.

Nikita joined them with sausage, thickly sliced ham, and a hamburger weighing down his plate. He sat next to Samantha and they shared a smile. Leisha noticed the way her friend's gaze lingered on Nikita and gave a mental groan. That was such a bad idea. She didn't even know where to start to talk Samantha out of it.

Turning to Leisha, Nikita searched her face. "How are you feeling today? It must be difficult to heal so slowly."

"Much better. I may be healing slowly, but I am still healing." She took a bite of crispy bacon. "Thanks for being such a great help last night." The man had always been good to Leisha.

Nikita had been there when Leisha discovered Ellery was dead and hadn't told anyone how upset she'd become. But now she wondered if his motivation to stay last night was more about impressing Samantha.

"Think nothing of it," he said and started eating.

If they were interested in each other, there wasn't much Leisha could do about it now, so she dug into her food. On her third bite, her lips started to tingle. She ignored the sensation, assuming it was related to her pain killers or some human reaction to the food. On her fourth bite, her fingers went numb. She dropped her fork.

Samantha was looking at her with her brows drawn together. "Are you okay, Leisha?"

Unable to find her voice, she nodded. Yet she clearly was not fine.

A clank filled the air. Both girls looked over at Nikita. He'd also dropped his utensil and was studying his hands, his head tilted to the side. Suddenly, the entire room was silent, the only noise forks and spoons clattering down on the tables and floor.

Leisha tried to look around, but found she could no longer move. Her body wasn't responding to her brain's commands.

That's when the pain began.

It felt like acid was slowly working its way up her legs, into her torso, then arms and head. She wanted to move, to scream, to somehow eradicate the fire rising through her. But she could do nothing. She realized that she was holding her breath and tried to release it. But her body still wouldn't respond.

Suddenly, her eyes teared up, the hot liquid streaking down her cheeks and dripping onto her arms. Then, whatever power was holding her seemed to let go. The agony was gone; she could finally breathe. She bent her head, gasping. She saw red splatters leaking down her arms.

Before she could process the bloody tears, every one of

her senses overloaded. The light was blinding, her clothes were chafing her skin. The body odor in the vicinity made her want to vomit.

The room suddenly filled with screams. Screams of every frequency and pitch that made her wish she were deaf.

Leisha felt paralyzed, in a different way now. She also felt something else. It was strong in her mind and her control over it was entirely too feeble.

The Hunger was back.

THE SILENCE IN THE ROOM was ominous. A foreboding crept up Samantha's spine as she glanced between Leisha and Nik. They both looked frozen in place, staring straight ahead, but they didn't seem to be seeing anything. When she saw bloody tears tracking down Leisha's face, she knew what was happening. They were turning back into vampires.

She sat motionless when the screaming began. It was as if a button was pushed, allowing all the vampires to move. They howled like tortured creatures, some covering their eyes, others their ears. Leisha fell into the latter, while Nikita had his eyes squeezed shut and was gripping the table, thick marble crumbling under his fingertips.

Something whooshed past her. She looked over and saw Jonathon on the floor, trying to fight off two vampires biting any flesh that they could reach. Samantha's blood ran chill. She knew they had to get out of there. She lightly touched Nik's arm. His other hand shot out faster than she could see and he roughly moved her hand off him. She knew that he was probably fighting off The Hunger and her touch provoked it.

Hesitating, Samantha leaned towards both her comrades, and spoke low, trying to sound as calm as possible. "I have to leave now, but I can't get past vampires here. Would you two come with me?"

Leisha and Nik both nodded their heads while keeping their eyes shut. Each hunched over when they stood; Samantha hoped that they were not in too much pain. She led the way, glancing back every few minutes to make sure they were following her trail. She wondered how they knew where to go since neither had their eyes open.

Samantha was almost to the door when something heavy slammed into her from the side. As the air whooshed out of her lungs, she fell to the ground, hitting her head on the floor. She looked up in time to see Annette, eyes unfocused and frenzied. Instinct kicking in, Samantha threw her arms over her head in a defensive position. Annette's teeth ripped into her right forearm. Samantha cried out in agony as searing pain ran all the way to her shoulder.

Annette had only gotten a few swallows in before Nik was there. He gripped Annette's jaw, forcing her teeth out of Samantha's arm. Samantha immediately scrambled to her feet. She saw Nik holding the vampire down, trying to avoid Annette's gnashing fangs.

"Go!" he yelled.

Samantha hesitated a second, but knew there was nothing she could do to help him. Besides, she'd seen a vision of him later in the future, so she knew he'd survive this night.

Leisha was still behind her as they made their way through the mayhem. The hallway wasn't nearly as crowded but there were a few human servants surrounded by several vampires. The creatures used their hands and teeth to rip off their clothes, exposing the servants' vulnerable flesh. One of human servants looked up at Samantha. She could see the sheer panic in the young woman's face. Samantha slowed, racking her brain to think of how she could save them. It was only a second before she felt herself being picked up. She screamed until she looked into Leisha's face, her friend's eyes still squeezed shut.

Nausea flooded her stomach as Leisha took off, moving faster than Samantha could track. They suddenly stopped at the elevators and one of the doors slid open at a snail's pace. As soon as there was enough space to squeeze through, Leisha moved them into the car and pressed the button to close the doors. Three vampires were rushing toward them when the elevator closed. The car moved slowly as they headed up, but at least they were alone.

"Are we going to be safe in our hotel room?" Samantha's voice quavered.

Leisha nodded. "They're not in their right frame of mind. They won't be thinking about stairs or elevators right now. They're basically wild animals. What you should be worried about are the people outside, in the street."

Samantha swallowed past a very dry throat and tried not to think about it, or what she had witnessed downstairs. "How are you and Nik able to think past The Hunger?"

Eyes still closed, Leisha shook her head. "Don't know. Maybe our instincts to protect you are stronger." She crouched down in the corner of the elevator and put her head in her hands. "Though you should definitely lock your door against me tonight. In fact, I don't think I should even enter our hotel room with you."

This is just getting better and better, Samantha thought, but she decided not to comment. Once at their floor, they swiftly went down the hall and to their room. As Samantha was putting their card through the lock, Leisha crouched down again. When the door opened, she looked down to see the vampire had fallen completely to the floor and was in the fetal position.

Chewing her lip, she tried to think of what she should do. Though Leisha was having a hard time controlling herself, Samantha knew she couldn't leave her friend out here like this. If any of the other vampires found Leisha this vulnerable, Samantha wasn't sure if her friend would see the next day.

Bending, Samantha pulled the vampire from under her shoulders, literally dragging her into their suite. Her arm screamed in protest, and Samantha was aware of the blood dripping from her wound. She left Leisha in the kitchen and snapped the dead bolt into place on their door, then went back and dragged Leisha into her bedroom. Once there, Samantha looked around as she debated trying to help her friend into bed. When she heard Leisha whimper, Samantha automatically bent to check on her.

That mistake made it all too easy for the vampire to pull her down. Samantha landed on her knees and over Leisha. Before Samantha realized what was happening, she felt sharp teeth biting into her throat, hard. Samantha knew struggling would only widen the wound at her jugular and possibly kill her, so she forced herself to stay still as she felt Leisha sucking through the stinging bite.

"Leisha, I'm glad to donate some blood," her voice cracked. "But please don't kill me!" The latter was said with an edge of hysteria; she hoped that Leisha understood.

As if in answer, the vampire raised a hand and placed it over her forehead. Her fingers tightened to an almost painful pressure on Samantha's head. Suddenly, there was tingling through her mind and at the wound on her throat. The sensation spread down her torso and through her limbs, making her feel heavy and fatigued. Time stood still; it seemed like that odd feeling would consume her body.

The tingling suddenly stopped, but then so did everything else.

As if through a fog, her head slowly fell towards the carpet, her vision gradually fading to black.

CHAPTER 12

Leisha woke up feeling wonderful. Her ribs were healed and there was no pain in her back. No sore muscles or aches of any kind. Her senses were back to normal and she smiled as she opened her eyes. It was so nice to be able to see so clearly, even in the shadows, and to have such clarity.

Turning on her side, she realized she was on the floor of her hotel room, and so was Samantha. The stench of dried blood almost consumed her sense of smell. Leisha looked down to see red-brown flakes all over her clothes and hands. As flashes of memory returned, she gasped and sat up.

Samantha was pale and cold to the touch. If Leisha didn't have her heightened hearing back, she'd think her friend dead. As it was, her heart beat steadily, if faintly.

Leisha was ashamed to see the savage wound at her neck. It was clotted and looked as if it had healed quickly, but it would be incredibly painful for a while.

Of course, now that she'd made Samantha a human servant, it would heal faster than normal. Leisha stopped at that thought. She had made Samantha her human servant.

Something she had never planned to do.

But she remembered how out of control she'd been last night. When she had bitten into her friend and the sweet ambrosia of coppery liquid had hit her tongue, all cohesive thought had fled.

At least, until she'd heard Samantha pleading that she not kill her. That was when she knew the only way her friend could survive. She would become a human servant. It was an act of desperation, but now Samantha would have to pay the price.

Her life, her humanity, was ultimately changed and it was all Leisha's fault.

Blinking back tears, she picked the teenager up off the floor, carried her to the other bedroom, and settled her comfortably on the bed. She noted the wound on her forearm was a lot deeper than the bite on her neck. Leisha could spot a bit of bone through the torn flesh. The vampire looked through Samantha's toiletry bag in her bathroom. She found a small bottle of hydrogen peroxide and cotton pads, along with some ointment.

She returned to Samantha and noted her breathing and the movement behind her eyes. Leisha wasn't sure if the girl was sleeping deeply enough. Sighing, she began cleaning the wound on her arm first with the peroxide. The girl whimpered but didn't wake. Once finished cleaning her arm, she bent and did the same to her neck. Leisha hadn't seen any bandages in the bathroom, but applied the ointment to both wounds. The maids could deal with the mess that got on the sheets. That is, if there were any left alive.

She exited the room, grabbed a candy bar, and sat on the couch. She was going to have to do some major groveling to Samantha. The poor girl should never have come with her.

Finishing the chocolate, Leisha leaned her head back and breathed deeply. It was at that moment she realized something was off. She was once again a vampire, and felt like her usual self, but her body didn't feel . . . right.

Frowning, Leisha tried to take an inventory of herself. Her feet and hands were fine and functioning properly. Her arms and legs were the same. Her heart was beating at the normal rate for a vampire . . .

She sat up with wide eyes. "There's no way," she whispered to herself. She looked down at her flat stomach, where the second heartbeat was coming from. "It's impossible." Leisha had never heard of vampires procreating—ever. Doing the math in her head, she knew that even if vampires could get pregnant, there's no way a baby could be developed enough in her belly to hear the heartbeat. The first time she'd had sex in ages was with Tafari, and that was only a week ago. *None of this makes any sense!*

A knock sounded at the door. It took Leisha a few minutes to tear her gaze away from her stomach. From the thing that couldn't possibly be true. Schooling her features into a stoic expression, she opened the door, knowing it was Nikita.

"I came to check on the two of you."

"We'll be alright," Leisha hedged. "What's the damage report downstairs?"

Nikita shrugged. "Only two human servants survived, and they'll be recovering for a while. Victor was able to keep most of the vampires contained, but a few got out. There are reports on the news of wild animals that killed a dozen citizens last night."

Leisha shook her head. There had been several thousand human servants in the hotel. Though, she'd rather have them die than the entire town. At least they knew the risks when they joined the vampires. "So what's Victor's next move?"

"He's called for an assembly tonight." Nikita checked his cell. "In about two hours. All vamps are required to attend. I assume he'll announce our next course of action."

He looked around behind Leisha. "Where's Samantha?"

"In her room, sleeping."

He walked into the suite and towards Leisha's room. "I smell her blood."

Leisha noted the strong tone and was taken aback. Nikita was never emotional.

Though it was hard to admit, she forced through her teeth, "I lost control last night, but she'll be okay."

Face grim, he strode into the girl's room and walked to her side. Leisha followed. Samantha's eyes were open and full of questions as she was looking up at Nikita.

Reaching out, Nikita gently moved her head to the side and inspected the wound. His expression softened as he studied the girl's face.

Nikita moved so fast he took Leisha completely by surprise. He whirled and punched her savagely across the face, sending her crashing into the wall.

"You said you wouldn't make her a human servant!" He strode to her and lifted her by her arm. "Look what you've done to her."

Samantha was out of bed in an instant, rushing over to them. "Stop, Nik! You probably would have done the same thing." Almost reaching his side, she teetered and fell toward the floor.

Nikita immediately let go of Leisha, and caught Samantha before she hit the ground. He scooped her up and smoothly placed her back on the bed. "You need to rest. It will take sleep and a lot of fluids to get you fully recovered."

Samantha nodded, her face pale. "Leave Leisha alone. She did the best she could."

Nikita breathed in deep and his body relaxed. After a moment he went to Leisha and offered a hand to help her up.

"Sorry," he muttered.

Leisha stood with his assistance. "I deserved worse than that."

He studied her swollen jaw for a second. "It should be healed by the time the assembly starts." He looked as if he were going to say something else, but he paused. His eyes grew wide and his head tilted to the side as if he were listening for something.

The shock on his face was the most expression Leisha had ever seen. "By God, it can't be." He stared at her stomach as if there were an alien in it.

"My sentiments as well."

With effort, Samantha sat up against the pillows. "Hello, remember me? Care to let me in on the conversation here?"

Nikita turned to her. "You didn't know she was pregnant?"

Samantha chuckled, then waited for the real explanation. After a moment, Samantha's eyes grew round and she looked at Leisha. "Tafari?"

"He's the only one I've had sex with in too many years to count."

Jaw dropping, Samantha tried to stand again. Nikita was by her side in an instant, urging her to stay down. She sat back, but kept her attention on Leisha. "You're carrying the prophecy child!"

Leisha glanced to Nikita. He wasn't running out to tell Victor. At least not yet. Trying to have this conversation outside of his hearing range would mean leaving him alone, and she couldn't do that. *If he tried to run, I'll have to kill him.* It would be difficult. After all, he'd almost been a friend to her for four hundred years, but she'd do what she had to. "What makes you think that?"

Samantha pulled her hair behind her back with her uninjured hand. "You guys were temporarily turned human so that Leisha could get pregnant with the prophecy child. Why else would I be present at his birth?" She touched her forehead. "All

the pieces are coming together. I can't believe I didn't think of it sooner."

"There's no way that we all turned human just so Tafari and I could, could . . . you know."

Samantha raised her eyebrows while smirking. "Get it on? Fool around? Have sex? Make a baby?"

Leisha shook her head. "How could the forces that be know that Tafari and I would get back together?"

"I have visions about the future all the time, Leisha. Of course someone in the universe could know."

Stepping back until she met the wall, Leisha threw her friend a helpless look. "But that still doesn't mean this is the prophecy child."

"Leisha," Nikita said as if she were slow. "In the history of vampires, no one has gotten pregnant. Now you conceive right when we know that the prophecy child is about to be born. That's too much of a coincidence for anyone to ignore."

Sighing, she looked at the floor. "What am I going to do?"

Face stoic, Nikita answered, "You'll have to get out of here as soon as possible."

Both girls looked over at him. Nikita shrugged. "Any vamp within five feet of her will know she's pregnant. They'll assume the same thing—that you're carrying the child of prophecy."

Leisha was nodding her head as she studied him. It genuinely looked as if he was not going to report them. She was grateful for that, but concerned about his reasoning at the same time. "And they'll kill us without a second thought." She glanced at Nikita. "You'll be branded a traitor by not reporting me."

He folded his arms. "Not necessarily. They don't have to know I was here."

Leisha accepted that, and saw that Samantha had opened her mouth to say something, then seemed to think the better of it and remained silent.

"You'd best go then. Text me or Samantha if you get word of anything?" She gave a small smile when he nodded. "Thanks for everything, Nikita. You've been a good friend to us."

He gave a closed-mouth smile, paused, then looked down at Samantha. His face was its usual impassiveness, but Leisha sensed emotion stirring within him.

"I wish you could come with us." The girl forced a light smile.

Nikita hesitated, and glanced at Leisha. She made it clear with one look that she wouldn't leave the two of them alone. He patted the top of Samantha's head, then he strode out of the room and was gone.

Leisha left the room so Samantha could have a moment to herself. She was secretly glad Nikita wouldn't be around Samantha anymore, but that didn't mean she couldn't feel sympathy for the teenager. It was hard for her to get deeply attached to people since their lives were in constant upheaval.

Leisha went into the kitchen and grabbed a bottle of water, apple juice, a bag of nuts, and some chocolate. She brought them in to Samantha and placed the refreshments at her bedside table. The girl was blinking tears from her eyes, but smiled appreciatively at the food.

"Eat and drink as much as you can. Then rest while I pack everything for us. We'll sneak out during the assembly. Hopefully, no one will notice."

Samantha grabbed her hand. "We won't die, Leisha. I had a vision about your baby's birth and the future doesn't change, remember?"

Leisha swallowed and nodded. No matter how cynical her thoughts, she wasn't going to contradict Samantha. Last year, when the teenager had had a vision about her mother's death, the girl had very maturely accepted it. Samantha would know better than anyone that once a vision was shown, it would happen.

Walking out of the room, she began packing up all of their

things. She double-checked their various identities and passports. They would be on the run, again, and couldn't afford for anyone to be able to track them.

When she was done packing, she sat on the couch to try and figure out their next destination. There was a whole world out there, but she needed to go somewhere Samantha would not stick out. It was school season, making it difficult to pass as tourists.

A twitch in her stomach interrupted her thoughts. She placed her hand over her belly, and wondered what kind of child would be born. She was a vampire and Tafari an immortal. *Not sure if I want him to be more like his dad, or like me.* Maybe that's what the prophecies meant when they said this child would be connected to both the immortals and vampires. Maybe he wouldn't have the power to destroy either race after all.

Massaging her temples, she wondered if she should tell Tafari. No, the question wasn't if, it was when. Would he remain loyal to the immortals even if it meant handing over his own child? Leisha wouldn't put it past him. He was loyal to a fault—almost fanatically so.

When it was finally time, she woke Samantha and helped her get ready. The girl was still very weak and her wounds looked terrible, but she was making good improvement. Leisha gathered their luggage and bit back her impatience as she waited for a sluggish Samantha to go out the door.

Raising her brows at the two carry-on bags, Samantha glanced at her. "What about our other stuff?"

Shaking her head, Leisha kept their pace. "It's too much to take. I packed all the necessary items and left the rest behind."

"And how many outfits do I have?"

The vampire pushed the button for the elevator. "Three, the same as me."

Sliding doors to their right opened and they walked inside. "How long do you think we'll be running, Leisha?"

"Don't worry. I have plenty of money to buy us stuff once we've found a good hiding place."

Samantha pressed her lips together. "I never said goodbye to Spencer or any of my other friends."

Knowing there was nothing to say, Leisha reached over and gently squeezed her shoulder. The elevator dinged their arrival. "Stay close to me," she cautioned. "We'll get a cab once we put some distance between us and the hotel."

The lobby was empty, and Leisha could hear Victor's voice faintly from down a corridor. She grabbed Samantha's hand and they walked as quickly as Samantha was able to. They were almost to the doors when Leisha felt another presence in the room. Hoping whoever it was wouldn't notice her, she kept on.

"Are you so ready to depart?" Ellery called out. It was never a good sign when a vampire sounded that amused.

CHAPTER 13

Leisha stopped and turned to face the fellow vampire, Samantha staying close to her side. "There's an emergency I must attend to," Leisha said. "No offense was meant toward you or Victor."

Ellery slowly walked toward them, her red evening gown swishing at her ankles. "If it was as innocent as that, my dear friend, you wouldn't be trying to sneak away." Her eyes narrowed. "And I have my powers back again. So I know how nervous you two are." She placed a hand on Leisha's cheek and looked into her eyes. "In all the years I've known you, I have never sensed such fear in you."

"That doesn't mean anything," Samantha said.

Ellery turned her attention to her. "Ah, little beauty. I'm glad to see you survived the night. Congratulations on becoming a human servant." Removing her hand from Leisha, she reached over and stroked the girl's hair. "Too bad you couldn't have been mine. I daresay I would have made the transition very enjoyable indeed." Ellery angled her head slightly. "Finally. My summons have been answered."

Leisha looked behind Ellery to see Annette and Victor striding toward them, a large group of vampires trailing behind. Leisha wished she had brought every weapon she owned. Unfortunately, all she had was a dagger strapped to her calf. Samantha didn't have anything, let alone the strength to fight.

"Leisha," Victor said. "Annette tells me you were trying to flee."

Eyebrows drawing together, Leisha met Nikita's gaze in the crowd. Very subtly, he shook his head. Ellery must have sensed Leisha's confusion, because she answered Leisha's unspoken question. "This morning, we discovered that Annette and I are able to communicate with each other telepathically. As a fellow telepath, you probably could too, if you were willing to let her into that complex little brain of yours."

"I think a resounding no would be answer enough," Leisha said. She looked at Victor and tried for ignorance. "What's the problem, Victor? Everything has gone back to normal now. And ordinarily, I'm doing my own thing, so I thought I'd go back to my life."

He gave a cold smile. "I believe we already had a conversation about your privileges changing to better serve me."

Leisha straightened and took a breath, preparing herself for the unavoidable altercation. "I'm finished being ruled, Victor. I'll not yield to anyone anymore."

A flush rose to his cheeks. "You've made your choice then. I hope you understand: your fate will be *much* worse than Leighanna's."

Leisha pulled Samantha behind her and went into a fighting stance. At Victor's nod, six vampires slowly began to approach.

"Wait a minute," called Ellery.

Everyone stopped and turned their attention to her. Leisha wondered if Ellery might actually try to save her.

The empath's eyes sparkled in the crystal lighting. "I think you've missed a crucial detail here."

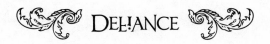

"What would that be?" snapped Annette.

Looking at everyone in the room, Ellery raised her voice. "Focus carefully, all of you. Direct your attention on our Leisha here, and simply listen."

It was a mere second before vampires started murmuring. Annette appeared thrilled. "It's unheard of for a vampire to get pregnant. Even if one of us got pregnant while human, there is no way a fetus would have survived the transformation back. This has to be the child who has been prophesied." She brought her hands together. "After all this time searching for him, and Leisha walks right into our lair with the babe nestled in her belly."

A vampire standing on her left glanced between Annette and Leisha. He was tall and handsome with a thick head of black hair. His eyes gave off a shrewd intelligence. "We don't know that this is the prophecy child. What if we kill it and then the true child is born later and destroys us while we sit in ignorance." Victor stared at the man, his eyes slightly squinted in thought. "We can always kill them and continue our search to be certain. No one can ever accuse me of not being thorough." Victor gestured to the six men who had halted. "I don't care about the servant, but don't kill Leisha. I want to know where that babe came from before I snuff out her existence."

There was a buzz of people muttering to each other as they stood by and watched.

Leisha pulled out her dagger as they approached. "If you see an opportunity to run," she whispered as quietly as she could to Samantha, "take it."

Leisha rushed forward and met the oncoming vampires halfway. A vampire with spiky hair came at her in a full frontal attack. She dropped down to avoid his sidekick and swept her leg through his standing one, making him fall. She quickly plunged the dagger into his heart, twisted, and yanked back. It wouldn't kill him, but he'd be down for a while.

Before she could stand, something grasped her hair and pulled her back flat on the ground. His mistake was when he proudly stood over her, both feet on either side of her waist. Arms reaching down, it looked like he was about to strangle her. She swung her weapon and castrated him, blood pouring over her. Spinning and quickly rising to her feet, Leisha faced her next assailant.

The vampire in front of her was named Carl. He smiled ruthlessly as two other vampires grabbed her from behind. She waited until Carl was close enough, then used the bodies holding her as leverage to jump and wrap her ankles around Carl's neck. His arms flailed as she squeezed tightly, but it was too late. She released the head and landed just as his neck made a sickly snap. She threw the vamp on her right over her back so he landed on the floor. Before he could recover, she stomped on his windpipe, snapping his neck as well.

There wasn't enough time to duck, so when the other vampire punched her in the eye, so she rolled with the force of it, flipping over backwards and jumping into the air. As she landed in front of her attacker, Leisha jabbed her weapon into his heart and twisted.

Turning, she smiled at the other challenger and beckoned him. The last vampire paused and looked to Victor for guidance. Leisha used that opportunity to rush back to Samantha, who looked like she didn't know what to do. Leisha grabbed her arm and propelled her forward. "Run! I'll find you."

Samantha ran out the sliding glass doors. Leisha turned just in time to defend herself from yet another group of vampires.

This time there were seven of them. They came at her two or three at a time. Leisha fought off the first wave, but the second attack was more organized. The vampires landed several blows to her jaw and eyes.

Allowing anger to fuel her, Leisha growled and reached out on either side of her. She poked her fingers through the

vampires' eyes to buy her time. When she regained her equilib-
rium, Leisha saw six more vampires rushing toward the fight.

Three came at her directly while the others surrounded
her from behind. Leisha brought her blade up and deflected
the three in front of her while trying to use her other arm to
punch behind her back. One of the vampires caught her free
hand as she swung back and the other two behind her used
that opportunity to grab her around the waist and neck. Her
throat was bruising quickly under the pressure and she in-
stinctively dropped her sword and clawed and the arm around
her neck. She began to panic, her movements becoming wild
and desperate.

Leisha could feel capillaries bursting in her eyes as more
hands grasped her legs and forced her on the floor. Darkness
threatened her vision and Leisha felt tears of defeat leaking
out the corners of her eyes.

Suddenly, the bruising grips were ripped away and three
vampires cried out in surprise as they were thrown into the
watching crowd. Sputtering, Leisha was surprised to see Nikita
there, fighting off the incoming vampires. He used a machete
to decapitate anyone who came near him. Moving with grace,
every motion of his arms brought a fresh spray of blood from
his attackers.

The assassin made eye contact with her and nodded. She
smiled at him and jumped up while fingering her dagger to
return to the battle. After a few minutes, Nikita spoke to her.
"We need to get out of here. There're too many."

Leisha nodded and looked around as she blocked one vampire with her arm while aiming a roundhouse kick at another's
head. Parrying another onslaught, she saw her opportunity.
"Be ready!" she called to him.

She beat off the two vampires attacking her and before
anyone else could challenge her, she turned toward Victor.
He was standing on the counter of the front desk a hundred

yards away to have a good vantage point, she assumed. He saw her look over and saluted her, trying to contain a smug grin.

Leisha copied his gesture with her left hand while she threw her dagger with her right. The blade flew swiftly, and Victor, caught off guard by such an aggressive move, didn't move fast enough. The dagger sunk into his chest with a meaty thunk. Surprise flickered across Victor's face as blood was blossomed outward from where the dagger struck — right into his heart.

The vampires in the room paused, their shock and disbelief evident.

Leisha used the diversion to make escape. She didn't have to look for Nikita; she knew he'd be right behind her. They were out the doors and down the street in no time. Following Samantha's scent, they caught up with her in moments. They didn't bother to slow down. Approaching from behind, Nikita scooped the girl up into his arms and kept racing by Leisha's side.

Samantha gasped when he picked her up, but calmed when she saw it was him. The girl closed her eyes tight and put her face into Nikita's neck. Leisha knew from experience that being carried at such speed made Samantha phenomenally motion sick.

Nikita was turning toward the airport, but Leisha stopped him and pointed toward the border. "We travel on foot until we reach France."

Shrugging, Nikita maneuvered Samantha to his back. Leisha ran to a tall building and climbed up the bricks, using her left foot as much as possible since her right leg was still healing. Her hands ached from the altercation with the vampires, but she still managed to ascend, with Nikita right behind her. Facing the direction Leisha indicated, they ran as fast as they could. Just before plummeting off the edge of the twenty-story building, they jumped. Wind blasted the vampire's cheeks and hair as they hurtled high. Exhilaration crashed over Leisha like a

tidal wave, sending tingling sensations up and down her spine, arms, and legs; she could hear Samantha whimper at Nikita's back, but didn't allow it to ruin the moment. Leisha couldn't help but savor the feeling absolute freedom when she propelled herself toward the clouds.

They landed hard on another rooftop. Leisha's knees buckled, but she recovered herself almost instantly. They continued on, leaping from building to building, working their way toward the edge of the city.

"We'll have to drink more frequently if we continue to exert this kind of energy." Nikita said after another long jump. "Though they might track us that way."

"No, they won't." Leisha wiped bloody sweat from her brow. Clear of the city, they dropped to the ground made a dash for a small forest. "I'll pick out our victims. They'll be the kind of thugs who don't get reported missing. Trust me."

CHAPTER 14

February 4th

Aarhus, Denmark had a beautiful old-country ambience, but Samantha simply wanted to be back in the United States. She had always thought travel would be fun, but when avoiding murderous vampires, it was just tiring.

After two weeks on the run across Europe, Samantha was relieved to hear that they were going home. That is, until Leisha explained that they would be starting a new life in Canada.

"I don't want to live there," protested Samantha. She got off the couch and looked out the window of their hotel room.

Leisha blew out a breath. "It's a good place to hide, Samantha. You don't have to learn a new language and can adapt to the culture easily enough."

"We could do that in the U.S. There's plenty of states to move between."

Leisha shook her head. "No. We spent too much time there and it's the first place anyone would look for us. Canada is the best place to go to ground."

Hugging herself, Samantha turned away so her friend wouldn't see the scowl on her face. She knew the vampire was right, but didn't want to accept it. She wanted to go back to Ohio and see her friends. She didn't want to have to start over again.

Leisha came up behind her and put a hand on her shoulder. "I know it's been hard on you, Samantha. And I know that you may never forgive me for changing you, but all I can offer is my protection. In order to do that, you're going to have to trust me in this."

Tears threatening, Samantha turned away. She only took two steps before she bumped into Nik's chest. Looking up at him, she felt a balm being in his presence. The vampire wasn't pulling her into his arms for comfort, but she sensed that he cared. Somehow, that made her feel less embarrassed about getting emotional.

She lingered close to his body heat, glancing away as she felt a few tears slipping. Taking a fortifying breath, she turned back to Leisha and nodded, "No arguing. We all know that you're right." Samantha hesitated. "But I would really like to go to Ohio once more, just to say goodbye."

Leisha was shaking her head before Samantha finished. "Absolutely not. It would be like handing ourselves over to them on a silver platter. There's no way we can go anyplace we've lived before, especially most recently. It's suicide."

"Maybe not," Samantha ventured. "It's so obvious, and they know how smart you are so they probably won't bother to look there. Or maybe they already have and are gone now."

Leisha's lips were set in a stubborn line.

"She has a point, Leisha." Nik put in. Leisha's jaw drooped in surprise. "If we were to visit for a day so that Samantha can get some closure, it would be safe enough."

"Not from you, too, Nikita." Leisha jabbed a finger in his direction. "You know better than anyone how to track people."

Samantha grimaced at the sentence.

Nik nodded. "I do, and my professional opinion is that there won't be any danger." He placed a hand on Samantha's shoulder. "She needs this, and it's within your power to give it to her." Throwing the vampire a pointed look, Nik added, "Considering what you've taken from her, I think that is the least you can do."

Samantha dropped her gaze to the floor. She wasn't sure how she felt about being a human servant. It had only taken a couple of days for the bite to heal, and she had more energy than she was used to. But Nik acted like he was deeply offended on her behalf. As they traveled, he had criticized Leisha at every opportunity for changing Samantha.

Samantha told Leisha she understood there had been no other choice, and didn't blame her. She still thought of Leisha as a sister. All of that was true, of course. But Samantha was nervous about how irreversible this change was. If Leisha were unable to feed herself, she would pull on Samantha's energy, or Samantha would have to drink by proxy. And Samantha knew she wouldn't be able to drink another person's blood.

It would be a strange existence. But she was already so different from other humans that maybe it wouldn't be so bad after all. Samantha shook her head at the internal argument. As far as she was concerned, the jury was still out on this latest development in her life.

"Samantha?" Leisha asked. "Is this something you want or something that you truly need?"

Samantha chewed her lip as she thought. A vivid image of Spencer popped into her head and she remembered the vision she'd had of him looking so forlorn. "I really do need this, Leisha. I don't think I can move on if I don't say goodbye." *I've lost too many people in my life to not have this.*

Shaking her head, the blonde vampire looked defeated.

"Fine. But can't stay long—one day, and that's it. Nikita will have to stay at the house, away from the sun. I'll shadow you at school to make sure there's no trouble."

Clearing his throat, Nik looked at Leisha. "If she goes early enough, I can handle being in the sun during the first hour of its rising."

"That would work." Samantha tried to keep her rising hope from showing. "The sun doesn't rise until halfway through first period."

Leisha mulled it over for a moment before responding. "Fine. Nikita, you'll shadow her at school. I'll go home and pack up some better weapons." She looked at Samantha, her brows drawn together. "Since Nikita will be with you, you won't have a lot of time to say goodbye. I hope it's enough."

Smiling broadly, Samantha gave her a tight hug. "Thank you, Leisha! This means a lot."

Leisha hugged her back, but her tone was gruff. "Don't blame me if we end up getting killed."

"They wouldn't kill you right away," Nik corrected. "You'd be thoroughly tortured first."

SAMANTHA WAS SERIOUSLY FEELING THE jet lag, but forced herself to drink the coffee she always swore she'd never touch. Even with the load of sugar she poured in, it was barely palatable. That task completed, she nodded to Nik and they left the house together.

Getting into the car, she drove her old Yugo to school for what would be the last time.

Teenagers were walking from their cars or buses to the main building, all of them talking animatedly to each other. Samantha parked near the football field. She could smell the fresh smoke from the kids who took drags under the bleachers.

They got out of the car and Samantha began walking toward the school. When Nik didn't follow, she turned and looked at him. "How exactly, are you planning to shadow me?"

"I'll stay in the parking lot, maybe scope around the outside of the building. But don't worry, I'll be inconspicuous."

"You're too handsome to go unnoticed." Samantha could feel her cheeks warming.

He gave her a rare smile. "While I appreciate the compliment, don't underestimate my stalking skills."

He walked in the other direction and she went into the building. Walking down the hall towards her first class, she weaved through groups of rowdy teenagers. After looking forward to getting back to school with her old friends for the last few days, it seemed incredibly anticlimactic. It was fifteen minutes before class started and she was able to spot her friend Stephanie in the crowded hallway.

"Hey, chica!" Stephanie's brown eyes lit up when she saw Samantha. "It seems like you were gone forever! Was everything alright with your little family emergency or whatever?"

They started walking together while Samantha recounted the lie Leisha had contrived. "Well, actually, my uncle's doing pretty bad and it turns out we have to move in and take care of him for a while." She shrugged. "It could be a few months, maybe even a couple of years. There's no way to know."

"That sucks." Stephanie gave her a look of sympathy. "You're going to miss all the awesome events! I know Spencer was going to ask you to the prom, and we girls are taking this way cool road trip for Spring Break. You won't be around for any of it!" She patted Samantha's arm. "When do you move? 'Cause you seriously have to come over and check out all the new outfits that I got for the road trip. And you totally should help us pick out our prom dresses before you go. It'll be a little party to say goodbye while you give us your much needed input!"

Grimacing, Samantha shook her head. "We fly out this afternoon. I came to school today so I could say goodbye."

"Aw." Stephanie gave her a hug. "In case I don't see you at lunch, I'll miss you! Text me whenever you want. And we're friends on Facebook, right? So we can still see what's going on in each other's lives." After an awkward pause, the girl smiled. "Well, bye then." She headed toward her class.

Samantha stood for a moment, looking at her retreating figure. That wasn't exactly what she thought it would be like. She realized she was expecting the kind of farewell she got when her mom died and she'd had to move in with her dad. But at that point, she'd lived in Florida her whole life and had grown up with those friends. She'd only been in Ohio for a few months. Apparently, that wasn't enough time to develop deep bonds with people.

After a few more minutes of contemplation, she decided Stephanie would spread the word for her and she didn't really need the goodbyes that she had begged Leisha for. She thought it was ironic that if she'd listened to Leisha, she would have pined for that closure with the friends she'd made. And now that she had gotten her way, she didn't actually need it.

Shaking her head, she swiveled to leave, and bumped right into Spencer.

"Whoa." He grabbing her arms to steady her. "Sorry, I was just about to say hello when you turned."

She gave him a reassuring smile. "It's fine. I'm glad I got to see you, 'cause I was heading out."

He frowned. "You're going? But school hasn't even started yet. Are you feeling okay?"

"Yeah, I'm fine." She bit her lip. "I'm moving today. We have to move in with my uncle to take care of him."

The light in his eyes dimmed.

The bell rang, echoing loudly and prompting students to hurry to their first period.

"Let's go someplace we can talk." Without waiting for her consent, he grabbed her hand and pulled her behind him. They ended up in the student lounge, squeezing through the quickly dispersing crowd. By the time they reached the sitting area, the vast room was empty.

As Samantha settled on a wooden bench, Spencer sat and turned to her. "What's going on with you?"

Her brows drew together. "I already told you, my uncle's really sick—"

"No, not that." He blew out a breath. "Sandy, how come you only left me a voicemail to tell me about your family emergency? Why didn't you call or text or something while you were away? And why am I just finding out you're moving?" The hurt in his eyes pierced her, but she didn't know what to say.

"Well . . . I guess I was just busy with everything, you know. There's been a lot going on."

His hands turned into fists on his lap. "That's no excuse. If I matter to you, then you'd be able to find the time to send me one damn text."

Swallowing, she looked into his eyes. "You're not my boyfriend, Spencer."

"I know, but... well," He looked away. "I thought we were headed in that direction."

She tentatively touched his fist. "If things were different, then I think we would have, but we're not going to. Not now."

Face turning slightly red, Spencer nodded without looking at her. "If you ever need anything, you've got my number."

She nodded and squeezed his arm, then let go. "Thanks, Spencer. You've been such a good friend."

He scoffed and stood. "I guess that's the big mistake I made, then." Looking down at her, his features softened momentarily. "Bye, Sandy." And with that, he walked away.

After he disappeared from her view, Samantha stood and headed to the parking lot. It was suddenly difficult to take a full breath, her eyes stinging with unshed tears.

While she felt bad about Spencer, she knew now that nothing more could have developed between them. He was great, but he didn't understand anything about her real life. No one did. *Spencer is my could-have-been, if I were a normal teenager.* If she could have a vision about her own future, she was positive it would look bleak and lonely. *If I can never be with a regular guy, then who can ever love me?*

With everyone in class, it took very little time to get to her car. She didn't get in, though. Just stood and stared at the keys in her hand without really seeing them. Nik came out of nowhere, his eyes sympathetic.

Looking into his hazel gaze, she couldn't stop the flow of tears that had been threatening to flow. Without a word, Nik stepped to her side and put his arm around her shoulders. Hesitantly, Samantha leaned into him and allowed a few tears to trek down her cheek.

She wasn't exactly sure what she was crying for. Maybe guilt about Spencer, or the life she should have had. It seemed like she didn't know a lot about her own feelings.

One thing she did know was that Nik felt wonderful and smelled delicious. He was her comfort and she couldn't give him up as easily as she had Spencer.

SPENCER STARED AT THE BROWN tile as he walked toward his class. He didn't really want to go to history right now, but couldn't bring himself to ditch school. Instead, he forced down the humiliating scene of only moments ago. He tried not to think about Sandy rejecting him so brutally.

He knew that he shouldn't be surprised. After all, she'd told him plenty of times that she didn't want a boyfriend. For some reason, he'd thought she would come around. He knew she was attracted to him but couldn't understand why she fought it.

And when she officially turned him down, it had felt like a punch to the gut. Without realizing it, he wandered outside. Looks like he was able to skip a class, after all.

Sitting on the grass, he stared at the sun just peaking over the horizon. He couldn't think of a time when he had felt more alone.

"Excuse me, but you're Spencer Hamblin, correct?"

Jerking in surprise, Spencer looked up to see a man in a dark suit and glasses standing over him.

"Yeah, that's me." Looking away, Spencer cursed himself for ditching. Now he was going to get into trouble.

The man reached into his jacket pocket and handed Spencer a wallet sized photo.

"Your principal informed us that you've been associating with this girl."

Looking at the smiling face of Sandy intensified the burning pain. She was a bit younger when the picture had been taken, but it was her alright.

Handing back the photo of the heartbreaker, he answered. "Yeah, I know Sandy."

"Would you help me find her class? I'm afraid there's been a family emergency and I need to talk to her."

Standing, Spencer looked into the man's eyes just as the sun hit them with its blaring light. "She already knows about her uncle. She's got a flight booked this afternoon"

The man studied Spencer's face for an uncomfortably long minute. For some reason, it made Spencer want to squirm. He suddenly felt like he was under a microscope and this guy was finding all of his secrets.

After a moment, the man gave a smile that didn't reach his cold eyes. "Thanks for your help anyway."

Spencer watched the man walk away, feeling unnerved. He

shook off the strange foreboding feeling, blaming it on his angst over Sandy. That man wasn't lying to him. Spencer caught the family resemblance almost immediately. They shared the exact same blue eyes, though hers held a lot more warmth.

CHAPTER 15

After putting up such a fuss, there was no way Leisha could admit out loud that she was actually glad they'd stopped in Ohio. She had just restocked her arsenal a few months ago and wasn't keen on having to do it all over again. It took time to acquire illegal weapons, and buying too many kinds of knives and other blades at once aroused suspicion.

The large canvas bag was loud as she zipped it, and she sighed in satisfaction. She was trying to think of anything else she'd like to pack when Samantha's Yugo pulled into the driveway.

"That was fast," she muttered as she carried her large bag downstairs to the entryway.

Samantha and Nikita walked in. Leisha paused when she noticed Samantha's red rimmed eyes, but knew better than to bring it up now. "Are you ready to go then?" She asked lightly, hoping to lift the atmosphere.

Samantha nodded.

"Alright. Well, instead of sitting around twiddling our

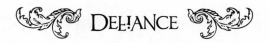

thumbs, let me see if we can change our booking." She pulled out her phone and looked up flights and availability, then transferred to a different itinerary. "Yep, if we leave now, we'll make it."

"But Nik can't be in the sun for more than a few minutes," protested Samantha.

"Leisha's tinted windows will be enough protection for me. I can manage at the airport easily enough and I can stay in the bathroom for most of the flight." He shrugged. "It wouldn't be the first time."

Samantha had a dubious expression, but Leisha rolled her eyes. "Trust me, Samantha. Vampires get around during the day much more easily now than they used to." She guided Samantha out the door.

They headed to Leisha's Audi, where she put her large bag in the trunk. Nikita climbed in the back, Samantha went in the passenger side, and then Leisha got in and started the car. The tires peeled out a bit as she put the car into gear and hit the gas.

It was an hour to the airport and the mood in the car was somber. As they were getting on the freeway, Leisha decided to turn on Samantha's favorite band to help her friend feel better. As the music played, she could see Samantha nodding her head to the beat from the corner of her eye. After a few songs, the teenager looked less sulky.

They were taking the freeway exit when Leisha noticed a black sedan behind them. She had seen it as they'd driven, but hadn't thought anything of it at the time. Now, her instincts sent up a red flag and she decided to turn into the downtown area. The sedan followed. When she made another abrupt turn, it stayed with her. Whoever was driving was definitely making their presence known. A black SUV turned from a Cross street to the right and stayed parallel to her side. Then one came in from the left. She pushed down hard on the gas and tried to outmaneuver them, but the streets were too crowded to do anything effective without hurting an innocent bystander.

Samantha looked pale, glancing among the three vehicles. Nikita appeared unperturbed, but Leisha didn't expect anything different from him.

Leisha steered towards the old industrial part of Cincinnati. This area was fairly deserted with a lot of rundown warehouses and abandoned factories. She floored the gas and pulled ahead of their pursuers enough to make a U-turn and drive on the sidewalk. They were two blocks away before the other cars turned around and continued their pursuit. Leisha had every confidence that she could lose them in the more crowded streets this time.

Nikita interrupted her planning. "We won't be able to outrun them." He pointed up. "They've got air support."

Leisha glanced up to see a black helicopter hovering above them. She cursed. "We're going to have to ditch the car."

Nikita nodded. She heard Samantha swallow hard.

Leisha stayed in the industrial section and looked around for a good place to run. Nikita found their escape route first.

"There." He was pointing at a large sewer entrance that stood perpendicular to the sidewalk. It was tall enough to stand upright as they ran underground.

Leisha nodded and swerved the car into an empty parking garage next to the sewer grate. Everyone jumped out as she cut the engine, and Leisha grabbed her weapons and their bags from the trunk before they jogged to the doorway. She gave Nikita a silent command. He nodded once and swooped Samantha into his arms. They would need to run too fast for the girl to keep up. They rushed to the sewer and Leisha yanked the heavy iron door from its frame. She put it back in hopes that their pursuers hadn't seen them go inside, but Leisha knew they wouldn't be so lucky. Their trail would be found, and soon.

Nikita put Samantha down and the three of them walked

speedily down the slope and into the overwhelming stench. The liquid waste came up to their shins. The putrid air was humid, the stink burning their nostrils.

Samantha started to gag, but kept her food down.

"Try not to think about the smell," Leisha advised. "You'll get used to it."

Samantha gave her an unbelieving look but stayed silent. She didn't splash much as she kept a good pace with them.

The sewers had openings and doorways here and there, letting in some dim illumination from the sun. After, a mile or so, Leisha heard several sets of feet pounding in their direction. Their assailants had used a different way to enter and were close.

They stopped at an open spot that led to several different tunnels. Leisha went behind a large, dry crate and ordered, "Nikita, take Samantha and go on. I'll jump them here where there's room to fight. I'll catch up in a bit."

"But if you can catch our scent, won't the other vamps be able to track us just as quickly?" Samantha trembled as she asked.

After a brief hesitation, Leisha answered. "They're humans, Samantha."

The girl's eyes widened in comprehension. "My father found us." She gulped as Nikita nodded.

As if summoned, a gate about forty feet down one of the tunnels opened and Mason Campbell jumped down, along with ten other soldiers trickling in behind him. Before any-one could respond, one of the soldiers pointed some kind of launcher toward them and fired. Within a second Nikita threw Samantha to the filthy ground and lay over her.

Leisha tried to dive away but wasn't fast enough. The blast threw her into a wall. A small, open pipe skewered through her back and stuck out the right side of her chest. She gave a ragged breath as she glanced at the dull object protruding from her. The damage wasn't permanent, but it was certainly painful and made her more vulnerable.

Samantha rushed over to her. "How can we help her?" She asked Nikita.

In response, Nikita grabbed Leisha by her shoulders and quickly pulled. She grunted as the pipe slid quickly, grinding against her organs and ribs. Looking down at the blood she was losing, Leisha knew she wouldn't have the fortitude to fight the men that were quickly splashing their way nearer and nearer by the second. If she was unable to exchange blows, then she wouldn't be able to protect Samantha. Coming to a decision she never thought she'd have to make, Leisha glanced at her young friend.

It was difficult to speak since her lung was practically non-existent, but she forced herself to talk over the pain. "Samantha," Her scratchy voice was lower than a whisper. "I need to draw your energy to heal." Blood threatened to choke her the more she spoke. "I have to do this so I can protect you, understand?"

Lips trembling, Samantha nodded without any hesitation. Nikita, meanwhile, had assembled a screw-served machine gun from Leisha's bag and was pouring rounds down the tunnel at the soldiers that were almost upon them.

Biting her lip, Leisha placed her left hand over Samantha's and began to pull in the girl's energy. As she did, she could feel the torn muscles and ligaments healing. Her lung and bones weaved themselves together until there was only raw skin where the wound had been. She was tempted to draw more energy to heal it completely, but forced herself to stop.

She looked up to see Samantha was pale and shaking. She helped the girl down to sit in the putrid water. "Wait here," she instructed before standing. "I'll keep you safe, Sam."

Eyes showing too much white, the teenager nodded.

Leisha stood and turned, meeting Mason's gaze across the way. His blue eyes were fiery with contempt. No doubt he'd witnessed what they'd done. Leisha wasn't sure if his research had covered the relationship between a vampire and her human servant, but he could probably deduce that Leisha had somehow used his daughter to heal.

The soldiers were almost upon them.

Leisha grabbed a handgun and a long, curved katana and joined Nikita.

"I've got this," she said as she eyed the men. "Get Samantha out of here right now. I'll catch up."

He was moving to obey before Leisha finished speaking. Her two companions grabbed their bags and hurried down a corridor to the right. Leisha surveyed the men and Mason. This would not take very long. They stopped about ten feet in front of her, positioned in two rows. Their guns pointed at her chest, she crouched into a defensive position. She wondered why they hadn't assaulted her yet.

"Remember, I want her alive."

Mason's order gave Leisha a vivid flashback to her capture six months ago. She promised herself she wouldn't endure Mason's sick experiments again. Especially now that a child was growing within her womb.

Their aim shifted slightly. A man on the end of the second line opened his mouth to give the order to fire. Just as his strong voice started to sound, Leisha rushed into the middle of their formation, making it impossible for them to shoot her.

Ignoring the protests of her still healing muscles, Leisha raised the sword in her left hand and decapitated two men before they had time to defend themselves. She heard a man stalking her from behind. Without turning, she slammed her sword into his sternum and up to his heart. He gurgled blood as he died, the weapon was still embedded in him. Another soldier kicked her sword hand, forcing her to lose her grip. Maybe it was because she was injured, but the impact felt stronger than it should have.

He raised his gun toward her when she turned. She shot him in the head at point blank range. His shot veered to the right as he toppled, the bullet hitting a pipe in the process. A thin stream of water hissed into the air.

Before she could make another move, two men grabbed her from both sides in bruising grips. They pulled her arms behind her at painful angles. One of the men tried to pry the weapon from her fingers, but she refused to let go of the gun. The other soldiers closed in around them, aiming their weapons.

Leisha kicked out to her right at the man's knee, his scream echoing over the sound of his bones crunching. He promptly let go of her gun hand and fell to the ground to clutch his broken leg.

She swiveled and shot the other man holding her. The bullet landed between his eyes, gray matter erupting behind him before he collapsed.

The last two soldiers began firing. Pitching to the side and down, she avoided being hit anywhere vital. One bullet lodged in her thigh and the rest grazed her arms. The old brick wall behind her exploded where the last of the bullets struck, bits of clay pelting her back.

Leisha sprang forward from a crouch, firing the rest of her rounds. She hit two men, but they must have only been flesh wounds since they continued to approach. Tossing the empty weapon, she targeted the man in the middle and brought her knee up to flip the gun out of his hands. Before he could respond, she punched his nose with the heel of her hand. He grunted as the cartilage cracked and blood gushed over his chin. Pressing her advantage, she hefted herself onto him and used him as an anchor. Her body parallel to the ground, she spun around her human pillar, her legs almost working

like scissors, kicking the other man squarely in the side of the head. His neck cracked.

A cacophony of yelling commenced as she knocked out the first two men. Some of the soldiers were grunting at the pain, and others were shouting orders that couldn't be deciphered through the chaos. As she kicked a third man in the chest, someone grabbed her from behind and spun, throwing her into the air.

Using that momentum, Leisha grabbed and held on to a brick beam from the low ceiling and slanted her legs forward to land on one of the men's shoulders. She squeezed her thighs together until the bones in his neck made a familiar crunching sound. Letting go of the ceiling, she used her hands to crush the throats of the men rushing in on both sides.

She landed on her feet and felt a bullet go through her side. She ran and darted into one of the corridors faster than a human could track. Just inside the archway, she jumped on the ceiling and pushed her weight into either side of the walls to prop herself up. Two men came through and shot their weapons every direction but up. She dropped and landed behind them, splashing in the sewage. The men turned. As they fired, she jabbed stiff fingers into their temples, coating her digits in sticky matter. They fell to the ground as the bullets hit both of her shoulders.

Three remaining men came behind her, firing. She rushed them in a frontal assault. Several bullets grazed her body, one hitting her in the elbow. Leisha kicked her leg up to knock their weapons out of their hands and flipped her leg around, collecting the guns in the crook of her knee. She stood up straight and let the guns clatter to the ground. Before they could attempt anything else, she bashed two of their heads together as hard as she could, the sound resembling smashing pumpkins.

The remaining man was the guy whose leg she broke. Despite his injury, he moved swiftly. He jumped on her, knocking her on her back to the filthy ground. His hands squeezed painfully around her neck, his legs straddling her body.

Leisha thrust her body to the side, lifting her arms up above her head, and pulling his hands off her. She then elbowed his head, which should have knocked him out. But it didn't.

Brown eyes blazing, he lifted his body off her slightly and punched her in the jaw. Leisha's head snapped to the side, half of her face becoming covered in the muck. She propelled her knee up into his butt, making the man fall forward. Before he could land on her head, Leisha stood and spun. The soldier was rising from his hands and knees. The vampire stepped forward and broke his neck with both of her hands. He fell into the murky water with a loud plop.

Her injuries burned, and she pressed her lips together to control her panting. She must have been slow with her reflexes. She shouldn't have been shot so many times. At least it was with regular bullets and no tranquilizers this time.

Walking over and pulling her sword out of the man she'd practically gutted, Leisha looked around. There were only eight lifeless bodies and the smell of smoke from the launcher. Nothing else. Mason and some of his men must have gotten past while she'd been fighting.

Cursing herself for killing all the humans before drinking from them, she limped after Samantha and Nikita.

CHAPTER 16

Samantha had no strength to walk, let alone run, but Nik said he didn't mind carrying her. She knew he wasn't moving as fast as he could and wondered if it was because there were so many twists and turns down here.

Leisha taking her energy had been, for lack of a better word, draining. Her mind felt fuzzy, and she was having a hard time focusing her eyes. Her body was fatigued to the point of shaking. However, it was nice that she could help Leisha. She often felt like a useless damsel in distress, sitting in the corner while everyone else fought, so being able to contribute was a great feeling. But Samantha hoped she wouldn't have to go through that experience again.

When they came to a fork in the tunnels, Nik stopped and looked at each corridor.

"How do you know which one we should take," she asked.

Nik shrugged. "I don't. But I'm trying to decide which direction would give us easier access to get above ground again." He paused and angled his head. "Some of them are catching up to us."

He went right, but again, didn't use his super vampire speed. After several more twists and turns, he put her down. "They're still keeping up with us," he explained. "I need to get rid of them. Stay here and wait for me."

She licked her suddenly dry lips. "Can't we simply outrun them?"

He shook his head. "It isn't working. But I can get rid of them quickly."

Even in their current circumstances, Samantha was surprised to discover that she actually condoned his intention to kill their pursuers.

She nodded and he moved to leave. On an impulse, she grabbed his shirt and pulled him down towards her face. She pressed her lips to his. Nik hesitated at first, then kissed her back. It was soft and tender, but it ended too soon and he returned to where they had come.

While waiting, she put her fingers to her lips. They still felt warm and tingly from the kiss. She sat thinking about that kiss, so engrossed that she didn't notice the minutes slipping by.

A sudden explosion ripped Samantha from her reverie. She jerked and almost fell, slapping her hand on the wall for balance. It took a moment for her sight to clear before she took a few steps forward. She could already smell the acrid scent of smoke mingled with the sewage.

"Nik?" She called softly. "Are you okay?"

No answer.

"Nik!" she called more loudly this time.

She exhaled at the sound of footsteps approaching. But it wasn't Nik who stepped into the light; it was her father. She gasped and stepped back.

"You know," Mason said, his brown hair covered with bits of debris, "it's sad to see such a reaction from my own daughter." He raised a gun and pointed it at her chest. "Of course,

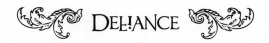

knowing that you serve those *creatures* makes me cringe when I see you, too."

Staring at the gun, she backed up until she felt the wall behind her. "So now you're going to kill me, is that it?"

Mason scoffed. "Hardly. No, I have something planned for you." He took a few more steps toward her. "And once it's all said and done, Samantha, I think you'll thank me for it."

"What did you do to Nik?"

"If you're referring to that male vampire, we took care of him." He smiled. "We've developed some weapons that even vampires aren't immune to."

Breathing was suddenly difficult as she leaned into the curved wall.

"Your beloved Leisha should be dead by now, too." He scratched his chin. "I wonder if you'd be as sad for my death as you are for those monsters."

Tears pouring down her face, she glared at her father. "You're just as much of a murderer! You have no morals, like some kind of government-approved sociopath!"

He pointed the gun at her again, shaking in anger. "Watch your mouth. The only reason I'm here is to save you!"

Frustration mounting, she burst out, "Why can't you just leave us alone?"

"We're family, my girl. I'll never leave you alone."

"You did a first rate job of it for ten years." Something was off, nagging at her brain, but Samantha couldn't figure out what it was. Her mind was still muddled.

"Things are different! You're with vampires. How can I ignore that fact? And look at what they've done to you!" Mason pushed a hand through his hair. "But don't worry, Samantha. I think I can fix it. You need to come with me."

"She's not going anywhere with you."

They both turned to see Nik slowly walking towards them.

He'd obviously been injured in the blast and was limping, but her heart lightened to see that he was alright. She smiled at him, and then it finally hit her. She'd had a vision about this.

She saw her father, glaring at Nik. She screamed a warning, even before he raised his gun, but it was too late. Mason fired. Samantha looked back at Nik to see him staring at his chest in surprise. The red liquid quickly oozed across his chest and down his stomach as the vampire fell to the ground.

"No!" Samantha cried and rushed toward him. A firm grip around her arm prevented her from reaching her destination. She pulled against Mason's grasp. "Let me go! I hate you! If I see you again, I'll be the one to pull the trigger!"

She saw a flash of hurt in his eyes, but they quickly turned back to steely resolve. "You don't know what you're saying." He turned and pulled her with him as he began walking.

Samantha continued to struggle and punched his arm and shoulder with her free hand. It seemed to have no impact on him while Samantha's strength quickly waned.

They had gone forward about twenty feet before something crashed into Mason from behind, making him lose his hold on her arm.

She looked down to see Leisha pinning Mason on his stomach, half his face in the dirty slime. The vampire reached toward his head, then hesitated and looked at Samantha.

The question in her eyes was evident. Should she kill him?

Even though moments ago, Samantha's dearest wish was to see her father dead, she now hesitated. Though Leisha would be the one to twist his neck, Samantha would be giving her the go ahead. She would be the one responsible for her father's death. She knew she wouldn't be able to live with that.

She shook her head.

Leisha turned back to Mason and lifted his head by his hair.

She slammed his face into the ground, making a loud smacking sound. Samantha grimaced but didn't say anything. Of course, they would have to knock him out so he couldn't to follow them.

She pivoted away from her father and searched out Nik. He was still lying in the same spot, covered in his own blood.

Moving over to him, she knelt by his side. "Are you okay?"

He was clearly in pain, but held on to his usual passive expression. "It will heal." He turned his head to Leisha. "He moved faster than a mere human."

Leisha nodded. "A couple of the men I fought were able to sneak up on me. They shouldn't have been able to."

Feeling the blood drain from her face, Samantha shuddered. "What has my father done to those men?"

They were quiet for a moment. Samantha figured they were all contemplating her question.

"We need to get out of here," Leisha said. "We'll have to find a different way to travel, since they'll be checking all the outgoing flights."

Samantha leaned down to help Nik, but Leisha stopped her. "You're still weak. I can handle Nikita." Grabbing their bags, Samantha turned to follow. She noticed that Leisha didn't look very well, either. Her friend had blood and filth all over her body and the girl couldn't tell how many injuries the vampire had taken.

After Leisha hefted a groaning Nik, they headed in a direction opposite of where they came from. It was slow moving, both vampires limping, Leisha's impairment more pronounced since Nik leaned on her.

Samantha was completely disoriented, but trusted Leisha to find the way. It took about twenty minutes until the vampire began climbing a metal ladder to get above ground. She came out of the manhole into an alley that reeked of garbage and rotting food. It was like fresh air blasting through her nostrils compared to the sewer. Samantha took a deep breath, filling her lungs as completely as she could.

The sun was still high in the sky. Leisha paused in the shadows, looking Nik over.

"Can't we find a place in the sewer where we can hide until sundown?" Samantha queried.

Nik shook his head. "We need to leave before backup arrives and combs every inch of the tunnels."

Grimacing, Leisha nodded. "They'll probably be expecting us to wait in the sewer. It would be better to get out of here now."

Putting her hand on Nik's shoulder, Samantha gave Leisha a hopeless look. "How?"

Nik gestured to his bag. "I have a jacket with a large hood that should cover most of me. There's also some gloves in the side pocket."

Samantha bent over, pulled out the items, and handed them over. Nik draped himself and insisted on walking without assistance.

Several construction workers stared at them as they ambled quickly down the sidewalk, and no wonder: they smelled horrible and looked worse, their appearance bloody and disheveled. Both Nik and Leisha were still bleeding from their injuries. Samantha hoped no one called the authorities and reported them.

Leisha stopped at a run-down motel. It took little convincing for the manager to give them a room, even though they looked a mess. Leisha merely had to pull out some cash and pay for two nights, regardless of the fact that they'd only be staying for a few hours.

They each took a turn to use the shower.

Nik came out in clean clothes and looking as handsome as ever, though he was still pale.

"Are you alright, Nik?" Samantha's brows drew together. "Shouldn't you be healed by now?"

Shrugging, Nik casually explained. "I'm not sure what was in the blast that Mason set off, but it knocked me out. I think there was something potent for vampires in the gas. Combine that and the fact that this is the longest I've gone without feeding, it's taking me a bit longer to heal. That's all."

Putting a hand to her throbbing temple, Samantha forced a light tone. "Looks like we're all feeling pretty bad today."

"Maybe we should stay here tonight," Nik suggested. "We can let everyone get some rest."

Leisha shook her head. "That guy at the front desk will give us away to the first person who asks. We're only here to clean up and regroup. We'll find a different place to stay." She studied Nik. "Then we'll let Samantha get some sleep while we go out and feed. You may need two feedings to bring you up to snuff."

Nik glanced at the stained and cracked wallpaper. "Good enough."

Less than an hour later, they were again walking the streets of downtown Cincinnati, only this time no one gave them a second glance. Once they were in the nicer part of town, Leisha pointed to a respectable looking hotel and told them to wait while she got a room. If word got out that officials were looking for two women and a man traveling together, she didn't want anyone to associate that with them.

They were in their room in no time, and Samantha barely managed to take off her shoes before collapsing onto one of the beds. Closing her dry eyes, Samantha listened to Nik and Leisha drop their bags on the carpet and walk around.

"See ya in a little while," the girl mumbled. She was already asleep when the door clicked shut behind the vampires.

CHAPTER 17

Walking the dark streets, Leisha was able to read almost every person's mind in this area. She needed to find the slimiest of people so she could justify killing them. Normally, she didn't feed this often. The only way to rejuvenate Samantha as well as fully heal from her own injuries was to drink blood so the energy would flow through their bond.

Leisha didn't miss the irony that she was now feeding more often and Nikita was feeding less. It was obvious to her that he didn't like Samantha seeing him killing humans.

"You and Samantha are getting too close," Leisha said to Nikita. She knew she was being abrupt, but couldn't stop herself from saying it. "It concerns me."

Uncharacteristically, he blew out a ragged breath. "I know."

"But," she prompted.

"But . . ." He glanced away. "I don't know. I can't seem to help myself. I care… deeply for her."

She squeezed his arm briefly. "I get it, Nikita, really. Samantha is special and I don't blame you. It's just that," she

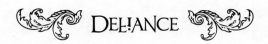

paused, trying to search for the right words, "it wouldn't be right. If you two were together, she'd have to condone your lifestyle. You murder for a living."

"You believe I would dim the light within her," Nikita murmured.

Leisha didn't disagree, so remained silent.

"You're right," he admitted. "I can't leave you guys now, though. Not while the other vampires search for us." He met her gaze and she was shocked to see the passion in his eyes. "I have to keep her safe." His face was almost blank, but the emotions swirling in the undertone caught her off guard.

Searching his face, Leisha nodded and they continued on.

It took some time to find the sort of scum Leisha was comfortable killing, especially enough for both Nikita and herself, so it was midnight when they returned to the hotel. Samantha was still down for the count. Though older vampires didn't need much sleep, Leisha decided that they both should get some rest. They needed energy to spare in case they found more trouble the following day.

Leisha shared a bed with Samantha and Nikita got the second one to himself.

In the morning, Leisha woke to blinding sunlight filtering through cracks in the curtains and Samantha stretching next to her.

"How are you feeling?" Leisha asked.

"Much better. I can't believe how tired I was. I must have slept for at least twelve hours."

Sitting up, Leisha nodded. Guilt filtered through her and she bit her lip. "I'm sorry I had to do that to you."

Samantha waved a hand. "It's in the past. But I hope we don't have to do the whole *chi*-sucking thing too much. It felt like having my insides sucked out through a straw." She looked around. "Where did Nik go?"

Getting out of bed, Leisha shrugged. "He couldn't have gone far with the sun up. Let's get ready so we can leave when he's back."

They changed their clothes and Leisha packed up their meager belongings. Nikita returned shortly with omelet-filled biscuits and scones with honey butter. He'd bought them from the restaurant downstairs. Samantha devoured her breakfast, and the three of them hung out in the room, waiting for twilight so they could leave. They'd slept late enough that they only had a few hours to wait.

As they were getting ready to leave, Leisha went to use the bathroom. After taking care of business, she noticed her pants were fitting rather snugly.

Inspecting her stomach, she could see it was already beginning to bulge. "This is going to be an adventure," she mumbled to herself and left the top button of her jeans open.

Once they were finally off, they took a taxi to a car rental place. There, Leisha made arrangements to get a recreational vehicle.

"We're going to drive up to Canada in that thing?" Samantha whispered to her. "I thought the point was to not be obvious."

"Nonsense. We're an average couple going on a trip to Niagara Falls with our daughter."

Samantha grimaced. "If I'm your daughter, then you guys had me when you were in junior high."

Unable to contain her grin, Leisha relented. "My niece, then. You've had a lot of bad behavior problems at school and got expelled, so we're taking you with us on our annual vacation."

Sighing, Samantha agreed to the cover story. Leisha looked over to see Nikita watching Samantha with amusement teasing the corners of his lips. Leisha hadn't seen him show so much expression in all the centuries she'd known him. A niggling remorse pushed at her for what she'd said to him last night,

but she pushed it aside. Samantha wasn't even an adult yet. A relationship between her and Nikita simply was not right.

They drove through the night with only a few brief stops. By the time the sun began to rise, they'd arrived at Niagara Falls.

Finding a spot in the crowded lot, Leisha parked the large vehicle. "We need to switch vehicles before continuing into Canada."

Samantha stood and stretched. "Fine by me, but can we get some food first? I'm dying here."

They walked over to a twenty-four-hour sit-down restaurant and went inside. As soon as Leisha smelled the delicious aromas, she realized that she was ravenous herself.

Frowning, she looked down at her stomach.

"What's the matter?" Nikita asked.

"Nothing, it's just… I think being pregnant is making me hungry for human food."

Both her companions wore thoughtful expressions, but no one said anything about it.

When their meal arrived, Leisha ate her own dish of steak, mashed potatoes, and sweet potato fries with the rapacity of a starving wolf. Unfortunately, the large plate didn't satisfy her cravings. Studying Nikita, she saw that he was only halfway through his platter of chicken fajitas. "Can I help you finish that off?" she asked.

Giving a small shrug, Nikita pushed the food toward her, and placed her empty plate in front of him.

Smiling gratefully at him, Leisha dug into the delicious food.

Samantha looked at her with wide eyes. "I don't think I've ever seen you eat so much."

Feeling heat creep into her cheeks, she mumbled, "Well, I am eating for two."

"Aren't you supposed to be sick at this point? My mom told

me she couldn't keep anything down for the first four months when she was pregnant with me."

Leisha shrugged. "I almost threw up on the plane that one time."

Samantha laughed. "That was, like, maybe five days after you conceived."

Licking her greasy lips, Leisha said, "Who knows what this pregnancy will be like. Besides, I'm already getting bigger. I wouldn't be surprised if I had to buy maternity pants next week."

Mouth shaping a small O, Samantha exhaled. "I didn't really think about that, but being a vampire could accelerate the development of the pregnancy, right?"

Leisha shrugged, but Nikita was the one who answered. "Not necessarily. I think this merely verifies that Leisha is carrying the prophecy child, and that he'll have some unique gifts in his genetic makeup."

Leisha touched her belly, wondering what this baby would do when he arrived. She brushed the thought aside. It was pointless to stress over something that far in the future; sufficient to the day, and all that.

Samantha and Nikita were patiently waiting while Leisha polished off the fajitas. Getting up, they paid the check and went about turning in their rental and taking a taxi to a run-down auto shop. Leisha talked the owner into selling them a car at an incredibly reasonable price. They ended up with a sedan. Leisha and Nik spent a frustrating fifteen minutes getting all their bags to fit into the trunk, but they finally managed it. They got through the border without a problem and were heading north to Sudbury.

The trip lasted another eight hours. Once the sun came up, Nikita had to lie down in the back with a blanket to cover

him. Luckily, it wasn't too long after his little transfer that they finally arrived.

Samantha complained about sore muscles, and Leisha now had more empathy for the poor human. She hadn't realized how easily muscles stiffened until she'd experienced it again.

Nikita waited in a shadowed corner of the lobby while Leisha got them a room. As they rode the elevator, Samantha commented, "We can't live in a hotel for however long we're going to stay here. We need to find a place with a basement for Nikita."

Leisha agreed. "That's the next phase of my plan. You two can stay here and rest while I look for a house to rent."

Samantha's brow wrinkled. "I thought you had a lawyer guy to do that kind of stuff for you."

"I usually do, but not when I'm trying to lay low. Things can always get leaked through a third party."

Leisha entered their room first to make sure the drapes were drawn tightly. Once it was dark enough inside, Nikita and Samantha came in. Leisha stayed just long enough to get their bags situated, then she was out the door again. Crossing the lobby, she walked to the front desk and asked the concierge where there was access to a computer. The concierge smiled and directed her to a cozy alcove off the main lobby that had computers with free WiFi. She mentally rolled her eyes at herself for not taking the time to get a new phone. She'd ditched her iPhone in Spain and hadn't bothered with getting a replacement. Once she found a new place to live, her next priority would be getting another smartphone .

Leisha looked up rental houses online, and then she checked where they were in reference to the city. She wanted it to be somewhat remote, but not in an obvious way, and it would still need to be close enough to the city that they wouldn't stand out.

Finding one that met her criteria, she called the number and scheduled an appointment to look at it in an hour. With time to kill, she drove to a French café that the concierge recommended and enjoyed a few chocolate-filled rolls. As she was finishing the last one, her stomach rumbled appreciatively.

She glanced down at her little baby bump. "I see you have great taste."

The woman at the counter across from Leisha gave her a knowing smile, and Leisha returned it. Checking the time, she got up and went to the house she hoped to rent.

It was older, but had a new furnace. The main floor had the original hardwood floors and it needed new windows. The basement had never been finished, and it was obvious the place didn't get much traffic. After thoroughly inspecting it, she decided it would suit their needs. It had three exits to the outside, giving them options of escape. The basement wasn't large, but Nikita could handle it.

Pivoting on the hardwood floor, she looked at the owner, who had introduced herself as Mrs. Begnoche. "I think this would be great. And the price is fair enough."

The older woman smiled broadly, and Leisha thought she detected relief from her eyes and the way the matron's heartbeat. "Wonderful. When would you like to move in?"

"Tomorrow, if that's suitable. My husband's company is putting us up in a hotel until we find a place, but I feel bad taking advantage of them for too long. Besides, we need a place we can call home."

Jaw dropping slightly, Mrs. Begnoche fidgeted with the long sleeves of her sweater. "It may be the day after that. After all, I must get the paper work ready and do a background check."

Giving her warmest smile, Leisha nodded. "I'm sorry if I've overwhelmed you."

"No darling. Everything's fine."

Tucking some strands of hair behind her ear, Leisha

lowered her voice. "The thing is, if we stay in the hotel for one more night, I won't have enough cash for the deposit you're asking for."

Mrs. Begnoche licked her lips. "Cash?"

"Yes."

"Well," the older woman said. "I suppose we could speed up this process if you're paying cash for the deposit and first and last month's rent."

"Thanks so much," Leisha gushed. "This will be wonderful for my family!"

She made the arrangements to sign the papers in the morning when Mrs. Begnoche would provide the keys to the house.

Feeling satisfied, she drove back to the hotel. Leisha was surprised to find Nikita sleeping, and even further startled to see Samantha resting her head on his arm as they napped. It appeared that they fell asleep watching a movie.

Leisha turned off the television and glanced over at the couple. "That better be as far as it went," she grumbled as she made her way into the bathroom to shower and change.

CHAPTER 18

February 9th

Moving into the little home that Leisha had found took exactly as much time as it took them to haul their bags in from the car. Samantha paused when she saw the place. It was a lot more run-down than Samantha had ever seen since she'd been moving around with Leisha. She tried not to be bothered by it. Besides, it was sufficient, and she knew Leisha chose this home for safety reasons. There were no furnishings , so the day after they'd moved in, Samantha and Leisha went shopping while Nik hung around in the basement.

Samantha hadn't liked the thought of him being in that small, dank place all day, but he had reassured her with a gentle squeeze on the shoulder. A large part of her wanted to stay with him and talk, like they had yesterday. Maybe even fall asleep on his shoulder again. Samantha would love to cuddle with him, and feel his arms around her, but she wasn't bold enough to try to make it happen.

She slid a glance at Leisha as they walked into a mattress store. She knew her friend did not approve of their burgeoning

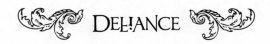

relationship and it saddened her that she couldn't confide these feelings to Leisha. It was all so new to her. Nothing like when she'd thought about Spencer.

So she kept it to herself, not ready to share her thoughts with Nik, either. Though she'd opened up to him at the hotel the day before, she was sure he wouldn't respond well if she talked about them having a romantic relationship . Besides, she didn't know what she'd call him if they did. The term boyfriend just seemed too . . . *juvenile* for what she felt for him. She smiled as she remembered laying on the bed with him last night, burrowing into his arms and smelling the shampoo from his hair as she talked about her mother.

"Even though she's been gone for over a year, I still have moments where it feels like she just died on me." She'd said. "I feel kinda dumb for crying about it time and again, so I try to remember the good times and enjoy what she means to me now."

His hand had come up and stroked her cheek. "I'm always amazed at how you look at things. You seem so young in many ways, then you say things like this and I think you have more wisdom than vampires who have lived for hundreds of years."

Cheeks warming, she'd glanced up at him and saw a tenderness that she never expected to see shining in his eyes. Her breathing had accelerated at the thought that he might kiss her. But he'd nudged her head back down on his shoulder and they'd fallen into a comfortable silence, sinking into sleep before Leisha'd returned.

"Please stop sighing like a moonstruck puppy and help me get these things ordered." Leisha was looking at her with a bemused expression, a frown tugging at one corner of her mouth.

Blinking her thoughts away, Samantha lightly stroked the mattress in front of her. "Sorry," she mumbled and set her mind to staying on task.

Sighing, Leisha sat on the mattress and met Samantha's

gaze. The vampire's face was tight, with no sign of emotion showing.

"You have something unpleasant to tell me," Samantha guessed.

"Look, Samantha, I've never tried to replace your mother. We act more like roommates than anything else, so I realize it may not be my place to say anything."

Samantha's shoulders tensed. "We also tell each other everything. So go ahead."

Leisha interlocked her fingers as she spoke. "You and Nikita are a bad idea. He's hundreds of years older than you, and has done things that would curdle your blood."

Speaking through stiff lips, Samantha did her best to keep her voice calm. "I know who he is and what he's done. But I also know that there's more to him than that. I think I may be the only one who's looked past the assassin side and seen his true depth."

Nostrils flaring slightly, Leisha stood and stepped closer. "I don't discount any of that, Samantha. And I won't stand in your way since you're certainly old enough to make your own decisions. But you should know that, along with his depth, is a darkness. And it will drag you down if you allow it."

Samantha blinked rapidly as Leisha turned away. *She doesn't understand.* The thought made her stomach sink. Her friend had always agreed with Samantha on just about everything. Samantha realized that they would never see eye to eye on this, and she could already feel the rift it caused between them.

Two hours later, they had finished buying all the furniture they'd need and grabbed a bite at the nearest restaurant. She'd noticed Leisha's appetite seemed insatiable lately, but chose not to say anything—she wasn't sure if Leisha would be amused or insulted.

"After this, I need to find a maternity store."

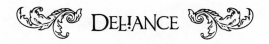

Samantha dropped her fork full of noodles. "Already? You're not showing yet."

"Well, you haven't seen me naked."

Samantha laughed. "No, and I don't plan to anytime soon."

Leisha chuckled with her, then grew serious. "But really, I can't even zip my pants anymore. I've been wearing long shirts to hide it."

Samantha shook her head. "At this rate, do you know when he'll be born?"

Leisha shook her head. "I've no idea. All I can do is hope that we don't get ambushed."

On that note, they paid their check and drove to a small shopping mall that had maternity clothes. Leisha bought enough for the duration of her pregnancy.

The sun was setting when they got home. Nik came up the stairs and gave her a small half-smile. "It's too bad we're not further up north, then we'd hardly have any daylight to contend with."

"The nights are still pretty long here," Leisha commented. "Do you need to feed anytime soon?"

Nik took a second to answer. "No, I think I'll be alright for another week."

"Good." Leisha said. "Speaking of food, we didn't go grocery shopping yet. Do you want to come with us?"

He nodded. "And we should get some board games or something as well. I have a feeling time will go by rather slowly while we're here."

Once in the car, with the heater blasting, Leisha spoke as she drove. "I've looked into homeschooling for you, Samantha. I don't think it's a good idea for you to attend public school since Nikita and I can't assure your safety. But you can still go out occasionally on field trips with other homeschoolers so you don't have to feel stifled all the time."

"Sounds fair enough." Samantha watched the snow covered trees they passed. "Maybe I should get my G.E.D. and not worry about this stuff anymore."

"We'll talk about that later," Leisha promised.

They drove into town and spent time picking out food at the local grocery store. Once they were back and had put away all the groceries, Nik treated them to some of his cooking. He didn't have any himself, but seemed pleased at the appreciative mmm that escaped Samantha's lips every now and then.

After dinner, they got out a deck of cards and played a few different games. Leisha's eyes were drooping by the end and she went off to bed.

Samantha looked after her in concern. "Leisha used to only need a couple of hours of sleep per day, if that. Now it seems like she needs a full eight hours, maybe more."

Nik tilted his head in the direction of Leisha's bedroom. "Don't worry about her. Pregnancy can wreak some crazy changes to a woman's body."

A smirk came to her lips. "Yeah? And you're an expert on the whole process?"

He shrugged. "When I was human, I was the oldest of twelve children. There were several births I had to assist with. Plus, I've been reading about it online so we'll be prepared when Leisha pops."

She giggled at the last sentence. "You don't talk much about your life when you were human. All I know is that you're from Russia and were a hired assassin. And now I've discovered that you had a huge family."

"Well, only four of my siblings survived childhood, so not that big of a family."

Frowning, she grabbed his hand. "Only five out of twelve? That's terrible, Nik."

He squeezed her fingers. "It was simply the way of life at that time. My mother was strong as an ox and always recovered,

though you could tell when she was thinking of her kids that didn't make it. She'd get this look of sorrow on her face and wouldn't respond to anyone for a while."

Shaking her head, she murmured. "I can't imagine."

He smiled at her. "You won't have to, not these days. When you have children, I'm sure they'll be strong and healthy."

Samantha tried to summon a smile, but couldn't. If she and Nik stayed together, they would never have children. "We could always adopt."

His hand jerked in hers. "What?"

She hadn't realized she'd spoken out loud. Her face flushed. "Nothing. I was just... thinking about something else."

Nik studied her face for a while, his lips downturned. On anyone else, it would look like a stoic expression, but Samantha could tell that he was thinking hard about something. He opened his mouth as if he would say something, then closed it. Laying down a card on the pile, he lightened his tone. "So, do you want to keep playing, or are you afraid I'll beat you again?"

"Hey," Samantha protested with a soft punch to his shoulder. "I won two games so far."

"Yes, but I've won four. I'd say the odds are in my favor."

Lips compressing in concentration, Samantha turned her attention to their card game.

TWO WEEKS WENT BY WITH little incident. Samantha was beginning to sleep in later and later in the day so she could stay up and spend time with Nik. Leisha never said anything, but her disapproval could easily be felt through the scowls she threw at Nik and her compressed lips when she was around them.

Leisha had been getting rather moody lately as well. The vampire would say she felt "cooped up" and go out for a walk or a drive to "clear her head". She was also definitely showing. She easily looked like she was four or five months pregnant.

"I can't hide my state anymore," Leisha complained to them

one day. "What if the vampires find me now that it's obvious to anyone I'm pregnant." She paced in the kitchen, the muscles in her cheeks twitching with agitation.

"This is an advantage," Nik argued. "No one is expecting such accelerated growth and will still be looking for you as you were, not with a rotund belly."

Leisha sighed and pressed her lips together into a flat line.

Taking Samantha's hand, Nik stood and gently tugged on her. "Let's go into the front room. We have some long overdue practicing to do."

Eyebrows knitting together, Samantha followed him, not sure what he was referring to.

Once in the main room, Nik let go of her and proceeded to move all their newly purchased furniture against one wall.

"What exactly are you thinking, Nik?"

Stepping in front of her, he waggled his eyebrows playfully. "What do you think I'm thinking?"

Blushing, Samantha giggled nervously. "No really. What's going on?"

"Well, you need to learn self-defense." Hands on her shoulders, he looked mildly concerned. "I certainly hope you'll never need to use it. But since there are all kinds of dangerous people looking for us, I thought it would be prudent to educate you."

Snorting, Samantha pulled out of his grasp and walked to the middle of the room. "I think 'all kinds of dangerous people' is putting it mildly." Without looking at him, she counted out on her fingers. "Vampires with crazy abilities, my father and his super-soldiers, not to mention the immortals with all their special powers, too." She turned to look at him. "How exactly am I supposed to fight people like that?"

Nik stepped close to her again. "I know the vampires and your father's soldiers have heightened strength and speed, but you should know a little about fighting anyway. If Leisha and I aren't there to protect you, I need to know that you're not

completely helpless. Besides, self-defense covers the way you think in an emergency. I can train your brain to be resourceful when the bad guys come around."

Raising her eyebrows, Samantha opted for a light tone. "You didn't mention the immortals. Is that because you think them beneath you?"

Shrugging, Nik explained conversationally, "Well, immortals are basically like humans. You'll have less trouble with them."

"Wait, I thought immortals were almost the same as vampires, except for the blood."

Giving a half smile, Nik pushed a stray hair from her face and behind her ear. Samantha hoped he'd ignore her fluttering heart. "No," he said. "They have some of the same psychic abilities as vampires, but physically, they are like humans. They simply heal quicker than anyone else. And they don't age or get sick."

Samantha didn't think she'd be fighting immortals anytime soon. They may hold a grudge against her for betraying them, but she felt they wouldn't actually seek her out and attack her. Nevertheless, she met Nik's hazel gaze and nodded her assent.

He started by showing her the proper fighting stance and basic punches and kicks — stuff that Leisha had tried to teach her several months ago. At that time, Samantha hadn't been interested and wasn't very good at it. She would accidentally turn a swipe kick into an arabesque.

But Nik was a lot stricter than Leisha had been. He was relentless, and after doing the fundamentals twice a day for a week, she was getting pretty good.

Once she'd gotten the basics down, Nik progressed to more detailed scenarios. "Now, if someone gets you in a grip from behind," Nik was saying as he wrapped an arm around her waist, pinning both of her arms to her sides, and placed his other hand around her throat. His natural scent and body heat surrounded her. "You have a few options. You could head-butt me, but I'm taller than you, and you don't want to give yourself a nasty headache. You could stomp on my feet or try to kick back and dislocate my knee."

Trying to stay focused on the conversation instead of Nik's proximity, Samantha glanced at the wall a few feet in front of them. "If we were closer to the wall, I could try to walk up it and flip over your back."

She could feel his chuckle vibrate through her. "It's a great thought, Samantha, but you may not always be in front of a wall, and you'd have to have more training to accomplish something as advanced as that." He gripped her tighter. "Try to think of more basics. Stuff your brain will remember when it's in a state of panic. Nothing fancy."

Sighing, Samantha tightened her core and raised her leg. She kicked back and down, trying to push Nik's kneecap off. Her foot barely grazed the inside of his leg.

Sudden laughter caught Samantha by surprise and she started like a skittish animal. Both Samantha and Nik looked over at Leisha, who was struggling to compose her mirth.

"Sorry," Leisha said. "It was too funny to not watch."

SAMANTHA AVOIDED MAKING FRIENDS WITH her home school group. Everyone thought she was shy and let her be. She met some people that she would have liked to befriend, but knew that she didn't want to have to say goodbye to them, so she kept to herself.

The home schooling wasn't merely a front, either. Leisha gave her homework and had her looking up tutorials online so she wouldn't fall behind in school when she went back. That was, *if* she went back.

"The way my life is going now, do you really think school is high on my priority list?" Samantha asked one day.

"Look," Leisha said. "I know that being around me has changed your world completely. But that doesn't mean you shouldn't try to have an education. Take it from someone who's walked this earth for over two thousand years."

Samantha didn't argue that point, but felt she could study online and get a GED. That was good enough for her.

The next week found Samantha coming home from another home school group activity to find Leisha napping. The teenager shook her head. That woman slept at least twelve hours a day.

She walked into the dark basement to see if Nik was sleeping. His scent hit her as she descended. The uniquely clean smell was a comfort to her now.

It was so dark and quiet that she couldn't tell whether he was awake or not. She thought about calling out, but even a whisper would wake him up.

As she turned to go back up, he called out. "Did you need something, Sam?"

Smiling, she turned back to where his voice had come from. "I thought I might hang out with you. I wasn't sure if you were sleeping, though."

His hands reached hers in the darkness and he steered her towards his bed. "I think Leisha is doing enough sleeping for all of us these days."

Chuckling, she sat back against the headboard. When he was next to her, she was immediately aware of the heat emanating from his body. Samantha marveled at how comfortable they'd become with each other. Nik would put a hand on her back or squeeze her hand at times, but they'd never actually held hands, or cuddled. The one kiss they shared in the sewer came back into her mind.

"Your heart is really starting to go up a few notches," Nik murmured. "What are you thinking about?"

Even though it was dark, Samantha could feel the flush burning up her neck and face. She gave herself a mental shake and tried to be flippant. "Well, we are on a bed in the dark together, Nik."

The vampire stiffened beside her.

"I mean," Samantha started, but couldn't think of how to finish. "Well, um. Never mind." She moved to stand, but Nik's large hand grasped her arm. Samantha waited, her fingers beginning to tremble.

Slowly, Nik's hand trailed up to her shoulder. Then he gently pulled her down next to him. Samantha ended up resting her head on his chest with one arm resting on his torso. Nik's toned muscles were surprisingly comfortable and his pleasant scent overwhelmed her. After a moment, they both relaxed into their more intimate position.

It was quiet for a few moments, then Nik broke the silence. "So how was the school session?"

Smiling into his body, Samantha was glad that there wouldn't be any conversations about determining what this new step meant. As he stroked her hair, she told him about her day and how easy her studies were for her. He would murmur here and there, but mainly listened. The conversation grew into a comfortable lull after a while, and before she knew it, she'd dozed off.

It was a few days later that Samantha was with her homeschool group and saw another girl looking at Facebook on her phone. She watched as the girl scrolled through pictures of friends at dances and hanging out.

Thinking about it, Samantha realized that prom had already taken place at her old school in Cincinnati. *Maybe Spencer went with someone.* A sudden desire to look up her friends and see how they were doing overwhelmed her.

When it was time to leave, she turned to the girl with

the smartphone. "Do you mind if I use your phone to check Facebook?"

"Sure." The girl tucked her dark hair behind an ear as she reached into her pocket to retrieve her phone. "Let me log out of my account real fast, then you can log in to yours." She quickly swiped a few commands across the screen and then handed it to Samantha.

Hesitating, Samantha chewed on her lower lip. She had an account, but wasn't sure if it was a good idea to log into it. *It's not like they can trace my account, right? And I'm not using my own phone or anything, so no one could track me.* Convinced, she quickly typed in her information and looked up Spencer's timeline. He had changed his profile picture to one of himself in a tux. He was smiling and looking into the camera as if he hadn't a care in the world. Using her finger to scroll down, Samantha saw that he'd taken a girl from her history class to the prom. The pictures posted portrayed a couple who had had a great time with their arms around each other in almost every one.

If I'd been an ordinary human, that would have been me. Samantha waited to feel the regret and sorrow that usually accompanied those types of thoughts. But she felt nothing. In fact, she was glad to see Spencer had moved on and looked happy.

"Are you done?" The girl's eyes were narrowed in annoyance.

Samantha handed over the phone. "Sorry, I guess I got caught up in the news feed."

The girl smiled in understanding, then left.

Leisha picked her up from the group a few minutes later. They didn't talk much, which suited Samantha since she felt introspective about what she'd just experienced. *I don't care about not having a normal life anymore.* The realization lifted an unnoticed pressure from her shoulders.

When they got home, Samantha immediately went into

the dark basement and found Nik sitting on the dirt floor, whittling a piece of wood.

She sat next to him and hugged him tightly.

"Um, hi." He paused before returning the hug. "Are you alright?"

Grinning, she wished it was lighter so she could see his expression. "Better than alright. I'm really happy with where I am right now." She could see his lips curving up through the dimness and felt happiness bubbling up through her chest. Leaning into him, she closed her eyes and listened to the sound of his knife carving through wood.

After several minutes, Nik put down the wood and the knife. "I'm glad that you're happy, Sam," Nik placed his hand over hers.

She squeezed his hand and stood, surprised when Nik stayed with her, his fingers lacing with hers.

"Come on," he said. "Let's see what Leisha is up to."

Leisha, as it happened was cooking, but paused to glance down at their entwined hands, tossed a pointed glare at Nik, and then resumed what she was doing.

"It smells delicious, Leisha," Samantha said. "I hope you made enough for us."

"Of course." The blonde pulled a pot of marinara sauce from the stove and poured it over a steaming bowl of angel hair pasta. "Why don't you get some plates and forks? I'm just about finished here." She looked at Nik. "Did you want any?"

He nodded. "I'll have a little."

In a few minutes they were all sitting around the table eating Leisha's cuisine. The vampire had made the sauce from scratch. She'd added some garlic, oregano and rosemary to make the flavors dance on the tongue.

After they'd finished, Samantha leaned back in her chair. "Now I wish we had some dessert to go with that."

Leisha nodded her agreement, but made no move to get up.

Chuckling to himself, Nik stood. "I'll go find something for you two. I could stand to get out of the house for a while anyway."

"Thanks, Nik." She smiled up at him.

"You should get something for yourself while you're out, Nikita." Leisha said.

He seemed to hesitate, then reluctantly nodded.

Smiling after him, Samantha turned back to Leisha holding a hand over her chest. "Are you okay?"

Leisha grimaced while rolling her eyes. "Heartburn."

"Oh. Should we call Nik and ask him to buy some antacids?"

She shook her head. "There'd be no point. My metabolism would process it too quickly for the relief to last long. You'd think it would be the same with the heartburn, but it tends to stick around for a while."

A thought struck her. "Is that why you're always so hungry? Your body isn't hanging on to the food fast enough for the baby?"

"I believe so, yes."

It was quiet for a moment before Samantha changed the subject. "So have you decided what you're going to name him? Calling him the prophecy child is getting pretty old."

Leisha smiled. "I don't know yet. I'm trying to decide if I want to give him an African name, or something more common these days."

"I think you should do both. Make his middle name an African one or something."

The vampire looked thoughtful. "Maybe. Where I grew up, our middle names were the day of the week we'd been born on." She smiled. "I didn't have one because no one was around when I was born."

That sobered them both. Samantha hesitated, then asked, "Do you ever think about what Ptah said to you the night you killed him? About him knowing who your real father was?"

The memory of that night was burned into Samantha's mind with perfect clarity. Ptah had orchestrated a scene that made it look like Leisha was loyal to him so Tafari wouldn't trust her anymore. It had worked all too well. Then, just before the vampires launched their assault on the immortals, Ptah had given Leisha a tantalizing clue about her biological father. Restrained by Ptah's vampire guards, Samantha had been there to see the whole conversation play out between them.

PTAH TURNED LEISHA'S FACE TO his. "There is much that I have kept hidden from you, but no longer. When you come back home with me, I will reveal to you everything about the world I come from and how that may relate to the prophecy child."

Leisha had told Samantha that Ptah originated from the same world that the prophecy child's spirit would come from. Samantha wondered if Leisha's curiosity would be enough for her to rejoin the vampires.

Abruptly changing the subject, Ptah whispered intimately, "I know your father."

Leisha shook her head in puzzlement. "Of course you do."

"No, not your foster father. I speak not of the shaman. I know your true, biological father."

"How could you know him?" she asked.

Ptah's smile was full of arrogance. "As I said, there is much you don't know. You have no concept of your true parentage, of how special you are." He stroked the side of her stomach to her rib cage. "You have powers and abilities that I could awaken for you. I could give you so much more, Leisha."

PULLING THE GIRL OUT OF her recollections, Leisha nodded. "Of course I do. It would be nice to unlock that mystery, but when I killed Ptah, that information died with him. There's no way for me to unearth it."

Unable to think of a response, Samantha got up and put the dishes in the dishwasher. After a few minutes of rinsing and arranging plates and silverware, she turned back to Leisha. Her friend was looking thoughtful.

"What is it?"

Leisha shook her head. "You don't want to hear it."

"You mean you were thinking something about Nik and me." It came out more bitter than she'd meant.

The vampire gave a helpless shrug. "I think you both know how I feel." She pulled her blonde hair from her face. "I already told you that you're old enough to make your own decisions and I don't want to interfere, but you do know that you could never be with him, right?"

Spine stiffening, Samantha leaned against the counter. "Why do you say that?"

Leisha walked over to Samantha and patted her shoulder while she mirrored the girl's stance. "That didn't come out right, I'm sorry. I don't want to make you feel defensive, Samantha, but he's done a lot of stuff in his life. He…" She seemed to be searching for the right word then sighed. "He's simply not good enough for you. He'll pull your morals down further than I already have."

"No, he won't," she practically snapped. "In fact, I think it's the other way around. He doesn't simply look for any old victim anymore. He's trying to take on your feeding standards instead. I think he's becoming a better person because of our relationship."

Leisha raised an eyebrow. "And it doesn't bother you that he was going to drain your blood the first time you met?"

Goosebumps broke out along the back of her neck when Leisha mentioned it, but she'd never acknowledge the discomfort. "But he didn't. And if we're bringing up moments from the past, he was there for me after Annette, you know…." Samantha shuddered. "If he hadn't been there and used his luring power to pull me out of that agony, I think I would have gone insane."

"Alright." Leisha pulled her hair off her shoulders and behind her back. "So he's a better vampire now. What about you?"

"What about me?"

"Would you say that you've become a better person being with Nikita?"

She opened her mouth to say yes, but she couldn't. The truth was that she didn't really know. Circumstances had turned her life upside-down. There was no way Samantha could judge things in black and white, not with what she's seen. She'd learned that there were times when killing was necessary. But how did she explain when it was okay? After some reflection, it occurred to her that she didn't truly understand who she was anymore.

Leisha was watching her with pity swelling from her eyes. Samantha closed her mouth. Without another word, she went into the next room and turned on the TV.

CHAPTER 19

March 3rd

A few days passed, and Leisha still didn't know if anything could be resolved. She truly didn't want Samantha to be hurt, but she couldn't just keep her thoughts to herself.

Leisha was in her room, trying to ignore the "lover's chatter". It bothered her on a few different levels. When it got quiet, she couldn't take it anymore. She could easily picture them snuggling against each other, comfortable in their silent company.

"I'm going for a walk," Leisha said as she passed them in the living room. This wasn't unusual. She went out nearly every night. For some reason, she felt cloistered in the house. Maybe because the baby was constantly moving. He never seemed to sleep or rest within her womb. She also felt a need for physical affection. Something she knew she wouldn't get any time in the near future, if ever.

She'd always been fine, being alone for a long time, so when she had moments like these—missing Tafari—she blamed it to her constantly changing hormones and tried to ignore the feeling.

Walking along her usual route, she came to a clearing in the woods within fifteen minutes. The nights were cold, and being a vampire didn't prevent the bite of the chill, but it wouldn't hurt her long term. Somehow, she liked to feel the icy air seep into her skin. It made her feel alive.

Leisha was still walking when she heard a peculiar sound. She focused on the noise for a few moments, and gasped as she realized it was a helicopter. The part that alarmed her the most was that it wasn't moving on. It sounded like it was circling around.

She immediately turned back towards the house. Then, she heard several heartbeats above her, getting closer. They'd jumped out and were about to drop almost on top of her.

Leisha took a fighting stance as she yelled out to Nikita that trouble was coming and jabbed at the first soldier square in the face, and he immediately went down. Another soldier dropped from the sky, and he swung at Leisha, but she dodged to the side. It was way too awkward to hunch down with a big belly, so Leisha fell completely to the ground and swept her leg under her opponent's.

He went down with a grunt and she jumped up as quickly as she could with her larger belly and stomped on his neck, snapping his bones.

Another man grabbed her from behind, his arms holding hers down. Leisha kicked his knee hard, snapping it backwards. The man bellowed and fell, letting go of Leisha. Just as he was crumpling, something sharp hit Leisha's neck, sending a burning sensation from that area toward her chest.

Leisha cursed, pulled the dart out, and began running as fast as she could.

"Nikita!" she yelled. "Get out, now! I'll find you."

She didn't need to go back to the house to find out if he'd

heard. She knew that even if he couldn't understand everything she'd said, he'd understand the context. His vampire hearing was enough to let him know.

Leisha headed toward the city. She could make it there in twenty minutes at a dead run normally, but with the drugs already in her system, and the burden of her baby, she was much slower.

If the soldiers had been regular humans, then she knew she could have made it. But they weren't normal. They had heightened strength and speed. She didn't know what kinds of experiments Mason had done with vampire blood, but was all too frightened of the testing he would do to her in her current state.

She was still running as fast as she could, but knew she wasn't fast enough. Her lungs were beginning to burn from the exertion and her legs felt so heavy. She hoped the drug wouldn't affect her son.

A strong arm came around from behind. Leisha immediately swung her elbow into his sternum. The man grunted, but didn't let go. Another soldier came into view with handcuffs dangling from one hand. Swiping her foot out, Leisha was able to knock the cuffs out of her opponent's hand. He bent to retrieve them while the man holding her punched the side of her jaw. It shouldn't have knocked her out, but the jarring impact mixed with the tranquilizers was too much.

THE NEXT THING LEISHA WAS aware of was the hard metal she was lying on. She didn't remember blacking out, but she was now in a small room instead of the forest. There was no lighting, but she could see into the shadows. It was more like a cell. There were no windows, and Leisha couldn't tell whether the room was underground or not. She could see fluorescent lights above her, but no switch to turn them on. Other than the metal slab used for a bed, there were two large drains in the floor and a door in the far wall that was shut so tightly that the edges were barely noticeable. The place had recently been sterilized. The scent of ammonia was practically burning her sensitive nose.

Leisha rubbed her stomach and realized that her baby wasn't moving. She poked at him gently, hoping to prod some kind of response, but got nothing.

Her pulse quickened and breathing suddenly became difficult. *My baby!* Leisha closed her eyes and willed herself not to cry or panic. She still heard his heart beating, so she assumed it was merely from the drugs.

Once she got herself under control and thinking logically, she got up and began feeling for any hidden panels in the walls and floor. Discovering only a couple of electrical outlets, she sat on the metal slab, closed her eyes, and tried to listen for anything.

After thirty minutes, she heard very faint footfalls, but she couldn't tell how many were coming. There was some electronic processing, then air hissed and swirled as the door opened.

Two soldiers filled the doorway with their rifles trained on her. Mason stood behind them. He clicked a remote in his hand and the harsh florescent lights turned on above.

Blinking through the brightness, she saw some cameras angled from the ceiling in the hall, but that was all she could see before Mason closed the door. He stayed behind the soldiers as he spoke.

"I have many questions I'd like you to answer. First of all, how long has Samantha been having visions?"

Leisha hid her surprise and almost barked a sarcastic snip, but then decided she was curious and wanted to get some answers herself. . "How did you find out?"

He tossed her a look that said she'd underestimated him. "Her mother left me some hints before she died. And after I

looked at the security tapes, I was able to puzzle things together to determine Samantha knew where to find you."

Pursing her lips, Leisha decided that it wouldn't hurt to tell him, and she wanted to see what his reaction would be. "She's been having them since she was really little. I think three or four ."

Mason closed his eyes as if she'd delivered a low blow. "That's why she left me," he murmured. It was so low, but she could hear it easily.

"Are you talking about your ex-wife, Mary?"

Glancing at her as if he'd forgotten she was there, he pressed his lips together.

Folding her arms, Leisha gave a half smile. "So you're saying that you didn't know why she'd left you all those years ago, huh?" She raised an eyebrow. "Now you know it's because she wanted to protect your daughter from you. I guess she knew what line of work you were in then."

How could both my wife and daughter think that I would allow Samantha to be hurt? Didn't Mary know that I would have protected our baby? The thought came from Mason. Leisha usually could only read people's minds if they were weak-willed or drunk. The fact that he'd projected so strongly spoke volumes about his emotions.

"That's not what I'm here to talk about," the man said tightly. He paced the width of the cell. "We were able to find you when Samantha logged into a Facebook account under one of her known aliases." He sighed. "I honestly didn't think I'd find you because I thought you were smart enough to stay off the grid." Mason gave another of those condescending looks. "Once we traced Samantha's login to a girl's phone, we checked any and all activities she engaged in that Samantha may have done with her. We sent in agents to scope out the area and search for Samantha based on her description. You weren't nearly as thorough as you should have been, you know."

Momentarily closing her eyes, Leisha couldn't believe that one act had been their undoing. She had no idea Samantha would want to login to her old Facebook account. If she got out of this, she'd definitely sit the girl down about what it meant to keep a low profile.

Mason stopped and shook his head as if to clear it. "But we're getting off subject. My next question." He glanced at her stomach. "How is it that you're procreating? Our studies of vampires show that all the men are sterile."

Leisha cocked her head. "Not the women?"

He waved a hand. "The women ovulate, but at a rapid speed. We thought it impossible for a human man to impregnate a female because of how quickly she ovulates. You don't even bleed at the end of the ovulation, so I'm sure you didn't even realize you ovulated or have a hormone cycle." He gestured to her. "Which begs the question of how you were able to get yourself in this condition."

When she didn't respond, he slowly stepped between the soldiers toward her. "What I'd like to know even more is where that creature has taken my daughter."

Forcing down a smile at this news, she gave him a blank stare.

"I wouldn't try to be so stoic if I were you. You know first-hand what we're capable of doing to you. I'm trying to avoid that so we can do some more experiments."

Schooling her features, Leisha inwardly cringed.

"But I will do whatever it takes to find Samantha, even if I have to kill you to get to her."

At that, she gave a bitter laugh. "If you kill me, then you kill your own daughter."

He roughly grabbed her hair and forced her to look into his eyes. "What did you do to her?" he spat.

"Samantha is my human servant. We're linked. If you torture me, it will drain her energy until one of us will have to feed

to be restored." Unable to move her head, she gestured with one hand to the men pointing guns at her. "I doubt you'd hand over one of your men to me, so that would mean that your little girl would have to find someone to kill and drink their blood." She glanced at him. "And she's still human, which means that her drinking blood will be quite a traumatic experience." Though Leisha sincerely hoped it wouldn't come to that.

Shoving her head away, he turned. "And she thought you actually cared about her. You're exactly what I thought: a blood sucking monster who's using her for your own gain."

"Not really." She reached up and smoothed her hair. "I love Samantha like a sister. I was merely telling you the facts about our situation and the consequences of hurting me."

He looked at her and nodded as if to acknowledge she'd won this match. "Very well. I'll leave you now, since I can't do what I'd originally planned." His eyes narrowed when she smirked slightly. "But don't get too comfortable. I'll come back tomorrow and we'll see what we can learn from your baby . . . without damaging *you*, of course. Since I'm assuming the child is half human, who knows if it will survive the ordeal."

He slid his card over a small scanner and the door popped open. The men backed out after Mason, keeping her in their guns' sights until the door closed.

Placing a hand over her belly, Leisha wondered how she would get out of this particular disaster.

CHAPTER 20

It felt like Samantha's nerves had been running high since the night before.

She and Nik had been talking quietly while Leisha went for her usual walk. He was telling her about his younger sister. Samantha chuckled at his stories, her heart warmed by the idea of Nik as an older brother.

Suddenly, Nik jumped up. "We need to leave. Now!"

Resisting his pull on her arm, Samantha glanced at him with wide eyes. "What about Leisha? Why do we have to go?"

"She can take care of herself." He paused as Samantha rose. "I just heard her. She said she'd find us later."

Still not sure what was going on, she put her shoes on.

"I'm going to grab my stuff. I'll be back." The vampire disappeared, moving faster than she could track.

Running into her bedroom, Samantha grabbed her traveling bag and quickly stuffed in whatever was easily accessible. Nik appeared and took her bag, zipping it for her as he led the way out to the car.

Before they reached the driveway, the vampire paused, then handed her their bags and the keys. "Start the car."

She saw his blurred form rush toward the trees. She couldn't see anything besides leaves shaking, but she could hear grunts and the sounds of skin smacking against skin. Hurrying, she opened the backseat and dumped their bags. Practically ripping the door from its hinge in her haste, Samantha sat in the driver's seat and started the car. She backed out onto the street and sat there, waiting for Nik.

Suddenly a man fell out of the sky and landed on the hood. She screamed as he pointed a gun at her. Without thinking, she slammed on the gas, propelling the car forward and hurling the man from the car. She screamed again when the passenger door opened, but it was Nik. He'd apparently been running alongside the car for a moment before jumping in.

"Let's go," he calmly ordered. "Drive as fast as you can. When we get into the city, we'll switch cars and then switch again before we drive back to the States."

Heart pounding and struggling to control her breathing, Samantha maneuvered through the streets. "We can't drive across the border in a stolen car. And what about Leisha? How will she know where to find us?"

Nik patted her shoulder. "I'll take care of everything. Don't worry. We won't be crossing the border tonight anyway. There's not enough time before sunrise."

So she'd gone along with his plan, Nik taking over the driving when they'd swapped to a "borrowed" car. They drove for a few hours, changed vehicles again, and then Nik found an abandoned house. He had dropped her there to settle in the basement while he ditched the car in a remote spot and ran back. She had just finished covering the windows when he'd returned.

They slept on the floor. Samantha rested fitfully, but was surprised that she'd slept at all.

Now, they were still at the house, and the sun was starting

its descent. Luckily, there had been a few water bottles in the car, but no food.

"I'm going to go out and get a legitimate car, as well as some food for you," Nik said, moving past her to grab a wallet from his bag.

"Can't we go together?" she asked as she eyed a large spider crawling across the wall.

"It'll be faster if I go alone. Besides, they won't be looking for a lone man. We'd stand out if we went together."

Samantha nodded. Nik went into another room to change.

When he came out, he hugged her. Samantha took solace in the embrace, and the way his arms felt around her.

Pulling away, Nik offered a small smile. "Why don't you pack up our stuff while I'm gone? It shouldn't take too long."

Though grimacing at how little there was to pack, she nodded. She surprised both of them when she went up on her toes to give him a soft kiss. His lips were cold, but quickly heated as their lips lingered over each other. "Try to hurry," she whispered.

His hazel eyes shone warmly as he lightly squeezed her hand, then left.

It only took her about ten minutes to have everything packed and ready to go. Knowing she shouldn't waste the batteries in her flashlight, she turned it off. She stood in the darkness for a few minutes, then turned the light back on. Making sure there were no spiders or other creepy crawlies near her, she sighed.

She was trying hard not to worry about Leisha. Samantha didn't have her smart phone anymore, and wasn't able to check online to see if Leisha sent an email or anything. It was frustrating not being able to get in touch with her dearest friend.

Nik had been gone for two hours before he finally returned in a beat up Suburban.

She hugged him, then wasted no time putting their stuff

in the car. It smelled of stale cigarettes, but Samantha was too tired to care at that moment.

Buckling herself in the passenger seat, Samantha let out a long breath as Nik put the car into gear and drove. "So what's the plan now?" she asked.

"We're heading to the border right now," Nik answered. "There's a road that travels through a national forest in Michigan. I think that's the best route."

"Is it a big forest? What if the drive goes into the day?" She brushed hair off her face. "Where could we rest?"

"We should be able to get through the forest before the end of the night. If not, I can toss a blanket over me while we rest in the car."

Samantha rolled her eyes. "That sounds awful. Sure hope it doesn't come to that."

"We should be alright."

"And what about Leisha? She should have caught up to us by now."

Nik sighed. "I really don't know. I thought she'd have caught up to us by now, but don't underestimate how good she is at taking care of herself."

"Her body is, like, five months pregnant. I'm sure that's got to put a damper on things. Plus, you said those soldiers have increased abilities, right?"

He hesitated, then nodded.

"What if my dad has her?" Samantha put her head in her hands. "He hates her, Nik. And what about the baby? He'll see it as some bug that needs dissecting."

She felt his warm hand cover her back. It was comforting, but he had no answers. Samantha was sure that something was wrong and felt that she was abandoning her best friend, but didn't know how to find her.

"You'll know if something bad is happening through your link to her," Nik said after a few minutes. "If she were injured, she would have to pull on your energy. Do you feel unusually fatigued?"

Sighing, Samantha shook her head. "I'm not sure. I haven't had much sleep, so yes I'm tired and worn out, but who knows if it's from Leisha drawing off me or from being on the run."

He removed his hand. "Why don't you crawl in the back and get some rest. It will help both you and Leisha, if she does actually need your energy."

She complied grudgingly. Samantha didn't really think she could sleep well on the lumpy cushioning, but the sounds and motions of the car lulled her to sleep before she knew it.

Her stiff neck finally pulled her from sleep. She had slept more deeply than she'd thought possible, and hadn't changed into a more comfortable position. It felt like there was a knot in her neck muscle the size of Texas.

"How do you feel?" Nik asked.

Sitting up and stretching, she answered, "Hungry. How long was I out?"

"Most of the night. I was surprised that you slept through the border check."

"You mean we're back in the US?" She crawled up to the front. When he nodded she asked, "How close is it to dawn?"

"Closer than I'd like it to be. I'm afraid there's nowhere close by to stop for food. We've just entered the Hiawatha National Forest. If we had an extra hour, we could find lodging in Gladstone, but the sun should be up in twenty minutes."

"What can we do?"

He shrugged. "I'll get under a blanket in the back. You can keep driving, if you're not too sleepy. But once you get into Gladstone, you should stop and get a room ." Nik grimaced. "I'll have to sneak into the hotel without anyone seeing."

Tossing him a look, Samantha added, "And without the sun touching your skin."

"We've done it before, but it certainly is risky. Since I'm an

older vampire, I've built some immunity to sunlight, but not enough to be directly exposed for more than a few minutes."

"Okay. I think this can work. I don't suppose you grabbed my other ID's and credit cards when we ran? "

Nodding, he pulled over and opened the glove compartment and brought out a driver's license for her. "Today you're going to be Gina Barratte from New York." He smiled at her as he handed it over. "I'm glad Leisha included credit cards along with your backup I.D.'s."

Taking it, she rolled her eyes and got out. Nik followed suit and she slid into the driver's side. Nik grabbed a large, thick blanket from the trunk and lay down on the floor in the back.

"Is there a map for me to look at?" she asked him as she maneuvered back onto the road.

"You don't need one. Simply follow the highway until you see the sign for Gladstone."

She drove for a while in silence, positive that Nik had fallen asleep. Since she'd slept a good while, she wasn't tired in the least. The sun was climbing steadily higher as they reached Gladstone. She was hungry, but decided that he'd sleep better if she didn't stop, so she kept going through the small city.

After an hour and a half, they'd reached Wisconsin and stopped in a place called Marinette to fill up on gas. She made sure Nik was completely covered, then went inside to pay and buy herself some food at the same time. They sold all-beef franks there, so she bought one along with some packaged snacks to eat in the car.

Once she was again sitting in the driver's seat, Nik spoke up. "I slept too long for us to be just getting into Gladstone."

"Yep." She said around a mouthful of hotdog. Starting the car, she drove back towards the highway. "We entered Wisconsin a few minutes ago. I figured if you were okay under that blanket, then we could make better time with me driving until sundown."

"Well, it's starting to get stuffy under here. Why don't you drive until we hit Chicago and we'll get a room there."

"Are we that close?" Trying to keep her eyes on the road, she pulled the map out of the glove compartment and calculated the distance. "That will take half the day. Are you sure you'll be alright back there for that long?"

He gave a long suffering sigh that she knew was fake. "I can tolerate it, if I must. But I think you may have to massage my poor, aching back."

She snorted and replied with a haughty tone. "Vampires don't ache, so there."

She heard him chuckle then murmur, "I guess I'll be fine, then, won't I?"

Smiling, she turned on the radio and found a station she liked. After a few hours of driving and chatting with Nik, she pulled out her bag of chips and slid another bag under his blanket. Two hours later, she went through the doughnuts and jerky. They were almost to Chicago and she had just under a fourth tank of gas.

A little later, she was pulling into the parking lot of a motel. Her license said that she was twenty one and hoped that the manager wouldn't question it. As she was about to get out of the car, she suddenly felt as though all the energy had been sucked out of her body. She couldn't bring herself to stand as she felt herself sagging against the steering wheel.

"Nik?" she called out weakly.

"What's wrong? I heard your heart stutter."

"Leisha's in trouble."

CHAPTER 21

After letting Leisha stay in the cell for another day, Mason and his goons returned. The guards were the same men from yesterday. One had orange-red hair and the other had lips so thin it looked like he didn't even have any.

Mason held up a large needle for her to see. It was twelve inches long and a quarter of an inch thick.

Mason watched her closely as he explained. "This will cause you little pain. However, I believe that inserting it through several spots in your stomach will cause your baby great agony. I've spent the last several hours studying the best way to do this without killing the fetus outright. So all I need to do is feel how the baby is positioned within you. We'll bring in an ultrasound machine and then we can proceed." He paused. "Unless you would like to tell me where my daughter is?"

Her lips felt dry. "I don't know." As she stared at the needle, she wondered if she would be able to conceal the information if she did know where Samantha was.

After studying her expression for a moment, Mason shook his head and gestured to the men.

Leisha had already thought this out. She knew that if they were to shoot her, it would cause her a great deal of pain. Enough that she would pull on her link to Samantha. Guilt stabbed through her at the thought of sucking away Samantha's energy, but she hoped that would incite Samantha and Nik to look for her, if they weren't already. It was the only way for her to send out an SOS.

She hoped that her plan would also delay Mason's demented plan to torture her baby. So as the men approached her, she lashed out with her foot. Facing the man to her right, she kicked the gun out of his grip and pulled him towards herself, just in time for him to be shot by the redheaded man.

Her victim screamed and she threw him at Redhead, but he jumped out of the way. Since he was quick and they were in a confined space, she wouldn't be able to fight him well. Instead, she rushed at Mason, and tried to throw him into Redhead, who was readying to fire at her again.

She missed Mason, but Redhead's shot was dead on. As searing pain exploded in her left shoulder, she forced herself to move on. She slammed opened the door and was two steps into the corridor beyond when more pain shot through her hip. Her leg gave out and she collapsed onto the tile floor .

"Don't kill her," Mason shouted from the room.

Redhead roughly yanked her up and dragged her back into her cell, but she had enough time to look around. She saw that they were above ground. There was only an elevator as an exit from the hall, which was not up to fire code regulations. That meant this building was probably off the radar and didn't need standard permits for operation, which also indicated that she probably couldn't wait to be rescued.

Redhead got her on the metal slab and was cuffing her wrists to the bed. She was kicking him hard on his temple before Mason pinned her legs and strapped them to the bed.

"You shouldn't be able to hold me down," she muttered through clenched teeth.

At the comment, Mason stood tall and smiled broadly. "I know. My superiors didn't think that I could accomplish it so quickly, but I figured out a way to infuse humans with your blood."

She shook her head. "That shouldn't be possible."

His blue eyes lit up. "It was difficult, let me tell you. A year ago, we had our first successful trial on animals with vampire genes and started experimenting on humans. Most of the subjects went insane and killed the majority of the doctors overseeing the experiments. I had some scars myself." He rubbed his stomach. "Luckily, they are completely healed, thanks to you." He gave her a pointed stare. "So far, your blood is the only sample able to see us through the transition. All the others we drained were a complete disaster."

Leisha had been one of many vampires taken last year to be experimented on. However, she was the only one who escaped. Eyebrows drawing together in confusion, she suddenly felt cold. What made her so special?

As if reading her mind, Mason said, "Your blood has an extra chromosome that the others don't have. I believe this is what enables you to withstand sunlight when the others can't."

Hoping to distract him, she continued the conversation. "Can you guys go out in the sun?" she asked, her curiosity peeked.

He teetered his hand through the air. "Sort of. We can, but the sun weakens us, so we're basically like normal humans in the daytime. At night, we're almost as fast and as strong as you are."

Lifting her eyebrow, she clarified. "Almost, but still you're not one of us."

"Thank the good Lord for that," muttered Redhead.

Mason nodded. "True. While we do need to have small infusions of blood via injection every once in a while to sustain us, we don't actually have to drink blood all the time like you do." He paused. "We also have lost our ability for scent and taste." He looked up with a quizzical expression. "Is that why it's so easy for you to drink blood? Because you can't really taste it anyway?"

That was interesting. Leisha wasn't sure how useful that information was to her, but stored it away and shrugged her shoulders. No way was she going to tell him that vampires had heightened senses. If he hadn't discovered it in his "research", that was his problem.

With a little testing, she could tell that the constraints would hold her down pretty well. She could possibly try to break through them, but she would need blood to restore her strength afterwards, and couldn't bring herself to draw so much on Samantha's energy.

She had stopped bleeding. Leisha could feel the bullet still in her hip. The one in her shoulder had exited out the other side. The bullet in her hip would need to be removed since it would recurrently damage tissue then heal again.

Rolling his shoulders, Mason pushed a button on the wall with his thumb. It scanned his print before opening a panel. He retrieved tweezers and a scalpel. "This wasn't the form of torture I was preparing for today, but we can take care of that bullet before we get to the main event."

Pulling her pants down to her knees, he dug right in.

Biting her lip to keep herself from screaming, she forced herself to see what he was doing to make sure there was no foul play.

She had to give the man props for efficiency. He cut straight to the bullet and used the tweezers to yank it out in no time. He didn't bother to staunch the bleeding, nor had he sterilized anything before he had begun.

Mason left the room, but returned a few minutes later with his hands cleaned up. "Now we can get on to the real reason why I'm here."

He went back to the panel and pulled out the thick needle.

Heart rate picking up speed, Leisha's mind raced. She had more strength in her legs than her arms, so maybe if she freed her feet and defended herself that way... no, it wouldn't work fast enough to prevent the redhead from keeping her pinned.

Mason was getting closer, his eyes focusing on her stomach. Once he reached her side, he pulled up her shirt. As her belly was bared, she felt a ripple of the baby's movement that could be seen under the skin, as if he were pushing an elbow out along her stomach.

Out of the corner of her eye, she saw Redhead grow pale. At least he had some kind of conscience. Mason showed no reaction. He put his empty hand over her belly and felt around. "I think we can do this without the ultrasound," he muttered.

After a few minutes of probing, he lifted his needle.

"I swear I don't know where they are," Leisha burst. She could feel perspiration beading up along her brow and upper lip. She hated herself for breaking, but it was her baby. She flashed back to when Ptah threatened her daughter, Adanne, so he could convince Leisha to become a vampire. It hadn't taken long before she'd broken under that pressure as well.

"Please," she whispered. "You must know that I'm telling you the truth by now."

Ignoring her plea, Mason aimed the needle at her side and towards the baby. Leisha feared it would impale her child completely.

"Stop!" she screamed. "I don't know, I swear on my child's life!"

With a steady hand, Mason pierced her skin. She sobbed for her baby more than at the pain. Leisha wasn't sure if she should hold completely still or try to struggle.

The needle was slowly pushing deeper into her stomach. Leisha was about to start squirming when she heard a subtle sound that she wasn't sure the others had heard.

"What the—" Mason cut off as he looked down at his procedure. "It won't go any farther." He pulled the instrument out.

Gasping at the searing pain, Leisha looked down at a large chunk of her flesh that had been ripped out with the needle.

The needle was no longer straight. It looked like someone had bent it backward.

Shuddering, Leisha glanced at her belly. She wasn't sure how an unborn child could do something like that, but was relieved.

Shaking his head, Mason opened his mouth to say something, but was interrupted by the buzz of his cell phone. Sighing, he pulled it out and looked at the screen. "Looks like you were saved by the bell," he muttered before answering the phone. "Hang on a minute. I need to get to a more secure location." His skin appeared a little pale as he turned to Leisha and removed the phone. "Don't think this is over. I will find a way get the answers I want." He nodded to Redhead, who promptly picked up his unconscious companion and followed Mason out the door.

Once she heard the door click, Leisha closed her eyes. Mason was a brilliant man with unlimited resources. He would figure out a way, and it would probably be incredibly painful. She had to get away before that happened.

CHAPTER 22

Samantha couldn't stop pacing, even though there was nothing she could do to help her friend. She knew she should try to store up as much energy as possible, but she couldn't seem to stop herself.

"You should probably take some more iron pills and have another fillet," Nik said.

Grimacing, she agreed. She'd been downing iron pills and eating rare steak for the last two days. She wouldn't miss the meat if she never saw it again, but it did seem to help a little.

If she went out with Nik and drank blood from a human, it would probably fix her fatigue problem as well as restore Leisha's strength, but she couldn't bring herself to do that. Not yet.

She followed Nik into the kitchen of their small apartment and watched him season the steak and get the stove ready. She poured herself some water, grabbed the bottle of iron pills, and swallowed two. "They should have been here by now."

Nik shrugged as he cooked, the steam rising to his sandy hair. "They'll get here when they get here." Studying her face, his brow crinkled slightly. "You need to calm yourself. That will help Leisha more than anything."

Sautéed spices wafted toward Samantha from the the skillet. "She can't feel my anxiety."

"No, she can't. But when you become overexcited, it pulls on your energy more. You need to reserve as much as you can."

Closing her eyes and taking a deep breath, she nodded her agreement. "Do you think the baby's okay?" It was not the first time she had asked.

"You witnessed his birth in your vision," Nik answered patiently. "Remember that." It wasn't the first time he'd given this answer, either. She nodded and went into the main room to sit on the horribly drooping couch that came with the apartment.

It had been two days since her episode in Chicago. When she'd collapsed in the car, poor Nik couldn't get out to help her because his big hoodie was in the trunk. She had rested her head on the steering wheel for thirty minutes before the manager of the motel had come out to investigate.

She had made up a story about having anemia. The manager wrote down her information and credit card number and filled in the paperwork so she could check in. Then he helped her walk to her room and sent his son out to buy iron supplements for her.

Nik had waited in the car until sundown before joining her in the room. He'd been able to figure out which one was hers by her smell. After he had told her that, she'd soaked in the bathtub for an hour. She'd needed to get cleaned up after staying in that abandoned house and being in the car for several hours, anyway. But for some reason, Nik's comment was the catalyst that sent her to the bath.

The iron pills had helped, and Nik had gone out for steaks from a local restaurant. She'd wanted to try some Chicago deep dish pizza, but he kept her on the beef, iron pills, and a spinach salad diet. Not to mention lots and lots of water.

While at that motel, she had emailed both Tafari and Rinwa, telling them that Leisha was in serious danger and she'd appreciate it if they could fly out to discuss it.

She and Nik had left the next night and had ended up in Kansas City. They had found a crappy, two bedroom apartment that rented by the month. Samantha had sent her location to Tafari and Rinwa. It was just an hour later that Tafari had emailed her back with their flight schedule.

Samantha wasn't sure how they could help, but she hoped that they could use their connection with the immortals to find her father's new compound. She knew he wouldn't be in Vegas anymore, not since that compound's security had been so easily breached by his teenage daughter.

Nik brought the steak to her and she forced herself to eat. Then she sat back and let her body digest. It was amazing how fast her metabolism was now that she was a human servant. It seemed as though she could eat all day and not gain any weight, but the downside was that she needed to eat more frequently.

A knock came at the door and Samantha quickly got up to answer. She didn't bother to check the peephole since Nik didn't protest her getting the door. As soon as she saw Tafari and Rinwa on the doorstep, she ushered them in. Tafari put his bags down and opened his arms. Without a word, Samantha walked into them, tears pouring over her cheeks.

She knew that Nik and Rinwa were watching but she couldn't seem to control herself. It stayed quiet for a few minutes. Once she pulled away, she gave Tafari a watery smile. He returned it, though his was more of a grimace than a smile.

"Thanks for coming so quickly," she said as she wiped her face. She gestured for them to sit on the only couch in the room.

"I'll stand," Rinwa said, giving a pointed look at Nik. "I'm assuming since that *thing* is here with you, you'd be pretty upset if I killed him?"

"You could try," Nik countered in his usual, unaffected way.

Folding her arms, Rinwa said, "I have a very good record when it comes to butchering your kind."

Not rising to the bait, Nik simply met her stare.

"Alright kids," Tafari said as he lowered himself down, then fell into the couch. He shifted a bit before muttering, "This thing just sucks you right in."

"I know." Samantha smirked. "I really have to work hard to get myself out of it."

He shifted his weight again, then seemed to give up and crossed an ankle over a knee. "Do you need a moment, Samantha, or shall we get straight to the point?"

Sighing, Samantha said, "My dad has Leisha."

Rinwa leaned a hip onto the armrest beside her father. "So? He's taken her before and she got away."

"Not without my help." Samantha hesitated. "Plus, her condition is different this time."

Lifting his eyebrows, Tafari asked, "What do you mean, her condition? Her circumstances?"

"That too," Nik said. "The soldiers containing her have found a way to give themselves extra strength and speed." He looked at Rinwa. "You'd be surprised at what a challenge they can be in a fight."

"There is that." Samantha continued. "She's also... well, that is..."

"What?" Rinwa asked with a bored expression. "Has she been sewn to a cow or something?"

Samantha couldn't help the chuckle that burst forth. "Where do you come up with these things?"

Waving a hand, Rinwa stared at Samantha. "Well? It sounded like you were about to tell us something."

Samantha chewed her lip and then met Tafari's gaze. "Leisha's pregnant."

Tafari was off the couch instantly. "What?" he barked at the same time Rinwa said, "You must be joking."

"It's true." Samantha continued to look at Tafari. "I think you very well know who the father is."

His silvery blue eyes intense, he shook his head. "It cannot be. Rinwa is right, it is impossible."

"Look, I don't know how it's possible, but technically, both of you were human when you, er… you know, did it."

Everyone started when Rinwa burst out laughing. "It's called sex, dearest. You can say it without being struck by lightning."

Samantha felt her cheeks heating, but gave a tight-lipped smile anyway.

Tafari shook his head, his mouth tight. "Plenty of immortals engaged in intercourse while we were human and not a single one became pregnant."

Rinwa rolled her eyes and touched her father's shoulder. "Your shock is blinding you to what everyone else has figured out by now." When he didn't respond, she continued. "Tafari, you and Leisha have most likely conceived the prophecy child." She looked up at Samantha with her eyebrows raised.

"Yes, we believe the same," answered Samantha.

Putting a hand to his head, Tafari slumped back into the couch. "Bloody hell."

"Actually, it makes sense." Rinwa looked thoughtful. "After all, the prophecies talk about him being connected to both the immortals and vampires in some way. I guess that's how." Suddenly her eyes widened. "I'm going to have a brother." She shook her head. "That's so bizarre."

"I think my situation is a lot more difficult to swallow than yours," Tafari mumbled.

"Look," Samantha interjected. "I know this is a crazy huge shock, but Leisha's in some serious danger, and…" Tears misted in her eyes once more. "And I don't know what my father will do to the baby, but I guarantee it will not be good."

Shaking his head as if to clear it, Tafari said, "You are right,

Samantha. I am glad that you reached out to us. Now, we will help get her out."

Nik finally spoke up. "I'm not sure if you really can help. But Samantha needed you guys here anyway. So I didn't protest when she contacted you."

Rinwa looked the vampire up and down. "You didn't protest? And when did you become her keeper, oh mighty one?"

Samantha waved a hand. "It's not like that. This is Nik, I mean Nikita. When the vampires found out about Leisha conceiving, they tried to kill her. Us. Anyway, we couldn't have escaped if it weren't for him, and he's been with us ever since."

Rinwa pursed her lips, studying Nik's features, but stayed quiet.

Tafari brought the issue back to hand. "Do you know where they're keeping her?"

"No. They attacked us in Canada, but I don't think they're up there. To be honest, I have no idea how to find my father's compound, and time is running out."

When the immortals asked her to explain how she knew time was short, she took a deep breath and looked away, unable to meet their eyes as she explained. "There was a little emergency when everyone changed back into vampires. In order to save me, Leisha sort of had to turn me into her human servant."

Tafari stared at her with cold eyes. "Could she not have done something else to save you?"

Rinwa's face was red and her lips were pressed together. "No." Samantha cleared her throat, relieved. She hadn't realized until that moment, but she'd been expecting them to ostracize her or something now that she was part of the vampire circle. "It was the only way. I promise that it was a last resort."

The immortals glanced over her shoulder and Samantha turned to see Nik's face passively not telling them anything. It was obvious to her that Nik didn't like addressing this subject again.

"Anyway, because of that link, I can feel her pulling on my energy. She's not doing well and I'm worried that if we don't get her soon, she won't survive." She blinked back tears.

Rinwa walked over to Samantha and patted her shoulder. "We'll get her out, Samantha." Her tone hardened. "Then I'll kill her for changing you."

"I told you she did what she had to do," Samantha insisted. She couldn't help defending Leisha, even though she knew Rinwa was at least partly joking. "I'm over it. Besides, I kinda like that I can eat whatever without gaining a pound."

Rinwa huffed. "If feeding you were all I had to do to convince you to become an immortal, I would have made that argument when you stayed with us last year."

Tafari had been quiet during their exchange, looking like he was contemplating something. Suddenly, he stood. "I think I may know of a way. It would be a considerable risk, but if we prepare for it properly, we would be able to overcome the odds."

Leaning against the wall, Nik said, "Do tell."

"Well, we could use me as the bait. I was exposed to those guys last year when they chased us in South America. I fought one of the men and he had to have noticed my quick healing."

"Yes, I remember," Samantha said.

"If I offered them my blood in exchange for some kind of political gain, I am certain they would take me to the same compound. Once we know the location, we can infiltrate it and get Leisha out."

"Tafari, that won't work," Rinwa protested. "Mason would accept your deal, and then lock you up and do whatever the hell he wanted. We'd have to rescue both of you after that."

Tafari shrugged and turned to Samantha. "We have a kit that we always take with us—in case we find vampires. It includes tracking equipment." As if just realizing Nik was there, he glanced at the vampire in alarm.

Nik waved a hand. "Oh, don't worry, your secret is safe with me. Besides, they probably already know that anyway."

"Oh, we weren't worried about that," said Rinwa as she put her arm around Tafari's waist. "There are other, less innocuous tools in there that we could use on you now."

"Rinwa," both Samantha and Tafari cautioned in the same tone.

Rinwa shrugged, pulled out a knife, and began twirling it deftly between her fingers.

"Let's jump on this plan, Tafari," Samantha said. "We still have hours until sunrise and I know we can get this thing moving along before then."

Looking up at Nik, Rinwa said somewhat arrogantly, "We could move a lot faster if we didn't have to wait around for you to sleep your lazy behind through the day."

Samantha threw a warning glance at Rinwa, but Nik spoke up. "You're right. Just give me some way to check in with you and I'll catch up when I can."

"But we need you," Samantha spurted. "I don't want us to get separated. What if the vampires or my dad's soldiers find you?"

Nik walked over and embraced her. "Then I'll be glad to know that you're safe while I fight my way out." He pulled back. "You don't need to worry about me, Sam. I always come out fine."

Conflicting emotions ran through her, but she knew this was the best course of action. "I'll miss you."

A laugh escaped him. "Hopefully, it'll only be one day. I'm sure you won't miss me."

Smiling shyly, she hugged him back. "I guess I got used to you being glued to my side." They pulled apart and Samantha saw Tafari's disapproving stare. It looked very similar to Leisha's.

CHAPTER 23

March 11th

Leisha was beginning to feel desperate. Luckily, Mason and his goons hadn't been back to see her in what she estimated to be about three days. She assumed that her enemy had been called away on some mission. While she didn't have to worry about them for the time being, she was starving, her bladder was full, and she was still strapped to the uncomfortable metal slab. Her pants were still pulled down and her belly was exposed. The worst part was that when she shifted, her skin stuck to the metal surface.

She had decided to conserve what strength she had left for when they came back. She couldn't escape without Mason's access card, so she had to wait for his return before she could try out her haphazard plan.

Obviously, there hadn't been much to do to occupy her time. She usually exercised when she was in a confined area to keep her sanity. But since she couldn't move, this time she'd had to get creative within her mind. She'd done all the times tables, counted how many minutes between the generators turning off and then on. Leisha had tried to ignore her own body odor as it became more and more pronounced.

She'd also tried to figure out what to name her son. Though she'd thought of several names she'd liked, she felt that it would be wrong to name him without Tafari's input. Of course, she had yet to contact him about the child. Now she wasn't sure if she would get that chance.

The baby had started kicking a lot. He was getting incredibly active and was very strong. Luckily, she was a vampire and healed quickly from the damage he inflicted. Though it still hurt pretty badly. Her ribs had been broken several times, and she was surprised the baby hadn't kick through the placenta since he'd damaged her organs time and again .

Sighing loudly, she pointed and flexed her toes while she rotated her wrists to keep her blood circulating. She didn't know when Mason would come back, but she had to be ready when he did.

As if summoned by her thoughts, footsteps echoed down the hallway. They stopped right outside her door. Licking her lips, Leisha looked over at the restraint on her right arm. One of the links in the chain was just loose enough from her yanking on it over the past few days. She simply needed to pull hard enough and it should break free.

Redhead and another guard with puppy-brown eyes entered as the door swung open, their weapons trained steadily on Leisha. Mason came behind, looking both impatient and excited at the same time.

"Well, Leisha, you'll have to excuse me for neglecting you." He grinned. "Turns out you're not the only special species on the planet." He leaned toward her, his spearmint breath whispering on her chin. "I have new specimens coming in and I have to say I'm thrilled to discover their secrets."

Leisha stiffened at his words. Had the government found

an immortal, or was there something else out there that she wasn't aware of?

"Anyway, back to where we left off, hmm?" Mason walked over to the hidden panel and the two guards held their weapons loosely, looking relaxed. "I'm afraid we'll need to hurry. I'm completely booked today, but I need to know where my Samantha is."

"I already told you all that I know," Leisha said as she squirmed against her restraints.

Mason shook his head as he held up a new needle. Leisha assumed this one had some kind of reinforced steel coating. "You were running away from that house in Canada. You were planning to catch up with her. How would you be able to do that if you didn't know where she'd be going?"

"I would have followed her trail." She began struggling against the bonds in earnest now, but was careful to not break the one on her wrist yet.

"No, that can't be it. She was canny enough to lose us, and we have the latest equipment and technology. There's no way you could have followed her."

"It's true! I was going to follow her scent."

Brow drawing up in confusion, Mason asked, "Her scent? But you don't smell anymore. Once turned into a vampire, you lose your sense of smell and taste."

Though she hadn't planned to divulge the information, Leisha couldn't help a smile coming to her lips. "Not true. I don't know why you guys lost those senses, but vampires have *everything* enhanced."

Eyes narrowed, he pointed the needle at her stomach. "That is a lie. When we're through, you'll be spouting everything you know, and then some."

The needle was about four inches away from her belly when Leisha used the little strength she'd reserved to pull up her right hand to snap the chain. She hit the needle out of Mason's hand and grabbed him, using him as a shield when Redhead fired at her. The blast echoed loudly in the small room and Mason gasped as his body jolted from the impact. The bullet hit him in his back, blood already spreading through his shirt.

Sending a warning look to both of the guards, she seized Mason's Adam's apple. "I realize you must be in a lot of pain right now, but you're going to unstrap my left arm." She squeezed his neck for emphasis. "Now."

Trembling fingers reached over and unbuckled the binding on her other arm. Leisha put both of her hands on Mason's neck and sat up, her ankles still bound, and kept him in front of her the whole time. Once upright, she gestured with her left hand to the new soldier. "Toss over your weapon or I'll snap his neck."

The guard glanced over to Redhead, who shook his head. When he didn't move, Leisha shrugged and dug her fingers into Mason's neck.

"Do it," Mason screamed. His voice was rising toward hysteria.

Redhead was still shaking his head, but the guard tossed the gun to Leisha. She caught it easily, and keeping her right hand on Mason's neck, pointed the gun at the redheaded guard.

"Now," she said to Mason. "You will free my legs."

It took little time to get them undone. As soon as the straps were off her ankles, she shot Redhead without even looking in his direction. The bullet hit him right in the heart. He was clearly surprised by it, and dropped his gun. Before his weapon fell to the floor, Leisha had taken Mason's key card and was over at Redhead's side, picking up his gun and strapping it over her shoulder while the man bled out behind her. Quickly yanking her pants up, she was ready for escape.

Mason was hidden behind the other solider. The guard had his gun out and aimed at her, but it looked like he was uncertain

if he should take the shot. Keeping her gun trained on the other two men, she went to the door and used Mason's card to get out. As she backed out of the room, she pulled the trigger and hit the other soldier in the gut. Mason jumped behind the metal slab and pulled the guard with him for cover.

Leisha fired several more rounds, hitting the man in the legs and blasting bullets into the metal slab. She could hear Mason's heavy breathing and erratic heart, but it was more important to escape than to make sure he was dead. She wasn't certain what kind of security awaited her outside.

She studied the outside panel for a minute before figuring out how to lock the door behind her. A quick scan with her eyes and strain of her ears told her that there was no one else in the hallway.

She rushed over to the elevator and pushed the button. She fixed her disheveled clothes so they fit more properly, though they were very wrinkled and crusted with blood.

Standing there and waiting for the lift to arrive seemed ridiculous, but she had no other choice. She could feel her hands beginning to shake, but she clamped down viciously on the urge to draw upon Samantha's strength.

Finally, the elevator dinged. Pointing her gun at the doors, she waited for them to open. Once they did, she blinked in surprise. Tafari was standing before her—the last person she expected to see. He stood passively while one guard held his upper arm and two other soldiers stood close to the door, their guns trained on Tafari.

Before anyone could react, Leisha quickly shot the man holding Tafari's arm, hitting him in the face and killing him instantly. The man closest to her chopped down on her arm, making her drop her weapon.

As her opponent started to raise his own gun, she punched his hands down and to the side with her right hand while simultaneously jabbing him in the face with her left. Blood sprayed from his nose but he stayed upright. His green eyes blazed with pain and anger as he lunged for her.

Leisha swerved to the side and kicked him in the chest. Unfortunately, it didn't have much power since she was pregnant and weak. Green Eyes rushed at her again, but this time Tafari was there. He gave an uncharacteristic growl and seized the soldier in a head lock. He pulled at an angle, and the man's neck snapped.

Leisha looked in the elevator to see the man she'd shot with the back of his skull gone, and the other guard was on the floor, his head gushing blood. Glancing back up at Tafari, she marveled at the storm that seemed to rage in those silvery blue eyes. "What are you doing here?" She demanded.

Stooping to drag the one with the head wound out of the car, he answered. "I came to get you out. Samantha contacted me when you did not turn up." He pulled the other man out and gestured for her to get into the elevator with him.

Inside, Leisha handed him the key card so they could move. His musky scent filled her nostrils and she took a deep breath before saying anything. "Thanks for coming." It came out awkwardly, but she didn't know what else to say. "Is Samantha alright?"

Tafari shrugged. "She is eating a lot of steak because she refuses to drink blood. Not that I can blame her." He gave her an accusing glare. "I cannot believe you made her your human servant."

Looking away, she nodded. "I never intended to."

"The road to Hell, and all that."

Leisha pressed her lips together and then met his stare. "But I'm already going there, right?"

She could feel his frustration in the small confines of their car. "Let me ask you this," he said. "Did you ever intend to tell me you were pregnant?"

Putting a hand over her large stomach, she looked down. "Eventually." She licked her lips. "I didn't know how to tell you. Seek you out in person, or try to call. Either way would have been hard considering how we left things."

"Yes, because this way is working much better, is it not?"

Leisha tried to find a retort, but was saved when they heard the elevator ding. "What's the security like?" she quickly asked as she gripped the gun from her shoulder.

"Fairly light, actually. This base is so secret that there are not that many people guarding it."

The doors opened to show a sizable army waiting for them in a large lobby. They all had guns trained on the couple.

"You call this light?" murmured Leisha. There must have been hundreds of soldiers filling up the two hundred yards between them and their escape. "These guys may all have heightened abilities. We'll be lucky if we can kill half of them."

Appearing unperturbed, Tafari stood there looking at the soldiers. "Wait for it."

Some of the soldiers had their fingers pressed halfway on the triggers. Leisha could see in their eyes and hear in their heartbeats how much they were anticipating this attack.

"We need to get the doors closed *now*," she muttered softly. "Maybe we can get out through a window or something on one of the higher levels."

Eyes still scanning the crowd of soldiers, Tafari shook his head slightly. Leisha swallowed and tried to see what he was looking for. But before she detected anything, an explosion crashed through the front doors of the lobby, felling the majority of the men. The blast reached the elevator, and Tafari wrapped his arms around Leisha from behind to keep her steady.

Before she could recover, he grabbed her elbow and was pulling her through the smoke. Though the blast had knocked a lot of men down, there were still enough left over to challenge them. Tafari let go of Leisha to rush at a man who was about to fire upon them. In one fluid movement, Leisha unslung her spare gun and pulled the trigger, spraying bullets in a wide arc. The smoke made accurate aiming difficult, but the room was so crowded with soldiers that she almost couldn't help but hit them.

Suddenly her weapon clicked on an empty chamber. Quick as a thought, she flipped the gun around and, grasping it by the muzzle like a baseball bat, she laid about her furiously, smashing in faces and cracking rib ages of anyone who got too close. Three had tried to sneak up on her from behind, but she was able to take out two of them with a combination jab and sidekick. She almost lost her balance from the move, but quickly recovered. The third got close enough to yank back a handful of her hair. She pivoted and clocked him in the jaw with her elbow, then kneed him in the groin hard enough to make him pass out.

The smoke was beginning to clear a little, and Leisha scanned the area for Tafari while she fought off two more soldiers. She didn't see him. The couple in front of her worked well as a team and got in a few swipes at her arms with their knives. She finally got a good hold on one and threw him at his partner . She wanted to feed on one of them, but the urgency she felt to get out of there overran her hunger .

Just as she was turning, there was a sharp jab at her lower ribs. Leisha grunted as she heard bones cracking. Tafari came out of nowhere. "Did they get you?" he asked as he tried to move her hand away from her side.

Shaking her head, she said through clenched teeth, "Don't worry about it. It was only the baby kicking." She gestured with her hand. "Bad guy."

Tafari quickly stepped in front of her and took little time to kill two soldiers trying to sneak up on them. Eyes wide, he glanced down at her stomach and spoke as if they hadn't been interrupted. "I thought I heard your bones breaking." He squinted through the smoke and grabbed her hand to maneuver through through the parts where there were less soldiers to fight.

"You did," she said dryly as she shot a man coming at them. "He's real strong and tends to break my ribs at least a few times a day."

Had there been time, Leisha would have laughed at the expression on Tafari's face; mortification and pride warring with each other. But the downed soldiers were already stirring from the explosion and time was not something they had. Instead, she grabbed his arm and went toward the outer doors. "So I'm assuming that you have some kind of escape planned for us, right?"

Blinking, he nodded. "We need to get to the beach, and we will be out of here shortly." He looked at her. "How well can you run with broken ribs?"

"I'll manage."

They fought off a few more groups of soldiers on their way out. This time, Tafari didn't leave her side and she could tell he was trying to take on of the bulk of their opponents. She knew she should be indignant about that, but at the moment, she really didn't mind.

Before she knew it, they were outside. The sun was just touching the horizon, which meant that the soldiers would soon be at their full power. Leisha sighed. They were hard enough to fight off when they weren't at full capacity.

The parking lot they were standing in was surrounded by palm trees. A saltwater breeze brushed over them. She nodded toward a single lane road that led east "Is that where we go?"

Shaking his head, he went in the other direction, still holding her hand. There were dozens of soldiers already coming after them, and Leisha could hear at least two helicopters nearby. As the pursuing footsteps drew closer, she tried to tug her hand free of Tafari's so they could fight off the men. Tafari just held tighter. "Keep running. They'll be taken care of," he said.

As if on cue, she saw Rinwa leap from a nearby palm tree onto the nearest group of soldiers. Leisha was running too fast to stay and watch, but she heard a good fight ensuing. It sounded like Rinwa was more than a match for the soldiers.

"Glad she's on my side right now," Leisha muttered.

Tafari grinned. "I trained her pretty well."

Grinning, she responded, "Typical man, you take all the credit for her natural talents."

He chuckled and before she knew it, they were slowing down.

"This is the rendezvous spot," Tafari said unnecessarily. They were standing on a white-sand beach. There was surprisingly little debris, and clear water was lapping at the shoreline.

Before they could look around much, a small pontoon plane landed in the water about thirty feet from the shore. Nikita called out the window. "Does she need assistance, or can you come out to us?"

"I can help her," Tafari called back. They walked into the water. He reached out to her when they were at waist level and fifteen feet from the plane.

"I'm fine, Tafari," she protested. "I can get there on my own."

Batting her hand away, he picked her up and kept walking. "You get to carry the precious cargo night and day. Let me have this moment for now."

A sudden well of emotion rose in her chest. Blinking back tears, she relaxed into his arms. She wasn't sure why that statement affected her so much, and blamed it on her hormones.

As soon as Leisha was inside the plane, Samantha grasped her from behind, hugging her fiercely. "I've been so worried!"

she nearly screeched. "Are you okay? What did my dad do to you? Did he hurt the baby?"

Leisha pulled out of the girl's embrace so that she could settle in next to her friend and patted her hand. "I'll be fine. I'll tell you everything once we're safe."

"And after you have fed and rested," Tafari put in.

Feeling sheepish, Leisha looked around. "Speaking of which, is there any food in here? I haven't eaten in days."

At Tafari's questioning glance, Samantha answered for her. "She needs real food as well as blood while she's pregnant." The teenager put her arm around Leisha. "She usually eats enough for about five normal people in a day, so she must really be starving right now if my dad didn't feed her."

Leisha didn't respond to that, but her stomach heartily agreed. The plane was starting to move, and Leisha's head came up. "What about Rinwa?"

Tafari smiled back at her. "She used a separate transport."

"But can we check on her before we take off? Just in case?"

Tafari shook his head. "She will text me when she leaves, but you must trust her. She has not failed in centuries."

Biting her lip, she nodded. Leisha really needed to sit down with Rinwa and hear about her life. The small plane hit some nasty turbulence as it was taking off. Samantha grabbed Leisha's hand. Leisha wasn't sure who it was to comfort, Samantha or herself, but squeezed back.

They'd been flying for about ten minutes when Tafari's phone beeped. After glancing at his screen, he smiled at Leisha. "Rinwa has left. She is staying a little behind us to be certain that no one is following."

Shoulders relaxing at the news, Leisha returned his smile and leaned back into her seat.

CHAPTER 24

Samantha was glad to see the landing strip. The high turbulence had made it feel like the small plane was going to come apart at any minute. She felt her stomach dropping as the craft descended. It jolted abruptly when the wheels touched the ground, making Samantha's teeth click.

She looked over to see that Leisha was still sleeping, her head lolling along the backrest. The vampire had fallen asleep almost immediately after takeoff and hadn't stirred the entire flight. Samantha nudged her.

"I don't feel like waking up yet," Leisha mumbled with her eyes still closed.

"Too bad," Samantha quipped. "You slept through the landing and we're about to park the plane."

Blinking her eyes open, Leisha sat up straighter and looked through the window. "Where are we?" she asked.

"Venezuela," Samantha informed her.

"So the compound I was held in was in South America?"

Tafari shook his head. "Not quite. It's on a private island southeast of the Virgin Islands."

Steering the conversation back on track, Samantha told Leisha, "Once we get you cleaned up and fed, we're going to a small city east of Caracas. Tafari set it all up."

Leisha glanced at the immortal in surprise. "It will be too close to daylight," she murmured. "We'll have to find a place to stay around here and then travel tomorrow night."

Nik spoke up at that. "They're going to stuff me into the trunk with a thick blanket."

Looking at his tall frame, Samantha knew that Nik wouldn't enjoy the ride at all—in fact, he looked like he would rather stick his hand down a wood chipper—but it had already been decided between him and Tafari.

Nik stopped the plane on a private tarmac and cut the engine. Tafari exited first, turning to help Leisha down. He extended his hand to Samantha as well and she took it. While she was definitely faring better than Leisha, Samantha was exhausted. She felt like she'd run a thousand miles while being pelted with rocks. Nik's presence behind her was soothing, and she slowed so she could walk alongside him. As if sensing her need for comfort, he put his hand at the small of her back and guided her along. Just that little touch and the heat of his hand made her feel better.

They left the airport in a taxi, which carried them to a Marriott hotel so that Leisha could clean up. Samantha went into the bathroom with her and helped. Leisha was shaking from what Samantha could only assume was extreme hunger, and who knew what else. It was tempting to ask what her father did to Leisha, but she choked back the questions. There was no need to make Leisha revisit the terrors yet. The pants that Samantha brought for Leisha to change into were a bit too small.

"I don't get how your stomach could have grown that much when you were starved the whole time," Samantha commented.

Frustrated, Leisha ripped the top of the maternity jeans on each side, and then slipped them on. "It does seem strange," she said, "but I think he'll simply keep taking what he needs from my body." She hesitated. "And I have a feeling that it's possible he used our bond to pull from you, too."

Tilting her head, Samantha said, "In a way, that's kind of sweet. I get to do something to keep him healthy and growing."

Leisha smiled halfheartedly.

Once they were out of the bathroom, the smell of food hit them and Samantha closed her eyes and breathed it in. "That smells amazing."

Gesturing for them to sit on the couch, Nik brought them plates piled high with some very spicy smelling food. Samantha recognized beans, rice, and some vegetables, but nothing else. She thought one of the toppings was some kind of cheese, but she'd never tasted that flavor before. Relishing each bite, she wasn't sure whether the food was really that delicious, or that her mouth was happy to consume something other than steak.

Both girls polished off their plates. The others had already eaten while Leisha and Samantha had been in the bathroom. Stomach full, Samantha sat back. Taking an inventory of how she felt physically, she knew there was still a problem. It was hard to describe exactly what was wrong. She only knew that her body wasn't fully rejuvenated yet. Then she understood.

Turning to Leisha, Samantha said, "You still need blood. As soon as possible. I can feel you pulling on our link." Plus, she was having the strangest craving for blood. A disgusting urge, but she longed for it nonetheless.

Leisha nodded and stood. "It shouldn't be too hard. Caracas is a big city with some dangerous people." She turned to Nik and Tafari. "How soon did you want to be on the road?"

Tafari looked grim. "I do not want to condone murder tonight."

"You've seen me do it before." Leisha pointed out, her voice sounding a little frosty. "In fact, you did condone it when that guy was going to kill us and steal your car."

Tafari shrugged. "I am not comfortable with it."

Rinwa came up next to Tafari. "Well, it could attract the kind of attention we don't want. But it seems kind of silly to let her starve to death after we went through the trouble of rescuing her."

Looking at the wall, Tafari said, "She can rejuvenate herself with immortal blood."

Rinwa wrinkled her nose and looked at Leisha. "No way am I going to let you drink my blood. I'd rather you went out and killed some rapist or drug dealer or something."

Samantha watched Tafari closely. To the normal eye, he was simply looking distant, but she could see that he seemed torn. She didn't think it was the fact that Leisha drank blood. Suddenly she remembered how jealous he had been when Ian had offered to let Leisha drink from him while they were staying with the immortals. Her brows drew together while she continued to watch the immortal. Did he like it when she drank blood from him?

Samantha stood abruptly. "I think we should let Leisha and Tafari have some privacy while they discuss this. How about the rest of us go for a walk or something?"

Nik frowned. "I thought you were still feeling weak."

Waving her hand, she answered, "Only a little. Besides, every time I go to a foreign country, I barely get to see any of the sights. May as well get it in while I can."

Rinwa gave her a bored look. "I could care less about the sights around here."

Trying to act casual, she said, "That's fine. Then it will be me and Nik while you get some alone time with your parents."

Rinwa's lips drew down at the corners. "No, I should escort you and make sure this vamp doesn't try anything with you."

Barely concealing her smile, Samantha grabbed a light jacket. "I thought you might say something like that."

The three of them left the room and headed down the stairs towards the exit. Samantha had no doubt that Tafari and Leisha would need at least an hour to . . . do whatever it was that needed doing. She turned to Nik. "So do you know your way around here?"

Nik shrugged. "Not really. The last time I was in this area was two hundred years ago. Things have changed a lot since then."

Samantha didn't have much of a response to that, so turned to Rinwa raising her brow.

Sighing, she said, "I know some places that play good music."

Samantha smiled. She and Nik followed Rinwa into a cab and they were in a small club twenty minutes later. Samantha was surprised the bouncers didn't card her at the entrance, but she didn't know what kind of limits applied to minors in this country. They moved through the smoke-filled room to a booth towards the back.

Not bothering to sit, Rinwa explained, "This place gets pretty busy, so you two stay at this table and I'll get some drinks."

Before she could leave, Nik said, "Would you see if they sell *Papelon Con Limon*? I haven't had that in a while."

Rinwa nodded and made her way through the crowd.

The music overwhelmed Samantha's senses. The beat had a definite Latino quality that Samantha found she was enjoying. She scooted until her arm was touching Nik's.

After a few seconds, Nik grabbed her hand and lightly stroked it. Feeling contented, even if she was still pretty tired, Samantha leaned against the backrest and smiled.

Rinwa came back with three beers along with the drink Nik had requested and set them on the table.

Nik's eyebrow raised. "She's underage."

Glaring back at Nik, Rinwa used her usual sarcasm. "Someone should have mentioned that before she befriended a bunch of bloodthirsty vamps."

Eyes widening, Samantha realized that Rinwa was right. If Samantha could handle being around all the supernaturals, didn't that make her old enough to drink? She had certainly been through a lot more than most people would experience in their entire lifetimes.

Feeling justified, Samantha grabbed a bottle and took a large swig. The beer was a little sour and had a yeasty flavor to it. She choked the mouthful down, but couldn't help the coughing afterwards. "Beer is gross!"

Nik smirked and Rinwa laughed outright. "No way," Rinwa said. "This is quality stuff." To prove her point, the blonde took two large swallows before putting her beer back on the table.

Nik let go of Samantha's hand and snaked his arm around her shoulders. "It's definitely an acquired taste. You don't have to drink it. Try the *Papelon Con Limon* instead."

"What is that?"

"It's a specialty drink I hear is very popular in this area." He grabbed it and offered it over to her.

Samantha took a tentative sip, and then a large gulp. "That's good!" It was like having sweet and tart in one drink.

"That's right, Samantha," Rinwa said. "Those drinks are more your style. I don't know what I was thinking getting you a beer."

"I could handle the beer," Samantha protested. If she had grown beyond high school and was really as grown up as she felt, Samantha wanted to show Rinwa that mild liquor was nothing to her.

"But you don't have to," Nik said. "Don't let her or anyone

else badger you into doing anything you're not comfortable with."

He doesn't see me as too young, does he? She appreciated that Nik was looking out for her, but at the same time, it felt too much like a big brother approach and she certainly didn't want him to see her in that way.

Samantha pursed her lips and rose to a self-imposed challenge, sipping at her bottle for the next half hour. After she finished the drink, she accepted another from Rinwa. Samantha still didn't love the taste, but she enjoyed the buzz the beer was starting to give her.

After her third beer, Samantha was pulling at Nik's arm. "Let's dance. This music makes me feel alive."

"I'm not sure it's a good idea," he protested.

After staring into his hazel eyes for a moment, Samantha blew a raspberry and stood. Going to the dance area she closed her eyes and let the music wash over her while she moved to its beat. Within minutes, she felt a large arm around her waist, pulling her into a warm body. At first, she thought it was Nik and smirked in her small victory. When she opened her eyes, she saw that it was a Latino with a small mustache and yellowing teeth. He looked to be her father's age. Before she could react, the man was suddenly pulled to the side and Nik took his place.

Smile returning, Samantha snuggled into his chest while continuing to dance to the rhythm. "Maybe there really is something to a jealously ploy," she mumbled.

Nik wrapped his arms around her and began to lead. She closed her eyes again and felt like she was in heaven. Their bodies swayed together in perfect unison, his hand pushing her in the direction she needed to turn. She was surprised at how graceful it felt. When she opened her eyes, it was to find that Nik had somehow steered them back toward their table.

Nik gestured to Rinwa. "I think we've given Leisha and Tafari plenty of alone time. Let's go."

"No!" Samantha pushed at his chest. "I want another drink." She brightened and looked at Rinwa. "I want to try a shot of Tequila!"

"That would be a definite no," Nik answered.

Before Samantha could make an argument, Rinwa stepped up to them. "I'll buy you one shot at the bar before we go." When Nik glared, the immortal shrugged. "May as well let her have the experience while we're here to watch out for her. If she waits until none of us are around, what do you think could happen?"

Samantha blinked, unable to follow the thought process that Rinwa argued on her behalf. But she saw that Nik was relenting, so she grabbed Rinwa's hand and weaved toward the bar.

Rinwa ordered the shot, then handed it to Samantha when she got it. Both Nik and Rinwa were watching her. Samantha had to stop her giggles before she was able to put the drink to her lips. She downed the whole thing in one swallow like she'd seen others do. At first, there was a rancid flavor, then the burning kicked in and Samantha thought she wouldn't be able to breathe again.

Between choking coughs, she ranted about Tequila. "Who ever thought to make that stuff in the first place?" Cough, hack. "It's the nastiest thing ever!" Cough, cough.

She looked up through watery eyes to see Nik trying very hard to contain a smile. "You're laughing at me." She pushed him as hard as she could, but he stayed in his place. "Couldn't you at least give me a courtesy budge or something?" Samantha griped.

That had Rinwa laughing outright. "Hey, you asked for it and you got it. Next time, I'll make sure you have a chaser so it goes down a little easier." She tipped her head toward the door. "Maybe the fresh air will help."

Nik pulled Samantha to his side and they headed out. The early morning air was cool and muggy. It didn't help Samantha clear her head at all. In fact, she could tell that the effects of her shot were beginning because she suddenly couldn't stop laughing.

Pushing her face into Nik's shoulder, she giggled some more, then stumbled. That only made her laugh harder. Face still neutral, Nik picked her up and continued walking. Samantha cooed and snuggled into his body.

"Well, we know what kind of a drunk she is," Rinwa said. It sounded like her friend was farther away than she should be.

"I still don't think that was a good idea," Nik commented. He sounded distant, too, but Samantha could feel the vibrations of his voice through his chest. She giggled again.

"You could have tried harder to stop her if you really wanted to."

Nik's hold tightened slightly. "I'm not her father. She has every right to make her own decisions. Even if they are stupid ones, they're still hers to make."

Samantha wanted to comment about how they were talking about her as if she wasn't there, but found she couldn't bring herself to speak. She suddenly realized that she'd closed her eyes sometime along their walk. ...

SAMANTHA WAS IN A LARGE room. This was how most of her visions started, but something was... off. She couldn't figure out what it was, but she felt more involved. As if this were a nightmare and a vision mixed together.

She had the impression that it was underground, even though the ceilings were cavernous. She walked over to a plush couch and sat down.

There was a boy sitting next to her. She didn't know his name, but knew that she loved him dearly.

They smiled at one another for some moments. Though they were not saying anything, a profound communication was happening between them. She knew this boy in a way she didn't know any other person. She also knew that he understood her more intimately than anyone on earth ever could. Tears of deep affection sprung from her eyes and the boy nodded in encouragement. He reached out as if to hug her. Samantha leaned into him, feeling an amazing sense of love.

Suddenly, Samantha raised her hand high as a scimitar appeared in it. As a high-pitched shriek strangled out of her throat, she roughly rammed the weapon into the boy's chest. He gave her a pitying look as she sliced into him again and again, putting her whole body into every slash. Finally, soaked in the boy's blood and heaving from her exertion, Samantha ended it by cutting off his head.

Staring at the bloody aftermath, she dropped the blade. Samantha stood and ran as far away as she could. She screamed in an anguish that could never be quelled. Her surroundings gave way and she was outside, running through the woods. She was crying. Brushing away tears, she looked and saw blood covering her hands.

A large commercial swimming pool appeared, and she quickly undressed and submerged herself. The blood slowly washed off and she began to feel better.

A warm, naked body slipped behind her and she turned to find Nik. He was giving her a tender look before he leaned down and kissed her gently. Samantha moaned and kissed him back.

"I've missed you," Nik murmured. "We can't be apart again. I'll always be with you from now on."

"From now on," Samantha agreed. She leaned up to kiss him again when his face distorted slightly. It was still Nik, but shadows cast over his face to make him look monstrous and frightening.

Samantha gasped and tried to pull away.

"Too late," Nik's voice sounded exactly like Ptah's. "You already

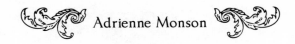
agreed to be with me." He opened his mouth and bit into her lower lip. His teeth ripped into her supple flesh and blood poured out over her chin, her mouth burning.

When he drew back, she looked around the pool, the water now blood. Nik began laughing and swung forward to savagely bite into her throat. He kept his hold while pushing them under the surface of the thick, red fluid. Samantha opened her mouth to scream but the blood filled her. It didn't simply pour into her mouth, but forced its way into her every opening and crevice. She could feel it invading her very pores, burning everything it touched until she was utterly consumed

CHAPTER 25

Leisha pushed herself out of bed. "We need to dress," she stated. "They'll be returning any moment."

Tafari leaned over and kissed her before complying. His lips left a pleasant aftertaste that she tried to ignore. She needed to think clearly, and had a very hard time doing that with Tafari's musky scent and flavor lingering on her body.

After the others had left, they had stood awkwardly for a moment before Leisha had spoken up. "I do need to feed, Tafari. Please tell me you aren't going to try to stop me."

Glancing at the door, he murmured, "I think Samantha knows."

"Knows what?"

After a slight hesitation he looked at her, his silvery blue eyes dancing with passion. "She knows how much I enjoy it when you drink from me."

Whatever Leisha had expected him to say, it definitely had not been that. They stood, looking into each other's eyes for what felt like several minutes. Then Tafari stepped forward until his stomach was against her belly. Leaning towards her, he tilted his head to the side, offering his neck.

The immortal blood called to her, beating its rhythm just under Tafari's skin. The heat of his body relaxed Leisha as she inched her face forward. Both of their breathing was uneven, Leisha's heart stuttering as well.

Slowly, she placed her lips on his neck, stroking her hands up his shoulders and resting them behind his back. Tafari's arms closed around her and Leisha reveled in the feeling. Opening her mouth, she licked his skin, tasting his natural flavor mixed with a hint of saltiness.

Tafari groaned and tightened his hold on her. Feeling encouraged, Leisha bit down. Tafari's sweet blood gushed into her mouth and she swallowed. It was ambrosia! As she drank, Tafari's hands caressed their way down her back and low on her sides, making her hunger for far more than just blood. Fatigue flushed out of her body. Aches and little wounds she hadn't even noticed healed instantly, leaving the vampire energetic and craving just one thing.

The immortal's wound healed all too quickly. Leisha suckled the spot, remorseful for their embrace to end. Finally, she pulled back, but Tafari wouldn't let go.

Looking up into his eyes, Leisha saw that he truly did enjoy the experience.

Her tongue circled her lips, rich blood flavoring them, and Tafari watched closely. Leaning her face upward, Tafari met her mouth in a consuming kiss. His lips encompassed her while his warm tongue grazed against hers, teasing her. Leisha moaned into him and felt her body melting into his embrace.

In the present, Leisha smiled and pulled on her ripped maternity pants. Sex had been a little awkward with her rotund belly, but it left her more satisfied than she had been in a long, long time.

Fully dressed, she headed back toward the main room. Tafari stopped her by putting his arms around her from behind

and nuzzling her neck. Unable to help herself, she leaned into his chest and closed her eyes, smiling radiantly.

After a few seconds, Leisha shook her head and stepped away from him. As enjoyable as it was to be with him, she needed to address some issues. "Tafari, we can't just pretend there aren't problems between us."

Sighing, Tafari went to the couch and sat down. He leaned his elbows on his knees and looked at her with barely concealed impatience. "And what, exactly, are these problems, Leisha?"

She felt fully restored and knew this was probably the best time to have this conversation. She only hoped the others didn't interrupt. Lowering herself into a chair opposite the couch, she looked at him directly. "I need to know where your loyalties lie."

He raised his eyebrows. "Do you really need to ask that?"

"Of course not." She sat back. "It will always be with the immortals. I guess the real question is, what are you going to tell them about our son?"

Resting his cheek on one hand, he looked lost in thought. It was several minutes before he spoke up. "Yes, you did need to ask."

Leisha angled her head. "What was that?"

"You are right to ask about my loyalties." His voice was distant.

Brows drawing together, she waited for him to continue.

He sat up, appearing more focused as he looked at her. "The truth is that I am feeling . . . *uncertain* about the immortals right now."

"How do you mean, uncertain?"

Heaving a deep sigh, he answered slowly. "Ever since I have found out about the baby," he nodded to her stomach, "I have been feeling protective, and maybe a little possessive. I do not like the idea of the immortals taking our child for their gain."

Leisha huffed out a breath. "That's the point I was trying make from the very beginning!"

Tafari shook his head. "That was before you discovered your pregnancy. Before he was even conceived."

"Tafari, it shouldn't matter if the prophecy child is ours or not. The point I was trying to make is that you can't stand idle while the society you serve exploits a helpless little boy."

Staring at her face, Tafari's mouth opened and closed several times before he was able to speak. "It seems so backwards that a vampire is telling me how to value life." His voice held a small tremor of irony.

Looking away, Leisha shifted in her seat. "Tafari, we both know that I'm as far from sainthood as can be." She pursed her lips, considering what she could tell him, what she should tell him. "Before I grew a backbone and finally stood up to Ptah, I did many horrible things that I'm not proud of. In fact, if there's a hell, I have a first class ticket there when I die." She met his eyes. "But I do have a conscience and I very much value human life. I like what humanity stands for and I will do what I can to help those around me when they're in need."

A moue tugged at his lips. "Would you not agree that a drug dealer needs help? What if a serial rapist were to change his ways? You take their lives before they have that chance."

Squaring her shoulders, she held his gaze. "You're exactly right, Tafari. I try to justify what I have to do, but in the end .. . It's like I said: I'm going straight to hell."

After a few silent minutes, Leisha raised her brow in challenge. Tafari appeared thrown by her confession. After blinking a few times, he changed the subject.

"We are getting off-track from what we really need to discuss. That I have made a decision to protect you and our child. My family takes priority over my service to the immortals."

Leisha's voice quavered when she asked, "What about your oath to them?"

Looking into her eyes to convey his grave sincerity, he answered. "I made an oath to you first. It has been too long since I have lived up to the promises I once made to you."

Standing, Leisha turned away so that Tafari would not see the tears.

He was behind her in an instant and pulled her into his arms. She turned and buried her face in his shoulder, trying to control her soft crying.

It was at that moment that Rinwa opened the door and held it for Nikita, who was holding an unconscious Samantha. Quickly wiping her face, Leisha ignored Rinwa's downturned mouth and rushed over to check on Samantha.

"What happened?"

Nikita looked at Rinwa. "Would you like to tell your mother what you did?" His tone was a combination of accusation and mockery.

After making sure that Samantha's vitals were alright, Leisha turned to Rinwa.

The immortal waved a hand. "Don't blame it on me. It was Samantha's choice to get drunk. I simply made sure she was in a safe and controlled environment when she did it."

"Excuse me?" Leisha glared at both Nikita and Rinwa. "She's only sixteen! You can't allow her to drink."

Looking totally unapologetic, Rinwa shrugged and went over to the couch and sat. "I'm pretty sure that everyone in this room tried alcohol in their early teens."

Tafari sat next to Rinwa. "Times were different in those days. In retrospect, it was very unhealthy for anyone to drink so young. In fact, drinking at all is bad for you."

Rinwa huffed. "You have wine on a regular basis."

"Yes, but it doesn't damage our organs like it does a human's. Immortals do not fall under the same health restrictions."

"We're getting way off topic here," Leisha interjected. She turned to Nikita. "Is she okay?"

He nodded. "I think so. I'm pretty sure she had a vision while she's been asleep."

"How do you know?"

He shrugged. "I can tell by her breathing and heartbeat." His lips pursed to the side. "The strange thing is that she usually wakes up after having a vision. This time, she's still asleep."

"It's probably just the alcohol," Leisha reasoned.

Tafari stood and focused a hostile expression towards Nikita. "And how would *you* know about her sleeping patterns?"

For the first time since she'd known him, Leisha saw Nikita bristle. "We haven't had sex, if that's what you're asking."

Keeping eye contact, Tafari said, "That is what I am asking. And now I am telling you that you better not. Understand?" It was the second time Leisha had seen him act like a father figure towards Samantha. It was that attitude, in fact, that had driven her to try and leave Samantha with the immortals last year to keep the girl safe.

Nikita curtly nodded and took Samantha into the bedroom and didn't come back out.

Rinwa picked up the remote and turned on the television. "We're going to have to get moving pretty soon here," she said while flipping through channels. She tossed a brief glance at Leisha. "I'm assuming that Tafari's blood did the trick?"

The room suddenly seemed devoid of oxygen. Leisha nodded, then changed the subject. "I'm not sure how Samantha will be feeling. She may be sick while we drive."

Tafari rubbed a hand over the back of his neck. "We could wait another day."

Turning off the TV, Rinwa stood. "No good. We should leave now, while Samantha is still sleeping soundly."

After a brief mental debate, Leisha agreed with her daughter. Walking over to the bedroom, she poked her head in.

Nikita was standing and lifting Samantha back into his

arms. He'd obviously heard their conversation and was ready to leave. He nodded to Leisha as she made a sweep of the bathroom and bedroom to be sure they weren't leaving anything behind. By the time she finished, everyone else was already situated in the car. Nikita was placing a blanket in the trunk.

Looking at the awkward space, Leisha couldn't contain her guilt. "We could wait until dusk, Nikita. It looks awfully cramped in there."

Nik gave her an amused grin and placed a reassuring hand on her shoulder. "I've done this plenty of times. Besides, we vampires should never get too accustomed to luxury. Not with our lifestyle."

He climbed into the rectangular space and contorted his body until it fit. Sighing, Leisha closed the trunk on him. She knew he wouldn't be permanently damaged back there, but it would certainly be uncomfortable.

Rinwa allowed Leisha to sit in the front. "Since I was the one who got her drunk, I should be back here when she has her hangover."

Snorting, Leisha climbed in and relaxed while Tafari drove. He looked like he knew where they were going, so she let her mind drift and watched the scenery transform from bustling city to tropical savanna landscape. The sun was high in the sky when Samantha finally awakened. Leisha glanced back at her and watched as her face went from pale to green.

"Pull over," she said to Tafari.

Samantha was out the door in an instant, Rinwa following and holding her hair out of the way.

Crinkling her nose, Leisha commented. "This would be one of those times when I wish I had regular human senses."

Smirking, Tafari looked at her. "You are not going to throw up, too, are you?"

Rubbing her belly, she replied, "I hope not."

There was a bottle of water in the front that Leisha handed to Samantha when the two girls climbed back into the car. After two long gulps, Samantha seemed a little better.

"I'm never going to drink again," she muttered.

Rinwa laughed. "That's what they all say."

Sitting up, Samantha looked adamant. "I'm serious. I have more sense than most people."

Leisha threw her a curious expression. "What is that supposed to mean?"

Samantha's eyes suddenly looked haunted. "I had a vision while I slept."

Lifting her brow, Leisha waited for the girl to explain. Visions didn't usually upset Samantha, even the darker ones. The girl had witnessed death from the time she was a toddler. Samantha seemed to be searching for the right words.

"I could tell it was a vision, but it was… skewed. It turned into one big nightmare, and now I don't know what's real and what was just the alcohol."

Brow crinkling in concern, Leisha said, "Why don't you tell me what you saw and we can decipher it together."

Crossing her arms across her body, Samantha shook her head. "It's too fresh to discuss right now. I need to let it settle for a while first."

Leisha nodded reluctantly. She just hoped the vision didn't show anything too pressing. They drove in silence for about thirty minutes before Samantha began to heave. Tafari slammed on the breaks and the girl was back outside. The third time they pulled over to let Samantha vomit, it had been about twenty minutes from the previous incident. When she wasn't vomiting, the girl was hunched over clutching her head.

"This is going to be some slow going," Rinwa grumbled.

"Hey, you're not allowed to complain about this," Leisha admonished. Rinwa rolled her eyes and slipped on her sunglasses.

Leisha shook her head and settled into the seat. Her lower back cramped, but she shifted and it soon went away.

They'd driven a bit further when Samantha piped up. "Is there any more water?"

"We'll stop when I find something," Tafari responded. An hour later, he stopped at a cart by the side of the road and bought more water and fresh fruit for everyone.

Everyone snacked and stretched their legs a little, then they were back on the road.

"So," a replenished looking Samantha asked, "where are we going?"

Rinwa answered in a bored tone. "San Cristobal."

Pulling a map out of the glove compartment, Leisha calculated. "This is going to be an all-day drive, isn't it?"

Tafari nodded.

Glad that their car had air conditioning, Leisha shifted into her seat and tried to sleep. It took a few tries before she found a spot comfortable enough. She ended up having to take off her seat belt, but she was finally able to drift off.

Leisha could hear the others talking now and then, but ignored the noise and forced herself to rest. It had been about two hours when the baby kicked, sending a searing pain plummeting to the bottom of her stomach.

Sitting up with a gasp, Leisha forced herself to breathe out slowly until the pain eased.

"Did you have a nightmare," Samantha asked. Before the Leisha could respond, the girl pursed her lips. "Can vampires dream? I don't know if we've ever discussed that."

Putting her seatbelt back on, Leisha glanced back at her friend. "No, I didn't have a nightmare. And yes, vampires dream."

"Then what happened?" Tafari's deep timbre resonated through the car.

Waving a hand, Leisha explained. "It was just the baby. He probably did some damage to my stomach lining or something, but it'll heal."

Directly behind Leisha, Rinwa spoke up. "So you've been pregnant for how long, exactly?"

Counting back to when Rinwa and Tafari were in Ohio, she replied, "Three months, give or take."

"Then why do you look like you're six or seven months along?"

"It's easy enough to guess, Rinwa," Samantha piped up. "A baby conceived by an immortal and a vampire is going to have some special powers. Maybe that's why he's got speedy development, too."

Leisha peered back to see Rinwa tossing Samantha a look through her sunglasses. "I realize that we're in uncharted territory here," the immortal responded. "But I still say this whole thing is just plain weird." She glanced back to Leisha. "By the way, we have a ceremony we'd like to perform. Just to confirm this is actually the prophecy child. Are you amenable, oro do I have to hold you down for it?"

"As long as you don't take the opportunity to kill me, I'm game" Leisha smiled. "I have to admit, I'm getting excited for him to arrive. Not only will it be nice to have my body back, but I can't wait to see what he looks like." Reaching back, she slid Rinwa's sunglasses down the bridge of her nose. "He might look like you did as a baby."

Appearing unimpressed, Rinwa put her glasses back into place and murmured, "Not likely."

Lapsing into an easy silence, the rest of the drive went by rather quickly for Leisha. She was glad to be among friends and allies and to not worry about escaping a secret government compound.

It was late afternoon, with the sun still somewhat high in the sky when a pounding was heard from the trunk.

Samantha sat up straight. Crinkling her brow, she looked at Leisha. "Do you think he's alright? The sun hasn't set, so he can't come out yet, can he?"

Leisha shrugged and waited until Tafari pulled over on the side of the road, then stepped out and made her way to the trunk. The lid made a distinct clicking sound when it unlatched and Leisha reached down to open it.

Before she could, it was thrown up and smoke rushed into her face. Coughing at the smoke and the smell of roasted skin, she waved her arm to clear the air and see into the trunk.

Nikita was there, and he didn't look very good. Not only was he contorted in an awkward position, but his skin was smoking and looking slightly charred.

"How are you burning?" Leisha asked. "You haven't been in the sun at all."

"I believe it's the heat," Nikita choked through blistered lips. "I may not be burning in the sun, but I'm literally baking back here."

Samantha came around and gasped when she saw the vampire. "Oh no, Nik! Are you okay?" She reached out to him, but Leisha grabbed her wrist.

"His skin is pretty tender right now," she informed the teenager. "It's probably not a good idea to touch him."

Samantha's skin paled several shades. "But he'll be alright, won't he?"

"Yes," Nikita answered. "I just need some water." He shifted until he sat up, his torso leaning far forward to avoid touching the top of the car. "In fact, I think I could get in the front of the car now."

Glancing at the sun, Leisha saw that it was still above the horizon. "Are you sure? Maybe we should just wait here for a while so you can air out, and then continue our journey."

Tafari and Rinwa exited the vehicle and joined them at the back.

Rinwa's nose wrinkled. "The only time that stench is pleasant is when the vampire actually dies."

Ignoring the comment, Nikita leaned up until he peeked over the trunk lid to see the sun. He settled down and met Leisha's gaze. "It's close enough to the horizon. I'll be fine."

"The sun is facing the left side of the car, so you should sit on the right. Maybe it will be shaded enough," Samantha said. The concern in her eyes was plain for anyone to see.

"So the three of us are going to squeeze in the back now?" Rinwa asked. She slipped off her sunglasses. "That means we'll all reek of charred vampire flesh by the time we get there."

"I'll sit in the middle, and you can have first dibs on the shower when we get there." Samantha glared at Rinwa. "You could be a little more sensitive, you know. The poor guy was being slowly baked in a hot car while you sat comfortably with the A.C. on."

Seemingly unrepentant, Rinwa shrugged and sidled over to the left side of the car and climbed back in. Cracking a half smile at Leisha, Tafari followed suit and got in the driver's seat. Leisha and Samantha escorted Nikita to his door. While his face was utterly expressionless, Leisha could tell he was in a lot of pain by the way he carried himself.

Samantha climbed in and Leisha murmured to her vampire friend, "You need to feed soon. These kinds of injuries will be harder to recover from the less frequently you drink."

"No need to worry about me. I'm perfectly capable of taking care of myself."

A hint of amusement flicked through his hazel eyes.

Nikita sat, and Samantha helped cover him with the blanket, just in case. Leisha closed his door for him. She quickly got in and Tafari resumed their drive.

Pulling down her visor, Leisha could see through the little mirror that Samantha kept glancing at Nikita. His skin was already healing, taking on an angry pink color. Though Leisha

wouldn't admit it, Rinwa was right. The car already smelled of burned flesh.

Besides a pit stop for gas and food, the rest of the drive was uneventful. It was close to midnight by the time they arrived in San Cristobal. Leisha had never been here before. The city was large and densely populated. Samantha even forgot her sickness and Nikita's injuries when they passed an area that housed four stadiums next to each other. Two separate games were in progress, the stadium lights blazing, and traffic was heavy.

Winding their way through the narrow streets, the city-scape eventually changed into more rural surroundings. Some of the homes looked quite old, while others were brand new. The house Tafari had arranged for was at the top of a steep incline. Parking on the street, Tafari turned off the car and gestured at the dwelling. "It may be a bit cramped with all of us in here, but I think we will be able to manage well enough."

"How many bedrooms?" Leisha asked as she climbed out into the humid night air.

"Three."

Looking at him from the corner of her eye, Leisha gave a suggestive smile. "We should share a room, to conserve the space."

"Nik and I can share, too," Samantha offered.

Answers resounding in the negative came from everyone, including Nikita. Staring at the vampire, Samantha looked hurt.

"It would not be wise in my current condition," Nikita explained.

When Samantha's eyebrows drew together, Leisha jumped in the conversation. "Remember when we were on Tafari's yacht last year and we couldn't share a room anymore because The Hunger had gotten too strong?"

Understanding dawned on the teenager's face. "You need to feed?" She asked Nikita.

"Don't worry about it," he said. He moved to the trunk and began unloading their meager belongings.

When Leisha stooped to pick up some bags, Tafari placed a hand on her arm. "I can get this."

Leisha shrugged, hiding the smile that threatened. It had certainly been a while since anyone had given her the chivalrous treatment.

Samantha was standing next to Nikita as he closed the lid. "You can drink from me," she offered.

Everyone stopped and stared at Samantha.

The girl took a defensive stance and a stubborn expression. "What? Leisha takes little snacks until she has to have the big feed. I can help Nik with that so he doesn't need to go out and hunt as soon."

Nikita threw Leisha a pointed look. Wordlessly, she shepherded Rinwa and Tafari toward the house so Nikita could have a private word with Samantha.

Pulling keys from her pocket, Rinwa unlocked the front door and led the way inside. As she walked into the foyer, Leisha could hear Nikita explaining that he didn't want to use Samantha in that way. She thought he was doing a great job of making sure the teenager didn't feel rejected.

Walking over the hardwood floors, she noted that, though the house was a bit small, it was lavish. The ceilings stood taller than the standard eight feet; delicate chandeliers hung in every room. Tasteful art lined the walls in symmetrical formations. Following Tafari into what she surmised was the master bedroom. The bed was standard queen size. Touching the pillow case, Leisha could tell the sheets were a high-thread count Egyptian cotton. The connecting bathroom had no shower, but a jetted tub beckoned.

Turning, she noticed Tafari studying her. "This is a really nice place," she told him. "I wasn't expecting something so extravagant."

Before he could reply, Riwna walked past, talking over her shoulder. "Yeah, Tafari's getting soft in his old age."

Crinkling at the corner of his eyes, Tafari closed the door to the bedroom. "I think you and I should turn in." He walked over and grabbed the hem of Leisha's shirt.

Placing a hand over his, Leisha asked, "What about the others? Should we go out there and help get Samantha settled?"

Leaning close, his breath tickled over her lips. "They will be fine without us."

Relaxing as he caressed the back of her neck, it was easy to relent. "Sounds good," she mumbled. Though they stayed up for a few more hours, they didn't talk for the rest of the night.

CHAPTER 26

March 19th

Samantha was wary of falling asleep. The nightmarish vision she'd had the previous evening loomed in the back of her mind. Instead of going to bed at the same time as Rinwa, she opted to stay up. "I just want to make sure Nik's fully healed," she said.

Rinwa shrugged and headed down the hall. "Guess that means I get the bed tonight. I'll leave a couple of blankets on the floor for you." Turning, she pinned Nik with a glare. "I don't care if she tries to give you a lap dance. You'd better leave her alone."

Heat flushed Samantha's cheeks. "Rinwa!" But the immortal had already disappeared into the bedroom.

Avoiding his gaze, Samantha walked to the couch where Nik was sitting. She perched herself next to him, but not close enough to touch. Rinwa's comment was making her feel a bit flustered.

Taking a swig from his water bottle, Nik looked her way. "Don't let her get to you, Sam. She likes pushing buttons, and if you let her get under your skin, she'll never let up."

Nodding, Samantha twisted her head to study the vampire. "Are you sure you're okay, Nik?"

He waved away her concern. "It's nothing I can't handle." He changed the subject. "So why don't you want to go to sleep?"

"I wanted to spend more time with you," she admitted. "After all, it's been so crazy this past week and we haven't really had a moment to ourselves."

Reaching over, Nik grabbed her hand and held it in a comforting grip. "That may be true, but it's not the real reason."

Samantha sighed and gave in. "It's that vision I had last night. The booze skewed it so it was one giant nightmare. Now I'm afraid to fall asleep. I don't want to go through that again."

Lightly stroking her shoulder, Nik pulled Samantha into him. Her muscles relaxed as she breathed in his familiar scent.

"Well," Nik began, "you're not drunk tonight, so I think you'll be fine."

"But what if drinking once will ruin my visions from now on? What if I get another vision tonight and I can't understand what it's trying to show me?"

"First of all," Nik said as he rubbed her back, "you don't have to fall asleep in order to have a vision, so if one is going to hit you, it will do so no matter if you're asleep or awake. Second, there's no point in losing sleep over this. How often do you get visions?"

She sat up straight so she could look at him. "They're pretty sporadic, but maybe once every month or two."

"So the likelihood of you having another vision tonight?"

Smiling, Samantha leaned in and kissed Nik's cheek. "Pretty slim."

"Then why stress over this when you can't control your visions? And when you do have another vision, I'll help you through it."

Warmth filtered through Samantha's heart and she hugged him tightly. "You're the best, Nik."

Nik kissed the top of her head. "Sleep well, Samantha."

She squeezed him one last time and got up to go to the bedroom. It was dark, but Samantha was able to make her way to the pile of blankets on the floor. Rinwa was already breathing deeply, so she tried to be quiet as she arranged a makeshift bed and snuggled in to sleep.

Thinking of Nik, she drifted off easily with only a tremor of anxiety.

The next morning, Samantha awoke feeling well rested but stiff. After stretching for a few minutes, she finally rolled over and stood. Rinwa was in the hall as Samantha made her way to the bathroom. "No way am I sleeping on the floor again," she grumbled. "You won't get muscle cramps from lying on a hardwood, so you can take the ground from now on."

"Fair enough," Rinwa grinned. "But what sounds even better is first come gets first choice. So if you don't stay up with *that*," she nodded in Nik's direction, "then you should have no problem landing the bed every night."

Walking into the bathroom, Samantha called out, "Very subtle, Rinwa."

"Who said I was going for subtlety?"

The shower was cramped, but Samantha felt a lot more refreshed when she stepped out clean. She towel dried her hair and put her clothes on. She'd noticed that, in South America, she didn't have to put on lotion after bathing and assumed it was the humidity.

Opening the door and stepping into the hall, Samantha smelled something cooking. Her stomach growled, and she wondered how long it had been since she'd had a square meal.

She hadn't eaten much the day before because she'd been too hung over. Thankfully, she was back to her healthy self.

"More than half the population must be masochistic," she said to no one in particular as she entered the kitchen. Tafari glanced up from the oven and tossed her a quizzical smile. Nik and Leisha were sitting at the dining room table. The furniture looked like it was carved from solid wood.

"What makes you say that?" Nik tilted his head toward her.

Sitting next to him, she said, "I just think that too many people get drunk, knowing that they're gonna be miserable the next day. Why would they do that unless they took at least a little bit of pleasure in hurting themselves?"

"They're not thinking like that when they drink," Leisha stated. "Most people think that alcohol will numb their sorrows, help them forget their problems." Folding her arms on the table, Leisha smiled. "Of course they still have to deal with the issues the next day, on top of the hangover. But it's worth it to them at the time."

Rinwa walked into the room. "What makes you such an expert on drunk humans?"

Taking a deep, patient breath, Leisha tapped her temple. "They're the easiest ones to read. I've heard about everything you can think of just walking into a bar."

The haughty expression on Rinwa's face melted off. It was as if she had forgotten her mother could read minds.

Tafari placed a steaming plate of crepes in the middle of the table. "What about people on drugs? I would assume they fall into the same category."

Leisha forked a crepe onto her plate and shook her head. "It depends on the drug." She piled sliced strawberries onto the flat hotcake and smothered them in whipped cream. "If they've got a hallucinogen in their system, then sure, I can read their mind, but nothing makes sense."

Following Leisha's lead, Samantha helped herself to a crepe

and loaded it with three different kinds of fruit, a large dollop of Nutella, and some cream cheese. Taking a bite, Samantha moaned at the bursting flavors in her mouth. "Thanks, Tafari," she said around her food. "This is great."

It grew quiet as everyone concentrated on their food for a few minutes. Even Nik helped himself to some.

Samantha noticed that Nik appeared more docile than usual, almost lethargic. She realized that he hadn't fed in quite some time, and had been badly burned yesterday. If he'd been human, she was positive his internal organs would have been cooked beyond repair.

Wiping her mouth with a cloth napkin, Samantha piped up. "Is there anything happening tonight? I mean, as far as I know, we only planned up to this point. Now that we're here, what are we going to do?"

"We're just going to lie low for a while," Rinwa answered. "I'd like to perform the Voodoo ceremony to be certain Leisha is carrying the prophecy child. Then, Tafari and I need to go back and report to the council soon, or they'll come looking for us. But you guys can stay here as long as you need. This house is one that Tafari purchased privately. No one knows he owns it."

"So, the same thing we did when we were hiding out in Canada." Samantha hoped it wouldn't get too boring. At least they were in a big city this time.

"Except you won't be going to school here," Leisha said. "In fact, I think we should dye our hair and work on our tans. We don't want to stand out around here."

Brushing fingers through her damp, chestnut colored hair, Samantha raised her brows. "What do you think would look good on me? Are you thinking of making my hair black?"

Pursing her lips to the side, Leisha studied the girl. "We'll see. I'll think about it."

"Can vampires dye their hair?" asked Samantha.

Tossing her golden tresses over a shoulder, Leisha nodded. "We can, but it doesn't last long—maybe a week."

Nik stood and began to clear the dishes while Leisha and Samantha discussed what they would do to alter their looks. Once they agreed, Tafari grabbed a pad of paper from the counter and wrote everything down.

"I'll run and get the things you need." He walked out the front door.

After he left, Rinwa went into their shared bedroom and Samantha hung out with the vampires in the main room. Tafari returned an hour later, carrying several sacks in his arms.

Leisha stood and kissed him on the cheek. "Thanks," she said.

Samantha noted the pleased look that Tafari was trying to hide.

Rinwa came into the room carrying thick candles and a long knife. The blade was carved with intricate patterns and the tip looked very sharp. "Before you go off being all girly, let's get this over with." She looked to her father, who nodded.

Samantha sat on the couch and watched as Rinwa herded her mother into a chair and Tafari placed the candles around the room. Rinwa pulled the curtains closed so it was very dim, then she handed Tafari her ceremonial knife.

Tafari glanced to Leisha. "You remember what these ceremonies are like?"

The pregnant vampire nodded. "Though I never knew you performed one like this. I didn't know there was a way to confirm it's the prophecy child."

Stripping off his shirt to reveal dark skin covering sculpted muscles, Tafari nodded. "There are many that the immortals designed. This one is quite simple, but it still requires me to use bloode rites."

Leisha nodded. "I understand."

239

Samantha felt like she'd entered the Twilight Zone when Rinwa sat on the floor with a small drum. She started tapping a rhythm and Tafari was suddenly jumping up and down, spinning in the air, while he chanted something Samantha couldn't understand. After a few flips and turns, Rinwa joined in the chanting without pausing in her beat.

Soon, a strange ambience filled the room and Samantha began to sweat. Tafari's movements looked more crazed, his eyes getting larger with every word he spoke. Then he brought the knife up and cut his forearm.

Samantha gasped as blood pooled from the man's wound, but he continued on as if there were no pain. Then he proceeded to cut more and more. His body jerked as he bounced his way towards Leisha. Samantha was surprised to see how easily the vampire took everything in. By the softening around her mouth, it even looked as if Leisha was feeling nostalgic.

When Tafari got close enough, he picked up Leisha's arm and cut her as well. Blood drips echoed between the chanting. Both Rinwa and Tafari continued to escalate their pitches, almost as if they were possessed. Tafari cut Leisha's arm more frantically until the slash marks matched the same pattern on his own arm. Suddenly, he stopped chanting and knelt. Tafari pushed Leisha's arm over her bulging belly and then put his bloody arm over hers. He sat for one long minute, studying the patterns created by the spilled blood while Rinwa continued to tap her beat and chant at the top of her lungs.

When Tafari stood, Rinwa stopped and looked up at him. "This is the prophecy child," he confirmed, pointing to the bloody patterns around him and Leisha.

Rinwa sighed and stood, gathering up her knife and drum from the floor. "Figured. I'm not cleaning this mess up." She walked back down the hall and into the room she and Samantha shared.

Swallowing, Samantha looked down at the blood on the

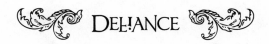

hardwood. It made a pattern on the floor. It if hadn't been blood, she might have stayed to study the beauty of it. Instead, she stood.

"I will clean this up while you two go through all the things I just got you." Tafari said as he helped Leisha to stand and kissed her cheek.

"Come on, Samantha." Leisha grabbed her hand and picked up the bags of merchandise. "We're going to spend the day doing makeovers!"

Tafari groaned as if it were a fate worse than death.

Samantha took a few deep breaths to recover from the strange ceremony. Of course, everyone else around her took it in stride as if that were completely normal. *It's funny how abnormal I feel sometimes, considering what they just did.*

Two hours later, Samantha was struggling not to scratch at her skin. Leisha had helped her apply a self-tanning lotion. They'd had to put five layers on to get her looking tanned. Samantha knew she was pretty pale, but hadn't realized how much work would go into getting her more bronzed.

"I hope we don't have to keep this up for long," she murmured as she studied the odd color of her arms.

"Hopefully not." Leisha brushed a dark curl from Samantha's forehead. "But you look pretty good this way. So it's not all bad."

Studying her reflection in the mirror, Samantha decided that the vampire was right. Not only was her hair raven black, but permed into medium curls. It caused her fine hair to look a lot thicker and made her face appear more heart-shaped than her usual oval. The darker tint of her face contrasted drastically with her blue eyes. The problem Samantha had was that she simply didn't look like herself. The person in the mirror was a stranger.

Glancing back at Leisha, Samantha cracked a bittersweet smile. "I may look cute, but you're absolutely centerfold magnificent as a redhead."

She'd helped the vampire dye her locks auburn. They hadn't done anything to her skin, but the more vibrant hair had brought out a pinker tone to Leisha. And her emerald green eyes were even more striking than before.

Smiling at each other, they walked out into the main room. Stopping in front of Nik, Samantha slowly turned. "What do you think?"

Placing his book in an end table, he studied her closely. "It's a very good disguise." He put his chin in the cup of his hand. "To be honest, I think you looked better as you were, but this will keep you well hidden."

Samantha smiled shyly. She was glad he felt the same as she did. She went over to the window and peeked through the curtain. "Guess we have more time to kill until sundown."

"And what happens at sundown?" Rinwa inquired.

Samantha glanced at Nik. "Nik's going to take me on a date."

The vampire didn't show any outward expression, but Samantha could see surprise flit across his eyes before it disappeared.

"Do you think that's wise?" Leisha was sitting next to Tafari on the couch, leaning against his chest.

Samantha gave a half shrug and made the argument she'd been preparing. "I don't see why not. After all, that's why we spent half the day making me look like a local. And Nik knows his way through any city in the world. He's the perfect person to take me out. I'll be safe with him."

"If you insist on going out," Tafari said, "then I can take you. I know San Cristobal like my own house."

Shaking her head, Samantha was about to argue further when Leisha spoke up.

"Samantha, you're old enough to make your own choices here. But I'd like to remind you that part of growing up has nothing to do with age and more to do with learning to make decisions with wisdom and foresight."

Brows drawing down, Samantha looked at her friend. "So are you going to support this decision I'm making, or tell me that I'm acting like a silly sixteen-year-old?"

"Like I said, you're old enough to make your own choices. I won't stand in your way."

"I'm glad that you're okay with this, but why do I get the royal treatment?"

Leisha's eyes danced with mirth. "Because I just realized that today is March twentieth."

Mouth popping open, Samantha stared. "No way."

"What happens on March twentieth?" Rinwa asked.

Gesturing to Samantha, Leisha answered all three curious looks. "As of today, Samantha is seventeen."

"It's your birthday?" Nik blinked.

Rinwa rolled her eyes. "Just because it's her birthday doesn't mean we can let her make stupid decisions for the day."

"This coming from the person who encouraged her to drink," Nik said with what Samantha guessed was annoyance.

Tafari shifted as if he were coming to a reluctant conclusion. "He has a point, Rinwa. Nikita was trying to be the voice of reason at that club."

Crossing her arms, Rinwa stared at her father with wide eyes. "Don't tell me you're suddenly okay with Samantha dating a vampire?"

"I did not say that. However, she deserves something special and I believe this date with him will provide it." He turned his blue-eyed-stare on Nik. "So long as he behaves as a *perfect* gentleman."

The vampire stiffened. "Of course I'd be a perfect gentleman."

Giggling, Samantha suddenly felt light-hearted. Today, she was a year older and Nik would take her out on a date. "Let's go." She walked into the front entry before she remembered that the sun was still up.

Biting her lip, she pivoted. "What I meant to say is that I'm going to take a shower and get ready for tonight

CHAPTER 27

Snuggled into Tafari's warmth, Leisha tried to contain her smile as Rinwa chuckled softly.

"Seventeen is so young," murmured Tafari. "If I could give her a birthday gift, it would be to let her have more of a childhood."

Remorse touching the deepest part of her soul, Leisha nodded.

Nikita rubbed his chin with his knuckles. "We may not be able to give her back her lost childhood, but we can try to make life more fun for her. I'll make sure she has a good time tonight."

Snorting, Rinwa pulled her long hair into a ponytail and wrapped a strand around it to keep it in place. "Nikita, you're going to take away even more of her childhood."

Sitting straight, Nikita glared at the blonde. "I told you, I don't plan to deflower her," he growled.

"I'm not only talking about sex here." The immortal's gaze bore into him. "You're a vampire and she's fallen in love with you. That means she'll do anything to justify your actions, to make you the hero, even though you're not one. You're the bad guy in this scenario."

Watching Nikita's face, Leisha could see the impact of her daughter's words. "That's a little harsh, Rinwa," Leisha said. "Nikita has saved both Samantha and me on several occasions."

"Sure." Rinwa readily acknowledged. "Because he *likes* you two. While he's nice to you and Samantha, his actions could be considered selfish. If he really wants to be a hero, then he has to stop whatever he may be doing to help a stranger in need. As far as I know, vampires aren't known for that kind of behavior." Rinwa looked back at the vampire, her brows raised in challenge. "Am I wrong?"

Face thoughtful, Nikita answered. "No, you're not. But that doesn't mean I'm a bad guy, either. I may have been in the past, but I'm changing. And one thing I know for certain," he stood and sauntered towards the hallway. "I will always protect Samantha. I can make her happy while you like to make jabs at her for the fun of it." He disappeared and Leisha heard him quietly close his bedroom door.

Tafari shifted, making Leisha move off him. "I don't disagree with you, Rinwa," Tafari stated softly. "But he also makes a valid point. You have little respect for those around you."

Rolling her eyes, Rinwa pulled one foot under the opposite knee. "Don't tell me we're going to have this conversation again. I think I've made myself very clear."

Squeezing Tafari's arm, Leisha gave him a small smile. "Will you make me something for lunch? Your cooking is divine."

Eyes dancing with indulgence, Tafari nodded and walked out of the room.

Leisha decided that tact would be a waste in this conversation with her daughter. "So why do you have to be so rude all the time? You do realize that you come off as a sulking teenager even more than Samantha does, don't you?"

Placing both feet on the floor, Rinwa sat forward. "I'm not a sulking teenager. I just don't bother putting on a show for people. They can see me for what I am, take it or leave it."

Leisha pursed her lips. "There's a difference between being comfortable with who you are and being antagonistic to others."

"I don't try to be mean."

Leisha scoffed.

"I'm honest and direct." Rinwa continued. "I just have a very sarcastic sense of humor. I'm really not going for rude . . . most of the time."

Raising an eyebrow, Leisha smirked. "Most of the time?"

Expression lightening, Rinwa leaned back. "Well, you have to admit, some people are just asking for it."

Covering her mouth, Leisha was unable to contain a snicker.

"See? You agree that sometimes my brutal honesty is welcome."

"Okay. But not always."

"Perhaps it's a good thing there are people in the world like me. We cynical commentators keep others on their toes." Rinwa laughed softly. "I remember when this guy, Willem, first joined the immortals. He didn't know what to make of me." Eyes glowing as she spoke, she grew more animated. "At first, he was polite and indifferent. Then, he'd try to draw me into his circle of friends. That didn't work out so well, though, because most of the guys would pick fights with me." She grinned. "I won every single one. And every time, I would taunt him and poke at him."

She wasn't certain why her daughter was suddenly opening up. But Leisha loved how freely the conversation flowed between them and became wrapped up in the memory. "So what happened with you and Willem?"

"After about a decade of me intimidating him, he finally challenged me. We fought in the sparring room with half of the immortals watching. I hadn't lost in more than fifty years."

"And?"

Looking into the distance with fondness, Rinwa answered. "He totally kicked my ass. I didn't have a chance."

Watching her face, the vampire noted, "And you liked it."

The immortal glanced at her mother. "Who wants to hang around men who cower at the sight of you?" She shrugged. "Of course, I had to deal with all kinds of blowback. It didn't last long, since no one else could best me. But I had to show Willem that he didn't impress me one bit."

Eyes narrowing in confusion, Leisha shifted on the couch. "But I thought he did."

"Yes, but I couldn't let him see it."

"Why not?"

Running fingers through her blonde locks, Rinwa pulled down her ponytail. "Just because. I may be upfront and blunt about things, but it doesn't mean that I'm going to let just anyone see my softer side."

Hesitating, Leisha debated her response. She knew all too well what it was like to have to prove she was untouchable but she also thought that Rinwa was sabotaging a chance at a great relationship.

"How long ago was this?"

"It's been a while." The immortal glanced at the ceiling as she thought. "I think Willem became an immortal around five hundred years ago. Maybe six hundred."

"And do you work well together?" Leisha asked in what she hoped was a neutral tone.

Rinwa saw through the questions. "Yes, Leisha," she said in a patronizing voice. "We work great together now. We even sleep together occasionally, if I allow it. But trust me when I say, I'm holding all the power in our partnership."

Becoming somber, the vampire licked her lips. "Be careful, Adanne. A partnership can't be one-sided. If it is going to survive, you not only have to share power, you have to let go of the concept of power. If you push him away much longer, he'll eventually give up—and there's no telling when."

Rinwa looked mollified by Leisha's serious statement. The immortal gave an uncertain nod.

"Rinwa, I've always wondered something." Leisha hesitated.

"Well, I was just promoting the benefits of brutal honesty," Rinwa said lightly. "May as well ask."

Watching closely, Leisha asked, "Why did Tafari turn you into an immortal? I saw the immortal council when we were there. They looked a bit... old-fashioned. I just can't imagine them approving a woman to become an immortal even today, much less a couple thousand years ago."

Eyes dropping, her daughter pursed her lips to the side. "I'm not sure if you want to know."

"What does that mean?" Leisha's eyebrows drew together. "I wouldn't have asked if I didn't want to hear the answer."

"Well," puffing out a breath, Rinwa glanced at her, "I grew up with a great love for my father. I knew that when he was away, it was to hunt down and kill vampires. Every time he came back, I'd ask him if he'd killed you yet."

"Oh." Leisha's breathing hitched, but she remained composed.

Rinwa leveled a sardonic smirk at her. "Yes, 'oh' could be an apt response. Anyway, as I got older, I could see he didn't have it in him to kill you. I began to fear for my father. After all, if he did find you, you could exploit his weakness and kill him."

"His weakness?" The redhead echoed.

"You know, all the old feelings for you that he carried around." She shifted her feet to the other side of the chair. "I should also point out that I wasn't the most well-liked woman in our little village." Rinwa picked at her chair. "I was a walking reminder that you left us all to become a vampire. Besides, from what I heard, you weren't all that well-liked before all the paranormal drama entered the town." She shrugged as if it were evident. "So I pushed Tafari to make me an immortal.

I wanted to be there to protect him, and I wasn't going to be missed by anyone in the village."

"I'm sure your grandpa missed you," Leisha interjected.

"He died when I was nineteen. There was no one for me but my father."

"Did it take much for Tafari to convince the others?"

"A lot." Rinwa huffed. "I had to challenge two immortals before I could join. But Tafari had been teaching me to fight since I was little—almost as soon as you left—so it wasn't too difficult."

Leisha imagined the kind of life the girl would have had to endure. The men probably hadn't thought of themselves as chauvinistic or sexist, but that was the mindset in those times. "It must have been a hard life with all those men judging you," she said.

The immortal waved her hand. "It's what has made me so strong now."

The room grew quiet, each woman reflecting on the conversation.

Rinwa cleared her throat, tilting her face in the direction of the kitchen. "I'll see how lunch is coming along. I feel a bit peckish myself."

Smiling after her daughter's retreating form, Leisha felt her chest lighten. She hadn't even realized it, but her muscles were always tense whenever she was alone with her daughter. Tonight, it felt like they'd had a nice, open discussion. It seemed to Leisha that Rinwa had actually enjoyed her company. She understood that it probably wouldn't happen again anytime soon, but she'd take what she could.

CHAPTER 28

After swishing the fruity liquid around in her cup, Samantha drank the last of her Diet Coke. A smile touched her lips: she was on a date, with Nik. It tickled her that he was her date tonight. She'd tried not to overdress for the occasion and was wearing a yellow summer dress with spaghetti straps.

"What are you thinking about?" Nik asked. He was sitting across from her at a table so small it was basically a glorified stool.

Shaking her head, Samantha smiled at him. "Nothing in particular. Just how happy I am to get out and be with you."

Warmth lit his hazel eyes, and the vampire reached across the table to hold her hand. "I'm glad you're having a good time."

And she really was. The sun hadn't even set yet when Nik drove her into the city. They'd had dinner at an Indian restaurant. Samantha had asked for the hottest spices with her order and was glad she hadn't worn mascara since her eyes watered through the entire meal. But the food had been delicious.

Then, Nik had driven them to a club to dance. Samantha was

starting to hold a special place in her heart for the combination of Latin and techno music they danced to. But something was off with her date. Nik acted the perfect gentleman and was incredibly attentive, but Samantha noted a tightness around his eyes the entire night. And his skin looked pasty as they danced.

"I need a rest," she said, knowing he'd keep going until she was done dancing.

Now, they were sipping drinks in a local café. The place was not large, and a long line of customers kept it loud and busy.

Suddenly Nik stood and glanced around. "We should probably go and free this table for others." His face wasn't as pale as when they'd danced, but there was still a tightness to it.

Samantha hopped up, and Nik took her cup and tossed it in the garbage. She wasn't certain, but it looked like his fingers were shaking. Returning to her side, he put his hand at the small of her back to guide her out the door.

The night air was hot and muggy on Samantha's bare shoulders, the feeling reminiscent of summer nights in Florida. She missed Florida; she'd grown up there, but she knew that returning wouldn't bring back the fond memories. Her friends had moved on with their lives, and her mother couldn't come back from the dead. Plus, nothing was the same now that she was wrapped up in both vampire and immortal politics.

As they stepped outside, Samantha went around the crowd to where it wasn't so loud.

"Where are you going?" Nik gently tugged on her arm. "The car is the other way," he explained.

Crossing her arms, she glared up at him. "Tell me honestly. You're starting to lose your grip on The Hunger, aren't you?"

The usual, impassive expression he showed to everyone else locked into place. "I'm fine, Samantha."

Samantha reached up and stroked his cheek. "I can see that you're not. You're pale and shaking. How much longer before you lose control and go on a murderous rampage?"

His hand came up to cover her own. "This isn't your problem."

Huffing, she lowered her arm and leaned against the side of the building. "Clearly, you should have fed days ago. Why are you pushing it off?"

Instead of answering, Nik's jaw clenched, the muscles on either side twitching. As she gazed up at him, she could see the tenderness shining in his eyes, and the shame.

"It's because of me." Her head felt almost dizzy as she thought it through. "You've become ashamed of yourself because of me."

Sighing, he brushed a hand through his hair. "I wouldn't have said 'ashamed.' You really don't need to worry about this, Samantha."

She shook her head. "How can I not worry?" Samantha straightened and grabbed his arm. "I always knew what you are, and what you've done. I know that there's so much more to you than being a vampire. I lo—" Her voice cracked. Heat flooded her face when she realized she'd almost said love. "I like you in spite of those things. I know that you need to drink blood. I'm not going to judge you for it."

Challenge emanated from his eyes. "Really? Because when I feed, I kill people. Can you honestly say that you condone that?"

Samantha was shocked at the strong emotion he showed. "You think I'll judge you?" She swallowed, uncertain of what to say. No, she didn't want to condone murder, but she knew Nik would lose control of The Hunger really soon. *That is worse than the death of one individual.* "Yes, I understand what you have to do to survive, Nik. I really do." She sighed. "You need to feed. Right now." She pointed to the west. "I'm sure you could find someone down that way who maybe deserves death."

He glanced to where she pointed. "That *is* a bad part of town." He nodded. "See how the street lights are mostly broken?" He glanced back down at her, frustration lacing his tone.

"Just because it's a seedy area doesn't mean you can suddenly justify murder, Sam."

The words felt like a slap in the face. "You think I don't know what it means for people to die?" Her voice was shaking but she couldn't keep it under control. "I foresaw my own mother's death, and then was the one who found her when she really did die." She blinked back tears. "I'm fully aware of what you're going to do. But I'm also very aware of what will happen if you don't feed." She gripped his hand. "Nik, we're being hunted. You have to stay strong. And you absolutely cannot allow The Hunger to take over. Otherwise, you may not be there to save me if they find us."

The tick in his jaw told her that Nik was grinding his teeth. "I don't think you really understand what you're asking."

"I do." She put as much conviction as she could muster behind her words. "You need to feed. End of conversation."

Glaring venomously at her, Nik sounded angrier than she'd ever heard. "Just like that? End of the conversation? What exactly do you want me to do, Sam?"

Blowing out a shaky breath, Samantha put her hand on his arm. "Just listen. Maybe you can hear a crime in progress and eat the bad guy."

Snorting, the vampire leaned back, his face hard. "This is not a superhero movie! I would be committing murder."

Samantha put all of the pleading she had in her expression. "What could it hurt to just listen and see?"

Body taut, he nodded grimly.

Samantha waited while the vampire stood before her. Nik stared at her as he listened, and Samantha was struck at how intense his gaze could be.

"There are a few prostitutes turning tricks a couple blocks over. Two drug deals, and one fist fight." He glared into her eyes. "The choice is yours: which of them deserves to die?" His tone was bitter and mocking.

Samantha swallowed. Now that she'd pressed him, he was forcing her to be part of this. Her throat felt swollen as she forced an answer. "Uh, the world could definitely stand to be rid of one more drug dealer."

"Fine." He grabbed her arm firmly and walked in that direction. She didn't know he could get this angry.

Maybe I shouldn't have pushed him so hard. She shook her head at herself. The vampire was suppressing his needs because she somehow made him ashamed. She had to show him that she could be with him and not judge.

They only went a block down a sloped street when Nik turned left. Tension boiled in her stomach with every step they took. A car was driving away, leaving a scruffy-looking Latino man in the shadows of a rundown building. He was putting something into his back pocket. Samantha could only assume that the drug deal had barely finished.

Thirty feet away, Nik stopped and turned to her. "You want me to feed? Look at that man. Are you saying you can look at him and still tell me to kill him? You think you can stand by while I drink his blood and not see me in a different light?"

The drug dealer looked harmless. He was probably about the same height as her and he was slim of build. When she started to take note of the scruff growing on his jaw and how long his hair was, she couldn't watch him anymore. She faced Nik instead, studied his sickly complexion that was becoming mottled with his rage. She knew he showed her more emotion than anyone else, but she knew that what she saw now was probably had more to do with exhaustion and malaise. Nik's eyes held the barest hint of dark shadows.

"You need to feed." Her eyes misted. "I can't stand the thought of you starving because of me." She sniffed. "I know there's more to you than being a killer I know you better than anyone else. Just because you drink blood doesn't mean I'll stop feeling that way."

A bitter laugh escaped, and Nik's features twisted in what she could only identify as anguish. "I'll drink that man's blood. You can watch. Then tell me you can handle being around vampires." He grabbed her shoulders. "Around me."

The steel in his eyes scared her, but she knew that's what he wanted. He was trying to push her away because he didn't think she could accept this side of him. Forcing herself to stay calm, she nodded. "I'll still be here when you're finished."

His mouth twisted and he stepped away. As he stared at her, his fists clenched and he opened his mouth to let out an angry snarl.

Nik vanished in a blur of movement, then suddenly appeared behind the drug dealer. The poor man never knew what hit him. Nik grabbed his head, clamping a hand over the man's mouth and pulling back, exposing the Latino's neck. Samantha winced when she saw him bite into the man's flesh, heard the Latino's anguished grunt. Nik fed quickly, and the man's arms flailed less and less.

Samantha could hear suckling and small splashes of blood hitting the pavement. Her stomach threatened to purge itself of the Indian food she'd eaten earlier, and she turned away, unable to watch the life leave the man's body. *He was a drug dealer. He deserved to die!* Yet she couldn't seem to convince herself in that moment.

She turned back in time to see Nik raise his head to the dark sky as he released the body. Even at his distance, she could see his body thrumming with energy. His back was straight and he was no longer shaking. After wiping the blood from his chin with his shirt sleeve, the vampire looked at her. It was as if he dared her to hate him now.

Swallowing down bile, Samantha forced a tremulous smile. "I'm still here." She said it softly, but knew he'd hear.

Once again, the vampire turned into a blur and was before her in an instant. Nik's eyes were a strange mixture of challenge and fierceness as he pulled her body into his as he leaned forward for a kiss. Unlike the tender ones they'd shared in the past, this was carnal. His tongue pushed its way into her mouth and Samantha could barely taste his natural flavor under the metallic taint of blood.

Sensations warred within her. The taste of blood was sickening, and she wasn't sure how she felt about Nik's blood lust turning into a different kind of lust. But she'd also never been kissed so passionately and had already told him that she accepted him for who he was. *If I push him away now, would he see it as rejection?*

"Papi!"

As if splashed by cold water, the two sprang apart. Samantha was gasping from the intensity of the kiss, but her mind felt numb from what she heard.

Crying. A little boy was sobbing over the fallen drug dealer. He was probably around eleven or twelve, looking every bit as unkempt as his deceased father.

"No," she murmured. "No, this can't be." Her legs gave way and she dropped painfully to the pavement.

Watching the boy, Nik pulled her upright. "We need to leave," he whispered.

The agonized cries echoed through the night as Nik steered her back to the car. The illness she'd felt earlier was replaced with a cold sense of shock. She moved woodenly, and if Nik hadn't been there to steer, she didn't think she'd be able to walk at all.

"What did we just do?" she murmured through stiff lips. "I told you to kill that man. We just took away that boy's father."

Looking exasperated, Nik snapped. "What did you expect, Sam? That only the good guys have kids? You of all people should know that's not true."

Images of her mother covered in blood pounded through her mind. Samantha struggled to breathe, but forced herself to keep going. She couldn't lose it in front of Nik. It would only prove his point, and she had to show him that she still saw the good in him.

When they reached their car, he opened the passenger door and Samantha slid in. She could see the wet blood on his sleeve as he closed the door. Nik climbed into the driver's side and pulled the vehicle out onto the street. They rode in silence for several minutes. Samantha was able to get her breathing under control, but felt practically claustrophobic in the confined space with Nik.

"Are you going to be okay?" Nik asked.

"Yeah, I guess I'm just processing." Squeezing her eyes shut, the image of the boy with his wretched grief popped into play. "I'm more naïve about this stuff than I thought."

"Rinwa was right," he murmured.

Opening her eyes, she glanced his way, suddenly back in the moment and alert. "Right about what?"

He didn't respond right away. When he did, Samantha wished he hadn't. "We can't be together, Sam. The fact that I'm a vampire is too destructive. I'll slowly strip you of your humanity. I'll take away the very spirit that I adore so much about you."

"No!" The protest came out forcefully. Samantha hoped it covered the hurt she deeply felt. Her fingers shook at the thought of losing Nik. "I'm fine, Nik. Like I said, I'm just processing. But really, I'm okay. I'm Leisha's human servant, for crying out loud! If you break up with me, I'll still be surrounded by the macabre!"

"It's not the same," he growled. "And you know it just as well as I do."

She opened her mouth to protest, but nothing came out. He was right—it wasn't the same. *But that doesn't mean it's over, right? What about love conquering all and everything that goes with it?* Samantha chewed on her lower lip as she thought about

it. If she wanted to be with Nik, she'd be sacrificing a part of herself. Was it worth it? Could she accept being with someone who took lives so easily? She thought she could, but after seeing everything tonight, her resolve was shattered.

After pulling into the gravel driveway, the vampire cut the engine. "Go on inside," he ordered. "I'll be in before the sun comes up."

Biting her lip, she hesitated. "You're not leaving, are you?"

He shook his head. "No. I'll stay until we're sure the vampires and your dad can't find you."

Nodding stiffly, she opened her mouth, but couldn't think of what to say. Tears were threatening to spill as Samantha got out and quickly walked into the house. She blew out a shaky sigh when she observed that the others were already in bed.

She went directly to the bathroom, locked the door, and sat on the toilet. She quietly sobbed, hoping that Nik would change his mind. But she'd seen the look on his face when he said they couldn't be together.

CHAPTER 29

April 25th

Four weeks had gone by since they'd arrived at Tafari's safe house. The time spent there had been wonderful for Leisha. She and Rinwa were slowly warming up to each other. She and Tafari were beginning to act like a genuine married couple, and the baby was growing ever larger.

Leisha had no hope of seeing her toes. Her stomach was huge, much bigger than she remembered being with Adanne. Her appetite was insatiable lately. For both blood and food. Luckily, Tafari was able to provide as much blood as she needed without being hurt. In fact, it had turned into a great foreplay for them.

Things were going so well that Leisha wondered when the ball would drop. Though, she'd noticed Samantha wasn't as happy. Clearly, something had happened when she had gone out with Nikita. Leisha had tried to pry the information out of both Nikita and Samantha, but neither would comment on the matter.

After watching the two of them over the last month, Leisha deduced that there had been some sort of quarrel and that they weren't romantically involved anymore. It was awful to see Samantha so down, but Leisha couldn't help but be relieved. That was probably why Samantha didn't want to talk about it; because she knew that Leisha never wanted them together in the first place.

Luckily, Rinwa was there to keep Samantha busy. She had taken Samantha under her wing, showing her around the city, teaching her Spanish, and helping her learn to fight. Samantha was picking up on the language quickly. The fighting was another story. When Leisha watched them practice, she could see the teenager was improving on her basic technique, but couldn't seem to get the hang of some of the finer points of hand-to-hand combat.

"Don't worry, Samantha," Rinwa said as she sat atop her. They'd just finished another sparring session and Samantha hadn't been able to land a single punch. It was easy to see that Rinwa was holding back, but she still bested the teenager easily. "One of these days, you're gonna get so sick of our sessions ending like this that you'll do something about it." She stood and offered Samatha a hand up.

Brushing dark hair off her sweaty, tanned face, Samantha got up on her own. "Maybe I'll kill you in your sleep."

Rinwa smiled as she patted her cheek patronizingly. "Oh, how I'd love to see you try."

Still breathing heavily, Samantha walked past Leisha and went into the bathroom. A minute later, Leisha heard the shower turn on. Leisha picked up a book about pregnancy and went into the front room. She awkwardly lowered herself onto the couch. Nikita walked in and sat in the chair opposite her.

As Leisha placed the book on the end table, she glanced at the other vampire and waited.

"It's time for me to go," he said.

Blinking, Leisha raised her eyebrows in question. "That's sudden. Where do you think you'll go?"

He shrugged as he leaned back into the cushions. "Not really sudden. I told Samantha that I would stay long enough to be sure you two were safe." He gestured around them. "It's been a while since there have been any incidents, and this place seems just as good as any hiding spot. Besides, Rinwa and Tafari are still around. So I feel my presence here is unnecessary."

"It may not be necessary, but we do enjoy having you."

Nikita didn't respond, showing his usual imperturbable composure.

Matching his body language, Leisha inquired, "So where do you plan to go? We'll need to figure out a way to contact each other in case any of us get into trouble."

"I haven't decided yet. I thought I would head north and see where I end up wandering."

Leisha chortled. "You sound like a hippie."

Nikita's lips twitched as he entwined his fingers. "Perhaps that's what I was supposed to be. If I'd been born in the last fifty years, I may have ended up doing something like that."

"No way." She shook her head. "I could never see you as a hippie, no matter what era you're born in."

"As for a way to get in touch," he said. "I have an email address that should be secure. Just send any messages there and I'll get back to you."

"Are you leaving tonight?"

"May as well." The vampire shrugged. "Now is as good a time as any, and it won't take me long to get my things ready."

"We'll miss you, Nikita."

He offered a soft smile as he stood and walked down the hall to his room.

Tafari entered with a tall glass in his hand. "Would you like

to try this new smoothie I made?" he asked. "It has spinach, mixed berries, and Greek yogurt."

Leisha hesitated as she eyed the cup warily. "Have you tasted it yet?"

"Yes. It is delicious, if I do say so myself."

She accepted the glass and took a tentative sip. The vampire swirled the thick, icy liquid over her tongue before she swallowed. "Not bad. Better than I thought it would be."

Tafari opened his mouth to say something, but was interrupted when their daughter came in. "I just got off the phone with the council," she stated. "They're getting restless. We need to go back and report to them in person very soon. We can only give them so many excuses before they figure out something is up."

"I know," Tafari answered. "I spoke with them today as well." He turned to Leisha. "But you will be safe here. I will try to return before the baby comes."

Raising her eyebrows, Leisha forced a light tone. "Oh, you know when that is, do you? Well, please enlighten me, because I'd love to have a timeline."

Her husband sat next to her and cuddled her into his chest. He addressed Rinwa. "Tell them we'll fly out tomorrow."

"I'll make all the arrangements." Turning on her heel, Rinwa walked into the kitchen.

Leisha laid her head on his shoulder, absorbing the heat of his body. "How long do you think you'll be?"

Lightly caressing her arm, Tafari shook his head. "I do not know. We must convince them that Rinwa and I are scouring the planet to find the prophecy child. Otherwise, they may send a team to keep their eyes on us. I do not need to tell you how disastrous that would be."

Swallowing past the ache in her throat, Leisha used a teasing tone. "Disastrous isn't exactly what it would be," Leisha protested. "More like, utterly devastating if I can't see you again."

His hand moved up to her hair. "It is lightening faster these days. You are almost completely blonde again."

Leisha picked up a strand of her hair for inspection. Tafari was right; it was a very pale strawberry blonde and would probably be back to her natural hair color by morning. "I think I should just get some wigs."

"But your hair is so long, and you have so much of it. I am not sure you could contain it all under a wig."

"I'll figure it out. It's not nearly as big of a problem as what you're dealing with right now."

Tracing his fingers over her distended belly, her husband asked, "How is the baby today?"

Leisha smiled. "He's good. He actually gave me a bit of a break this evening. I've only felt him moving a few times."

"That is unusual." Tafari had felt some of the baby's kicks over the past weeks. If he'd been human, some of those kicks would have seriously bruised his hand. It helped him have more empathy for the injuries Leisha sustained from their baby on a daily basis.

"It may be different, but I'll take what I can get."

Samantha came out of the bathroom wearing fresh clothes, her hair hanging damp around her shoulders. "I'm starving," she announced. "Is there anything handy in the kitchen?"

Offering her cup, Leisha said, "You can finish this off. It should help revive you after the beating Rinwa gave you."

The girl took it and drank it without question. "That's pretty good," she murmured.

Just then, Nikita entered the room, slinging a large duffel bag over his shoulder.

"Do you want a ride to the airport or something?" Leisha asked.

Samantha dropped her glass. Nikita caught it easily before it could shatter over the hardwood. "Airport? Why would you need a ride to the airport?" she asked.

Glancing at Leisha, Nikita stated, "Actually, I don't think I'll need a ride. But thanks." He stood up and addressed the teenager. "The reason Leisha offered is because I told her I'm leaving tonight."

Leisha could hear Samantha's heartbeat increase a few notches. "But you said you wouldn't leave."

"I said I would stay until I was certain you were safe." He gestured around them. "You are. My services are no longer required."

"Your services," Samantha echoed. A mélange of hurt and churlishness crossed over her features. "Well, if you are here only to serve, then shouldn't it be up to me to decide when you should be dismissed?"

Nikita remained composed. "Don't do this, Samantha. It's best for everyone that I go. You know that."

Shaking her head, she protested. "I don't know that at all. And neither do you! You're just running like a coward."

Nikita's lips tightened, but didn't say anything.

Tafari shifted and stood, helping Leisha to her feet as well.

"Samantha," Tafari said. "Try taking a deep breath. We can sit down and discuss this at the table. I will cook something for you."

Leisha didn't hear what the girl's response was. She was suddenly aware of many different heartbeats coming into range. Focusing her hearing, she made out groups of heartbeats approaching both the front and back doors. The worst part was that they weren't human. The heightened rhythm was definitely the heartbeats of vampires.

She grabbed Tafari's hand and pulled him into the kitchen.

"What is it?" He sounded impatient, but went with her.

"Vampires. They're surrounding the house right now."

At Leisha's declaration, Rinwa's head popped up from the counter, where she had been writing on a pad of paper. "How did they find us?" She asked as she darted for the family room. She returned with several swords and machetes.

Taking a machete for herself, Leisha answered. "No idea. But there are too many for us to stay and fight."

Rinwa spoke as if Leisha were slow. "If they have this place surrounded, then we'll have to fight." She smiled in anticipation. "I've been dying for some real action lately anyway."

Heading to the front entrance, Leisha tossed a sword to Nikita, who caught it effortlessly. By his bearing, he obviously knew the situation and had clued Samantha in on what was happening. Holding Nikita's duffel bag, Samantha looked pale under the coat of tan lotion.

"Stay with Samantha," Tafari ordered Nikita. "I will cover Leisha. Rinwa will take the lead. Our goal is to reach the car and get away as fast as possible." Everyone nodded. Looking at Leisha, the immortal asked, "How close are they?"

"It sounds like about fifty feet."

He fished the car keys out of his pocket and handed them to Nikita. "Get Samantha to the car as fast as possible. I will help Leisha there behind you."

Leisha huffed. "I'm a perfectly good warrior, Tafari. Don't treat me like an invalid."

"There's no time for hurt feelings, Leisha," Rinwa said as she opened the door. "You're a blimp, and they want you more than any of us. End of discussion." With that she was out the door, Nikita and Samantha following. She heard Rinwa's battle cry and the clash of weapons.

Tafari gestured for her to go before him. She complied, knowing now the best thing to do was follow his commands.

As the humid air snaked along her skin, Leisha studied

her surroundings. Rinwa was already fighting the closest vampires with her usual speed and accuracy. She was turning into a bloody mess, but Leisha had to remind herself that her daughter knew what she was doing.

Nikita and Samantha were five feet away from the car when a group of six vampires came at them. Without hesitating, Leisha headed in that direction.

Hearing attackers coming from behind, she whirled with her machete held ready. Tafari was already taking care of them. He had already beheaded one, and the others were trying to close in on him, but he was keeping them back with aggressive thrusts and lunges while parrying their attacks.

Leisha continued towards Samantha and the car. Nikita was battling with his usual precision, keeping Samantha behind him. They were slowly working their way closer to the vehicle.

Leisha reached them just as a third wave of vampires poured onto the front lawn. It looked like there were more than a hundred of them. Pointing her weapon in the direction of the closest vampire, she murmured to her companions, "We can't fight all of them."

Nodding, Nikita answered. "You two must get away. I promise we'll find you later."

"If you survive this." Leisha blocked a blow from her opponent and lunged, hacking through his rib cage and heart. Her bulbous stomach was throwing her off balance, but she was able to defeat the next vampire who came after her.

Two more were charging her way, and Leisha jumped back to dodge their swords. She did her best to avoid ducking; she'd learned from the last fight that she wouldn't be able to bounce up easily with the weight of the baby. She parried and gained ground between the two of them, taking cuts up and down her arms. She could handle the wounds. Besides, she was also landing in her fair share of attacks.

As she was blocking the sword from the vampire on her right, the one to the left punched her in the temple. Ignoring the blunt pain, Leisha swirled her machete around the other man's sword while pushing toward his body. Finally, the man dropped his blade, just as an angry slash burned into Leisha's back. She kicked behind her and landed a solid strike to a vampire's crotch as she decapitated the one in front of her.

She spun, beheading the man who'd punched her, before he could make another advance.

Leisha saw that Samantha was inside the car. Nikita was in front of her door, killing two or three attackers at a time.

"Get your butt over here and help me, Nikita," yelled Rinwa.

Leisha turned to see if her daughter was alright, but she couldn't tell because four more vampires surrounded Leisha. Grabbing a dropped sword, Leisha wielded both weapons as she twirled between her attackers. She decapitated two of the vampires while the other two moved in. The one from behind pulled on her shoulders, trying to kick her feet out from under her. The one in front grabbed her wrists, crushing them together in an effort to get her to drop her weapons.

Leisha clung to her sword and machete. Her balance, however, wasn't as easy to hang on to. She started falling onto the body of the vampire who'd tripped her. He began to move out of her way, but Leisha swung the sword in an arc, cutting off his head as she went down. The head landed on her face. The vampire blood choked her as it slipped into her mouth and down her cheek onto the grass.

Three vampires rushed towards her. Leisha decided trying to get up would only hinder her defense, so she lay back and brought the blades to her chest, ready to strike.

Rinwa's voice called urgently. "Get down, it's coming!"

Leisha wanted to see what was happening, but couldn't take her eyes off the vampires approaching. Suddenly, flames appeared as if from nowhere, consuming everything in their path. Screams of agony rang out from all around. Boiling heat singed Leisha's skin as she rolled to the side and got up as quickly as her awkward body would allow.

Leisha rushed back to the car. She noted that more than half of their attackers were writhing all over. The fire engulfed them, melting their hair and skin until muscles and bone protruded.

Rinwa and Nikita were manning the giant flame thrower. Leisha wondered where it had come from, considering it was attached to a fuel tank half the size of the house. Nikita threw out a clear liquid over the vampires and Rinwa speedily pointed the flame thrower at them. Once again, agonizing cries broke into the air and the victims fell, trying to roll and pull off their blazing clothes.

Leisha tapped on the window and waited for Samantha to unlock the door. Samantha did, and Leisha climbed in. It wasn't until she was inside that she noticed passenger-side door was gone.

Studying her friend, she found that Samantha bore bite marks on her shoulder and deep gouges in her cheek.

"Are you alright?"

Samantha said in a shaking voice, "Let's just get out of here." She pointed to the ignition, where the keys were waiting.

Leisha reached out and turned the keys, but the engine didn't start. She tried again; nothing happened. "They sabotaged the car." She muttered. "Come on." Grabbing the teenager's hand, Leisha led the way out of the car. Heat immediately met her face as she hurried to the sidewalk and down the street.

It was a miracle that no one tried to stop them as they fled. Leisha was grateful because she just realized that she'd left both of her weapons in the car. Silently calling herself a few nasty names, she urged Samantha to keep up.

They'd gone about two blocks before she let Samantha rest.

Leisha could see the flames easily from the corner where they stood. From the sound of it, most of the vampires had been wiped out by Rinwa's surprise attack. Leisha assumed there was some kind of special chemical in the mix that made the vampires burn up so quickly.

"We need to hotwire a car." Leisha studied the street. The vehicles in this area were fairly modern, but she was certain she could start one of them.

Samantha pressed a hand to her still-bleeding cheek as she muttered, "This will be my second auto theft."

A mixture of amusement and guilt flooded Leisha, but she knew this was no time to reflect on Samantha's morals becoming desensitized.

Just a little farther down the street, Leisha spotted a car that she could start. Not bothering with stealth, Leisha punched the window in. The loud, whining sound of the car alarm pierced her ears. Knuckles stinging, she opened the door and found the proper wires to cut. Once she snipped them, the alarm silenced and she was able to focus on getting the vehicle started.

Samantha climbed in on the other side just as the engine roared to life. Putting the car into gear, Leisha pulled out onto the road. She headed in the direction of the house so she could get the others.

The sound of two vampire heartbeats was Leisha's only warning. They were heading in her direction at jet-like speed. Before Leisha could veer out of the way, Annette crashed into the front fender, smashing it into a jumbled mess and forcing them into a tailspin.

Leisha maneuvered the steering wheel with the brakes, gaining control of the car after a second or two. But not fast enough to prevent Annette from ripping open the driver's door.

Annette grabbed Leisha by the hair and dragged her out of the vehicle. Leisha heard Samantha screech and angled her

eyes awkwardly to see Ellery pulling the teenager out by her ear, as if she were a naughty little girl.

Leisha's pants scraped around her bottom as she was dragged to the sidewalk. Annette released her before Leisha could put up much of a fight. Straddling her chest, the vampire plopped down and grabbed Leisha's chin.

"Now," Annette said coldly. "You are going to tell me everything about this baby and who the father is." With no further warning, Annette's twisted darkness invaded Leisha's mind. The filth forcefully consumed every crevice of her consciousness until all Leisha knew was the smut that Annette represented.

The breach receded and the blonde's vision came back into focus. Leisha panted from the exertion of having her mind raped.

"How are you pregnant?" Annette demanded.

Still reeling from the brutal attack, it was easy for Leisha to keep herself from answering.

"Think you're tough, do you?" Annette narrowed her arctic blue eyes. "I may not have been able to torture you *psychically* before, but things have changed and I'm more than ready to tear your mind to shreds." Seizing Leisha By the throat, the vampire squeezed. "Would you like another round of mind play or are you ready to give me what I want?"

"I don't see Victor," Leisha craokedcroaked out. "Did I actually kill him when I threw that knife in his heart, or is he licking his wounds while you're doing the dirty work?" Speaking that much made her gasp for air.

"He's simply being the ruler he was always meant to be. Unlike Ptah, Victor rules from a throne and doesn't trouble himself with pathetic peons like you!"

Wetting her dry mouth, Leisha gathered what saliva she could and spit in Annette's face. The brunette's pale features became mottled in the darkness as she crushed Leisha's windpipe. Through the haze of pulsing agony, Leisha could hear Ellery berating Annette.

"How can she talk if you crush her neck? We don't have much time, and Victor will not be happy with either of us if you ruin this!"

"She'll heal." Annette stood and hoisted Leisha in her arms. "Come on, we'll get out of here and question her on the plane. She'll be able to give me answers in an hour or so."

Glancing over, Leisha saw that Ellery was keeping a tight hold on Samantha. The girl had a new bruise around her neck and was sobbing quietly.

It was difficult to suck air through her ragged windpipe. Leisha pushed as much energy as she could into her arms as she reached up. With her right hand, she punched Annette in the jaw, snapping the woman's head back. With her left hand, she clawed down as deeply as she could into the vampire's cheek.

Annette screamed and slammed Leisha back onto the pavement. Bending over, the vampire once again grabbed Leisha by her hair, and smashed her skull into the concrete.

Searing light blinded Leisha. She was certain she'd heard her skull crack.

"Leisha!" Samantha cried.

Ellery spoke calmly. "Annette, why don't we switch? You can have all the fun with dearest Leisha once we are on our way. But for now, I think it's best that we leave as soon as possible."

Annette let go of Leisha and walked away. Blinking through fuzzy vision, Leisha rolled onto her side and pushed herself up. She knew that now would be the perfect time to fight and try to escape, but she simply couldn't make the connection between her brain and her limbs.

Blood tickled the back of her neck as she rose. Ellery's soft hand wrapped around her upper arm. "Sorry, friend," she

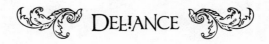

said. "But we need information only you can give." As an after-thought, she muttered, "And your child. He has to die before he can be born."

Leisha felt Ellery's other hand snake over her distended belly. "His emotions are already strong," the empath whispered. "So complex. I'm glad he'll die soon. I wouldn't want to feel those strange sensations for much longer."

CHAPTER 30

Samantha didn't think they could survive this. Leisha's skin was pale and clammy, and it appeared that her friend's eyes kept losing focus.

The feel of Annette's petite, bony fingers on her arms brought back all the horrible sensations from when the vampire had raped her mind last year. Samantha's throat threatened to close up, and her stomach twisted violently. She'd had nightmares about Annette's horrible psychic attack for months. Feeling the pull through her connection to Leisha, Samantha was beginning to feel weak. She trudged along with Annette, her spine straight so that she wouldn't lean into the horrible vampire.

As Ellery walked with them, Leisha in tow, the empath spoke casually. "I think we would get better results if we tortured Samantha first. After all, we both know that's how she broke when Ptah first kidnapped her all those years ago."

Forcing herself to breathe out slowly, Samantha made her face as impassive as she could. She knew if she gave in to her fear right now, it would only make matters worse. That was one of the first things Nik had taught her about self-defense.

"Just think of the book, Hitchhikers' Guide to the Galaxy," he'd said. "Don't panic."

It was a lot harder to apply in real life than in theory. She thought about trying to break away and run, but knew she had no chance against a vampire. Especially one as ruthless as Annette.

Leisha didn't appear to have the same fatalistic instincts as Samantha. Instead, she turned suddenly and punched Ellery in the nose with the heel of her hand. It must have broken some cartilage because Samantha heard a snap, and blood gushed over Ellery's lips and chin. It didn't do any good, however. Ellery calmly backhanded Leisha and continued on without breaking stride.

Glancing behind them, all Samantha could see were flames and smoke in the distance. There was not a soul in sight. She and Leisha had no hope.

They approached a black Lexus.

A vampire Samantha didn't recognize climbed out of the driver's seat and walked around to open the back door for them. As they approached the vehicle, Samantha felt a sudden dread, all the way down to her toes, that if they entered the car, they wouldn't survive.

Panic bubbled into her throat and Samantha began to struggle. Twisting her arms, she tried to throw her knee into Annette's stomach. The vampire's grip tightened to the point that it cut off Samantha's circulation. Grunting, Samantha tried to kick out, but Annette was unphased. She couldn't suppress a sob as Annette softened her hold.

"You'll never get away from me now, pet." Annette smiled, her teeth gleaming in the night. "The sooner you accept this, the easier your life will be."

Ellery stood behind them with Leisha. "Go on," the empath urged. "We don't have much time. They're on their way."

Resisting Annette's shove was pointless. Samantha fell

into the car, the vampire directly behind her, scooting her to the far side. Just as Ellery was pushing Leisha in, the blonde vampire stopped and whirled. She grabbed the driver's head and twisted viciously. Samantha heard a distinct snapping noise and watched as the man slid down the car and onto the pavement.

Samantha couldn't see what was happening, but could hear flesh smashing against flesh and various grunts. Leisha disappeared and Samantha felt a moment of abandonment. It didn't improve as Annette shifted toward her, an icy glare marring her features.

Annette grabbed her arm with one hand and opened the door on Samantha's side with the other. Just as the door cracked open, there was a jolt as something landed on the trunk. "Move it!" Annette growled. Before Samantha could react, the sound of tearing metal and breaking glass pierced her ears and she covered them with an agonized squeal. The roof of the car was ripped open. Nik stood over them with a crazy glint in his eyes Samantha had never seen before. He looked downright mad—and not the angry kind.

Nik snarled like a wild animal as he jumped on Annette. The brunette bellowed and made to grab his face. Nik got her wrists first and held them back. He was trying to look into her eyes and Annette twisted her head to avoid it. Letting go of her wrists, Nik pinned her down with one arm while he clutched her chin with his other hand. Annette's expression became determined and she met his eyes.

Samantha wasn't sure what to think about what happened next. The two seemed to be in a twisted kind of staring contest. A red sheen of sweat appeared on both their faces. Suddenly, Nik whimpered and Annette grinned. Samantha gasped. Annette was raping his mind right in front of her. His hold on her face faltered.

"No!" the girl screamed. Samantha's hands flew as if of

their own accord. Her fingernails clawed at whatever skin they could scrape through. Annette continued boring her gaze into Nik, unfazed by Samantha's wild assault.

Shrieking in fury and helpless frustration, Samantha braced her index finger and jabbed as hard as she could into Annette's eye. Soft, warm tissue collapsed around her finger. The vampire howled as Samantha pulled back. The girl thought she might throw up at the sight of the white and red mess on her finger. Annette's hand clamped around Samantha's throat and suddenly she couldn't breathe. As the skinny fingers tightened, Samantha's vision began to fade to black.

Bones crunched loudly, and then Annette's hand slid away. Samantha gasped deeply and coughed.

Glancing over, she saw Annette's unconscious form draped on the seat. And then Nik was there, crouched over Samantha, his hazel eyes shining with concern.

"Are you alright?" he asked.

Still choking with tears streaming, the teenager nodded.

Gathering her in his arms, Nik picked her up and cradled her to his chest. Then he stood and jumped over the mess to land in the street.

Tafari was supporting Leisha just a few feet away. Rinwa ran towards them, bloody and winded, but apparently not badly hurt. Though her clothes were practically shredded and dried blood caked her body, Rinwa looked more exhilarated than anything. And maybe a little frustrated. "Ellery got away from me."

"Let's get moving." Nik's voice vibrated against Samantha's cheek. "Some of the vampires didn't die in the fire and I can hear them coming."

Rinwa went to the nearest vehicle that wasn't totaled and broke in. Unlike her mother, Rinwa didn't break any windows. Instead, she pulled some sort of kit from her bag her bag and went to work. In just a few seconds, the door was open, and

Rinwa climbed in the driver's side. Nik settled Samantha in the back, next to Tafari and Leisha, then climbed into the passenger seat.

Rinwa headed toward the freeway. "What direction should we go?"

"West, toward Columbia," Tafari answered. "There are plenty of forests to hide in around there."

Gently touching her bruised neck, Samantha came to a horrifying realization. "This is never going to end, is it?" Her voice was hoarse from strangulation. "We're always going to be hiding and running. And fighting. It's going to be like this for the rest of my life." Her eyes misted.

Leisha's face was a mixture of concern and guilt as she placed a hand over Samantha's knee. "I wish I could change things for you," her friend whispered.

"But you can't." The girl's tone was as bitter as her tears. "No matter how much you love me, you can't do a thing!"

"I'm sorry, Samantha."

Exhaustion filled her bones and Samantha deflated. She couldn't deal with it now. Her reality was too depressing to face.

CHAPTER 31

R inwa pulled into a gravel parking lot just as the sun was rising. Leisha moved to wake Samantha, but Tafari stopped her.

"Let me," he said.

Leisha understood. Samantha needed time away from the vampire who had destroyed her world half a year ago. Chest tight, she watched Tafari crawl over her and lean into Samantha's face.

Leisha climbed out and stretched her back. The muscles around her spine were sore. It was a curious sensation for a vampire, but with all the fighting and her pregnancy, Leisha wasn't surprised. Still too worn out to think much, she watched as her daughter broke into a different car with perfect skill. Rinwa popped the trunk and Leisha walked over to inspect how large it was. It looked about the same as the last one Nik had ridden in.

"Will you be okay in here?" Leisha asked as Nik approached. "Won't you boil like you did the last time?"

"Probably," he answered. "But I'll heal. We need to keep

moving. As soon as I get out of there," he gestured to the trunk, "I'll feed."

Rinwa came back to them holding a wool blanket. "Don't know if this will do you any good, but in case there's any sun streaming through cracks, here you go."

Murmuring his thanks, Nikita climbed in and contorted his tall frame to fit. Leisha placed the blanket over him.

Wishing there was another way for him to travel, she sighed as she closed the lid.

"Let's get going." Rinwa gave one pat on Leisha's back and climbed in the back seat, by Samantha. Folding her enormous belly into the passenger side, Leisha closed her door. Tafari put the car in gear and they were once again on their way to nowhere.

They'd traveled for a few hours before Tafari spotted a small food cart at the side of the road and stopped. The sun wasn't even at its peak and it was already getting hot. Leisha hoped that Nikita wouldn't bake again, but knew it would happen anyway.

The pain in her lower back was becoming more intense. The vampire's eyebrows drew together. What was wrong with her?

She didn't bother to get out with the others. Leisha simply sat and waited until they would be ready to go. Interestingly enough, she wasn't very hungry at the moment. Tafari opened her door and squatted in front of her, holding out a bottle of water. "I bought you some fruit." He offered up a papaya, but Leisha shook her head. The vampire didn't feel like talking much. She forced herself to sip at the water, but dropped it when she felt a sudden cramping low in her belly.

"What's the matter?" Tafari asked. She could hear the apprehension in his voice, but was in too much pain to comfort him.

Another contraction hit and she bit her lip. After it faded a bit, she met Tafari's gaze. "Can you find us a place to crash?"

After pulling a map out of the glove compartment and consulting it, he answered. "It does not look like we are close

to much civilization right now, but there is a small town close by. We should be there in about forty five minutes."

Leisha shook her head, then doubled over her protruding belly as another cramp overtook her. "Drive like the devil's on your tail. This baby might be here before then."

Tafari's face paled a bit. "Bloody hell!" He practically dove into the driver's seat, slammed his door closed, and started the engine. Rinwa and Samantha barely got in before the car was spitting gravel and zooming down the highway.

The contractions were about the same for the rest of the ride. They were more painful than she'd had with Adanne, and they were very close together. But they didn't seem to be coming any more frequently, so she hoped that meant they had time to reach whatever place Tafari could find. Sweat sprouted over her forehead and upper lip, but Leisha concentrated on taking deep breaths through the pain.

It took another twenty five minutes before Tafari pulled off the highway and onto a small gravel road. "I spotted a house through the trees," he explained. "It looks like it may be abandoned."

Pulling up to the house, Leisha thought it looked like a glorified wood shack, but under the circumstances she couldn't complain too much. She didn't pay much attention to the de-tails, since the contractions were too much. They were starting to get closer.

Opening the car door, Leisha was met with a rush of humid, hot air. It made breathing even more difficult than before, and she found that it was almost impossible to walk. She took about two steps from the car and started to fall.

Tafari was there instantly and lifted her into his arms. Leisha grabbed his shirt and twisted it while she buried her face into his chest. Even through the haze of pain, she was able to draw some comfort from his musky scent.

The next thing she knew, Tafari was laying her on a small,

creaky bed. She realized she had temporarily lost consciousness after Tafari had picked her up. Samantha was propping
dusty pillows behind her back so she was in a sitting position.
Rinwa was pulling Leisha's pants and underwear off and also
found a blanket to put over Leisha's legs for modesty.

Leisha's body was almost completely covered in bloody
sweat, no doubt making her a gruesome sight. Not only were
the contractions getting worse, but the pressure she felt low
in her abdomen was almost too intense to bear.

There was a sudden gush of her water breaking and Rinwa
jumped back. "Now that's just nasty." The blonde grimaced and
wrinkled her nose. "Smells horrid, too."

Unclenching her jaw, Leisha looked at her daughter. "How
do you think you came into this world? On a magic flower?"

Rinwa turned away and went down the short hall into the
little kitchen.

Leisha couldn't keep herself from screaming with the
next contraction. Tafari grabbed her hand and allowed her to
squeeze it.

"There's too much pressure," Leisha got out between gasps.
"He's coming. I can feel it."

Samantha ran into the kitchen, and then came back. "We
still need to boil water. You're gonna have to wait."

Leisha snorted. "Like hell! Tell that to the one who's forcing his way out." Screaming again, Leisha let go of Tafari and
grabbed her knees. Clutching them as high as she could, she
started to push.

She could feel and hear her skin tear apart as she hollered
through another contraction.

Tafari was at her feet, ready to catch the baby. It looked
like his eyes were about to bug out of his head. He glanced at
Leisha, and then down again.

"What?" Leisha ground out. "Is he coming?"

Licking his lips, Tafari nodded, but she could see he wasn't

telling her something. Rinwa walked in with a large bowl. When she saw what was happening, she dropped the steaming water. Leisha glanced at Samantha. The girl wasn't simply pale, but had a yellow cast to her skin.

"Wha—" Leisha was interrupted by another of her own agony-induced shrieks. "It feels like he's clawing my body into hamburger meat!"

Tafari swallowed, then cleared his throat. "What it looks like, too."

Before Leisha could comprehend what he meant, the need to push again overwhelmed her. Grunting, she bore down as hard as she could. She wasn't sure how much time had passed when suddenly, there was a wet plopping sound. The pressure was instantly gone.

Her loins felt as if they were on fire, but even that was driven from her mind when she heard a high pitched wail. Looking up, she saw Tafari holding their squirming baby while Rinwa cut the umbilical cord. When Rinwa stepped away, Leisha could see that Tafari was holding their son's wrists away from the man's body while he carefully cradled the child. And then she saw sharp, bloody claws slowly retracting into the newborn's fingertips.

Jaw dropping at the realization, Leisha was suddenly very glad she couldn't see the damage done to her body. She shook off the sick sensation before she looked back up and studied her baby. He was crying ceaselessly. The babe had a full head of dark hair, matted with drying fluid, and creamy, chocolate-brown skin. While he was small, his body was nice and plump.

"He's beautiful," she croaked.

The sound of his mother's voice caught the baby's attention. He stopped crying and opened his eyes to look at her. Her breath stopped when she saw his tiny arms reach for her. It was utterly bizarre to see such an action from a newborn.

Leisha held her arms out and Tafari handed him to her. The

boy started to root at her chest and Leisha pulled her shirt up. Once she had bared a nipple, the baby smiled to show a full set of teeth. He promptly bit down and started to suck, drawing both milk and blood.

Leisha jumped, but forced herself to keep him snuggled against her.

Tafari watched with a horrified expression. "What have we created?" he whispered.

Giving a one shoulder shrug, she said, "It looks like he needs blood as well as regular food." She tried to shift, but her lower body was still in too much pain to move.

"You can accept it that easily? This is okay to you?" Tafari asked.

Narrowing her eyes, Leisha answered. "Of course it is. How can I have a problem when I drink blood to sustain myself?" Looking down, she lightly stroked the side of her son's face. The babe's eyes were fully alert, studying her face. Instead of the typical newborn blue eyes, they were the same vivid green as Leisha's. She smiled. "Don't you think he's beautiful, Tafari?" She looked up again to see her husband swallowing. He didn't answer.

Samantha broke the tension when she came forward and grinned at the newborn. "Congratulations, you guys. He's gorgeous!"

Rinwa was studying the baby. Her voice wavered as she spoke. "I don't care if he is my brother. There's no way he's sucking my blood."

Leisha was able to read between the lines and see the tender emotion that her daughter tried to hide. She sent Rinwa a tender smile. Rinwa gave a brief one in return, then looked away when tears misted her eyes.

Putting a hand on Samantha's shoulder, Rinwa steered her

toward the bedroom door. "Let's boil some more water so we can give that slimy thing a bath."

The girls left the room, and Leisha was surprised to find that her son was already giving signs to switch sides. Again, he bit through her skin and sucked both milk and blood at the same time.

"So," Tafari said. "Have you thought of a name? I really do not want to call him Prophecy Child anymore."

"I wanted to talk to you about it first, but I guess I was too distracted this last month we were together." She paused to focus her fatigued mind, before she continued. "I was thinking of Liam Mudiwa."

Looking thoughtful, he took her hand. "Does Liam mean protection?"

"Something like that."

Tafari studied their child. "Do you think that is the boy's purpose? It seemed the prophecies spoke more about destruction when they mentioned the child."

Leisha shook her head. "They're too vague to really understand. But I can't imagine our child being something bad."

He changed the subject. "Mudiwa means beloved."

Nodding, she studied the man's features. "He is beloved, isn't he, Tafari?"

After an awkward hesitation, he cleared his throat and answered. "Of course. Though, I must admit to feeling a bit confused right now."

Uncertain of what to say, she looked down at her son. "What do you think? Does Liam sound like a good name to you?"

The babe unlatched and gave a drowsy smile as his eyelids slid lower and lower until he was soundly sleeping.

"I think that settles it," Tafari said quietly. "I like the name Liam also."

Surprised at the warmth and tenderness in his voice, Leisha looked up and smiled at Tafari. He looked into her eyes for a moment before leaning down to kiss her softly.

"Seriously, can you guys not paw each other every two minutes?"

They both looked at Rinwa with tolerant expressions. She ignored them and placed a large bowl on the floor beside Leisha. "Is it alright if I wash him now?" She held her hands toward Liam.

After kissing his head, Leisha handed the baby over to her daughter. "Try not to wake him," she said.

Rinwa nodded and handled her brother with gentle care. Leaning back against the pillows, Leisha closed her eyes. Lethargy was hitting her in full force, and she gave into it, hoping that she would be healed by the time she woke.

CHAPTER 32

Samantha couldn't bring herself to put Liam down. He was wrapped in a blanket that Tafari had cut down to size so it would fit around Liam's tiny body. The babe seemed to be sleeping peacefully and was the perfect picture of innocence.

The image of his small hand literally clawing its way out of Leisha's body briefly flashed into her mind, but she pushed it aside. She admitted that Liam made her a bit nervous. No one knew what to expect from him, but at the moment she simply cradled the baby and smiled at his sleeping form.

Tafari had shooed everyone out of the bedroom so Leisha could get some rest. The vampire was so exhausted that she didn't even stir when her husband shifted her to a prone position.

Samantha could relate. She was pretty tired herself. She hadn't slept much, and was still recovering from her injuries. On top of that, she could feel Leisha pulling on her energy through their bond. She was certain that her vampire friend didn't even know she was doing it.

Rinwa and Tafari had taken the opportunity to clean up and

change out of their ragged, bloody clothes. They were reclining on the old couch in the tiny front room.

The door flew open, and all three occupants looked up as a smoking Nik rushed through with a wool blanket covering him. He closed the door, peeked through the blanket, then sat on the floor in the shadows, taking the covering off. Bloody sweat lined the part of his shirt beneath his armpits and the hollow of his throat was flaking.

Rinwa raised a brow from her spot on the couch. "Looks like you couldn't take the heat." She made a show of sniffing. "Glad this rundown shack has plumbing, 'cause you need a shower before you do anything else."

As usual, Nik remained unperturbed. "Actually, I need a lot of water." He glanced to Samantha.

She nodded and held the baby out to Rinwa.

The immortal shook her head and gestured toward Tafari. "He can hold him."

Samantha threw her an insistent gaze, and Rinwa reluctantly took the sleeping infant and rolled her eyes, but Samantha could see the softening of her features as she looked down at her brother.

Samantha grabbed four water bottles from the kitchen and handed them to Nik. Then she slid down next to him. "So I guess you've figured out that Leisha had her baby."

After taking a swig, Nik glanced down the hall. "And after I brushed up on my midwife skills, you guys didn't even invite me."

Smiling, Samantha replied, "Blame it on Liam. He's the one who decided to come out in the daytime."

They both glanced at the baby snuggled into Rinwa's shoulder. Tafari was in his own world, watching his children with a small smile.

Turning his attention back to Samantha, Nik asked, "And

how are you doing? I didn't get the chance to ask you if Annette, you know, hurt you."

Blood draining from her cheeks, Samantha's lips thinned. "She did it to Leisha, not me." Brow furrowing, she remembered, "Ptah told me if I became Leisha's human servant, then Annette couldn't hurt me in that way anymore."

The vampire nodded. "We used to be safe from Annette's psychic assault, but I think her powers grew when we became vampires again. I shouldn't have been able to lure her, either." She studied Nik. "I could tell she was doing it to you last night, in the car."

As he examined the rotted wood floor, the vampire nodded. "She won our little staring contest."

Blinking, Samantha commented, "I didn't really understand what you were trying to do to each other."

"We both have psychic powers," he explained. "If I could have forced my power on her, she would have been temporarily in love with me, which means she would have done anything I asked of her."

"So when you two were glaring each other down, you were trying to be the first to use your power?"

"That's a close enough description. I guess you could say it was a battle of metaphysical wills." Suddenly, Nik tilted his head to the side and looked at Tafari. "Leisha's awake," he stated. "It sounds like she's trying to get up."

Shaking his head, Tafari stood. "She has not had enough time to heal yet." He walked down the short hallway and into the bedroom.

Rinwa got up as well. "Samantha, I think I'm going to go for a walk." She lifted the sleeping baby in her arms. "Can you take him back now?"

"Sure." Samantha got up from the floor and went to Rinwa. Liam stirred a little when Rinwa handed him back to Samantha, but continued to slumber. "I'm glad you cleaned him," Samantha commented. "Now he has that new baby smell. Isn't it nice?"

Slipping her sunglasses on, Rinwa smirked. "Yeah, so? Are you going to burst into song over it or something?"

Samantha glared at her and gently bounced her bundle while Rinwa walked out the door.

A few minutes later, Tafari strode into the room. "Leisha wishes to take a sponge bath, but I must help her as she is not recovered yet." He looked at Samantha questioningly. "Would you tend to Liam?"

Samantha smiled in relief. She'd thought he was going to ask her to help bathe Leisha. As tired as she felt, she really didn't think she could handle doing something as awkward as that yet. "Sure, that's no problem."

Tafari smiled his gratitude and headed back into the room. "Let us know when he needs to feed again," he called over his shoulder.

Snuggling Liam closer, Samantha glanced down at Nik. He'd downed three bottles of water and was resting his head against the wall.

"You look exhausted," she observed.

Nik shrugged and closed his eyes briefly. "Yeah, battling off a horde of my associates and then spending the day being baked in a car can do that."

He'd said it casually, but Samantha could tell the vampire was hiding a hint of agitation. She hoped it was because of his situation and not her. It was quiet for a while. Samantha focused her attention on Liam.

After a moment of contemplation, she offered, "What if I get the blanket from the bedroom to cover the window in here? That way you could lie on the couch and take a nap."

After mulling it over for a second, Nik nodded and tentatively smiled. "That's thoughtful of you. Thanks."

Her body flushing at his compliment, Samantha went into

the bedroom and grabbed the black cotton blanket covering the bed. She could hear small splashes in the bathroom and assumed Tafari was handling the situation fine in there.

Handing the baby to Nik, she climbed onto the couch to hang the blanket over the window. She pierced the edge of the material with the nail heads sticking out of the wall. Once she finished, it was almost too dark to see.

She started when Nik touched her arm. She hadn't even gotten off the couch yet.

Nik helped her down. "Thanks," he murmured as he handed her the baby.

Goosebumps rose on her arms at the idea of being alone in the dark with him. She mentally slapped herself; she knew thoughts like that would only make things between them more difficult. It was obvious that Nik wasn't going to change his mind about the two of them.

She watched Nik's silhouette settle on his makeshift bed, then went into the kitchen. As she was sitting in one of the wood chairs, Liam began to stir. Knowing that Leisha and Tafari would need more time with the bath, Samantha stood back up and bounced as she paced back and forth across the small room. It was enough to coax the little one back into his slumber.

Samantha felt like she was getting the hang of being a good aunt already. It made her smile. As she was passing the window, Samantha noticed Rinwa on her way back from her walk.

When she saw the immortal pause in her peripheral vision, she didn't think much of it and continued her pacing. But then the girl heard Rinwa talking and stopped. She stepped back to the window, and peered through it. Rinwa looked surprised and a bit pale, whoever was out there with her was hidden by a tree.

Keeping Liam comfortably snuggled, Samantha stepped closer to the casement, practically pressing her ear against the pane.

"What are you doing here?" That was Rinwa's voice. It was

difficult to listen, but she concentrated and was just able to make out what Rinwa and the stranger were saying.

"It was easy enough to track you." It was a male with a Cockney accent. Samantha recognized the voice, but couldn't place him. "The council was getting curious about where you and Tafari kept disappearing to. You didn't return today like you said you would."

"We already told them," Rinwa stated. "We're searching for the child. There's a lot of leads to go through. Anyway, we missed our flight because we came out here on a bogus trail. I don't understand why the council is so upset. We're not the only ones out investigating."

"No, but you're the only ones who are acting strangely."

Samantha swallowed, uncertain what she should do. Should she wake Nik? She brushed the thought aside. Nik would probably *want* a confrontation with this unknown immortal, and Samantha definitely didn't want to deal with that today.

"Everyone has been different ever since that debacle last year."

The man retorted, "No, that's not it and they know it. Ever since we turned human, you two have been off. It didn't change once we turned back into immortals again."

Rinwa spoke up, her attitude coming through clearly. "Why don't you spell it out, Willem? I'm under suspicion? Of what exactly, besides doing my job?"

"I don't know." He sounded frustrated. "I'm just supposed to find you and Tafari and see what you're up to."

"The same thing everyone else is up to." Rinwa took off her sunglasses and looked in Willem's direction. "Now that you've discovered us, Sherlock, why don't you go report and let me get on with my work."

There was a brief silence. Samantha pulled her head back

a little so that she could get a better vantage point through the window.

Liam began squirming and Samantha pushed her finger into the baby's mouth. He immediately bit down, puncturing the skin, and suckled her blood. Clenching her jaw, Samantha tried to pretend she wasn't really donating her blood to a newborn.

Baby appeased, Samantha looked up to continue her spying.

Rinwa turned to leave, striding toward the house while Willem caught up to her and stopped Rinwa by touching her hand. He was gently stroking his fingertips along hers, his expression intense.

"I don't know how much more I can take, Rinwa."

Putting her glasses back on with her free hand, the immortal was nonchalant. "Don't know what you're talking about, Willem." Her tone was cool, and clearly meant for him to drop the subject.

Releasing her hand, the fellow immortal pushed his longish hair out of his eyes. "Sometimes, I think you're bipolar, the way you treat me." He grabbed her shoulders and pulled her in close until their noses touched. "Do you forget how amazing it can be between us? It's been a few months. Maybe I should refresh your memory."

Samantha watched Rinwa take a step back and give a half smirk. "Sounds like a hot invite, but I'll have to rain check after I'm done looking into our latest lead."

Willem didn't try to stop her as she walked away. "Do I really mean so little to you, Rinwa? Am I deluding myself in thinking that we have something here?"

While Rinwa had her back on Willem, Samantha could see the pained expression on her friend's face. Shaking her head, Samantha didn't understand why Rinwa pushed Willem away.

Liam's frustrated yowl brought her out of the moment. Looking down, Samantha could see Liam was no longer appeased with only her finger to suckle. He was hungry, and he was just getting started with his tantrum.

"There's a baby *here*?" She heard Willem ask.

Liam howled again. Samantha tried to put her finger back in the baby's mouth. She winced when the newborn bit down again, and gulped the blood with vigor.

"I told you that I was looking into it." That was Rinwa, and it sounded like she was closer.

Samantha peeked through the window again to see what was happening.

Willem was keeping stride with Rinwa, and she stopped and turned to him.

Hands on hips, Willem furrowed his brows. "This is where you're staying. And the baby is here, too."

Rinwa shrugged and shook her head. "Yes, we've figured out that you're great at stating the obvious."

The man's mouth opened slightly before he recovered. "It's the prophecy child, isn't it? You actually found him."

"Please," Rinwa said. "Why would you think that?"

Chuckling, Willem reached over and rubbed her shoulder. "Because I know you. You wouldn't be wasting your time here if it wasn't. All you have to do is investigate him and the mother before you decide to move on. You had to have already looked into paternity and performed the ritual to see if the child holds an otherworldly essence. Now you're babysitting for a couple of days or something? I don't think so."

Samantha held her breath as she watched Rinwa's reaction. Her friend was gazing up into the sky, as if she were contemplating something. After a few moments, she looked at Willem. "Okay, you're right. It is the prophecy child."

Willem seemed to vibrate with excitement. "Well, why haven't you taken him yet? We can fly him to the base tonight."

"Because," Rinwa answered. "The mother is dangerous. I

need to placate her for now and find an opportunity to take the baby when her guard is down."

Biting her lip, Samantha was uncertain if Rinwa really meant it. It sounded sincere. Was that why Rinwa had been so accommodating lately?

Deciding she'd heard enough, she walked as quickly as she could out of the kitchen and into Leisha's bedroom.

Leisha was in bed, her long hair in a wet braid down her back. Tafari was sitting next to her, his fingers trailing over the inside of her forearm.

As soon as Liam spotted his mother, he released Samantha's finger to let out a piercing wail.

Tafari was quick to get up and grab the baby, handing his son to Leisha. The vampire pulled down a sheet to reveal her nakedness for a second before Liam's little head covered it.

Leisha flinched slightly when the baby bit down, but her face quickly relaxed.

"We have a problem," Samantha said. Now that the infant wasn't crying, she was finally able to bring herself to speak up. "Willem is outside and he knows that the prophecy child is in here. Rinwa's trying to stall him. I think."

CHAPTER 33

Leisha's heart constricted at Samantha's news. "What do you mean, 'you think'? You don't know?"

The girl simply shrugged. "She made it sound like she's playing our side to help the immortals."

"Rinwa is a good actress when she wants to be," Tafari intoned. "I believe she is doing her best to keep Willem out."

Closing her eyes, Leisha tuned out Samantha and Tafari and strained her ears to listen for the immortals outside. It didn't take long to hone in on their conservation because their voices were rising.

Willem was speaking. "Leisha, the *vampire*, is the mother of the prophecy child?"

"I told you I was handling this, Willem. There's a reason I'm biding my time and waiting for the right moment to take the baby."

"But you don't need to do that now." There was a pause before Willem spoke again. "Yes, this is Willem. Lock in on my location. The prophecy child is here, being held by vampires. We will retrieve the baby in exactly thirty minutes."

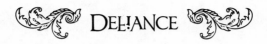

Leisha cursed. She could hear Rinwa protesting.

"I told you I was dealing with this, Willem. How dare you take over my operation!"

The vampire had heard enough and opened her eyes to see Tafari and Samantha staring at her. "We don't have much time. Willem just called in a team to kidnap Liam."

Closing his eyes, Tafari looked disappointed, yet unsurprised.

"What should we do?" Samantha asked. The whites of her eyes showed more than usual.

Switching Liam to her other side, Leisha watched him nurse as she contemplated her next move. After a moment, she finally answered. "We don't really have many options here," she said. "We'll have to make a run through the trees and try to lose them." Keeping the baby latched, she scooted to the edge of the bed and stood. Her body wasn't remotely close to healing yet, but there was no time to coddle herself.

Putting a warm hand on her shoulder, Tafari stopped her from moving. "You are in no condition to run right now." His eyes were dancing with emotion. "There must be another way."

"The only other choices are to stay and fight or simply give up our baby." Leisha shook her head. "The only one that makes sense is to run for it. As you've said, I'm still weak and wouldn't fight well. And you and Rinwa won't attack your comrades."

Her husband's hand drifted from her arm, his silvery blue eyes unfocused as he thought. Leisha stepped over the soiled sheets that Tafari had pulled off the bed earlier and went to the doorless closet. Rummaging through old clothes, she pulled out pants and a button-up shirt. They belonged to a man, but Leisha would make do with them. "You know I'm right Tafari. Come on, we need to get moving."

"We can't," Samantha spoke up, her face ashen. "Nik will burn in the woods."

That stopped Leisha mid motion. She'd forgotten about him. Turning to Tafari, she asked, "How long until sundown?"

"Too long. Probably three hours or so."

Leisha swore. She continued to the bed to lay the clothes down. Liam was finished, and she handed her baby to Samantha. "Could you burp him, please?" she asked.

Nodding as she took him, Samantha said, "I'm going to take him in the front room and see if Nik can think of anything."

Dressing was slow as her muscles and wounds screamed at her, but Leisha ignored the pain and put the clothes on. At least she wasn't bleeding anymore. Now she needed to find her shoes. Where did they get thrown in her frenzy to birth?

"Leisha," Tafari interrupted her scattering thoughts. "We need to discuss this. I have an idea."

Easing herself onto the bed, she looked up at him. "What is it?"

The immortal blew out a breath and came over to sit next to her, their shoulders touching. "Rinwa and I will need to stay behind. With the immortals."

Stomach dropping, Leisha stared at him. "I'm not sure I understand. I thought you decided to put Liam's needs, my needs, above the immortals."

His eyes widened in earnest as he squeezed her thigh. "I have. This will help you."

Brows drawing together, she waited for him to continue.

"You, Samantha, and Nik can take the baby and make a run for it. Meanwhile, I will stay behind and tell them that you escaped in a different direction. I can easily lead an attack that way, giving you time to find a safe place to hide."

Leisha mulled over the plan and realized it was as good a diversion as they were going to get. But there was one problem she wasn't sure she wanted to deal with. "If we do this, then that means I won't be able to contact you at all." She pulled her wet braid from her collar. "The immortals will be be watching everything you do." She gazed at him. "It means that we'll have to separate permanently."

He shook his head and he leaned closer. "Not permanently." His breath whispered across her cheek. "But it will be for a while."

His lips met hers and Leisha couldn't hold back the emotion as she kissed him. Two bloody tears trekked down her cheeks.

"It's like fate is doing everything to keep us apart," she said when he leaned back. It was meant as a joke, but came out all too seriously.

Tafari nodded solemnly. "I wish things were different."

Forcing a smile, she feigned a lighter attitude. "You and me both." She stood as a thought occurred to her. "We should have a chat room where we can meet online."

Tafari looked as if he'd disagree, but Leisha plunged on. "Just in case we really need to contact each other. Only for emergencies, okay?"

"Alright." Tafari conceded. "What chat room?"

"What do you frequent online? Is there something you could look up that wouldn't be suspicious?"

Eyes moving to the side as he thought, he finally came up with an answer. "The few times I do get online for fun, I like to research classical authors. So maybe a chat room for Alexandre Dumas or Victor Hugo."

"There's bound to be plenty of chat rooms about them." As she thought, Leisha looked around the room to see if there was anything to take with her. Grabbing the blanket from the bed, along with the pillow, she said, "Okay, here's what we're going to do. Three weeks from now, we'll both use Google and do a search for Alexandre Dumas. The first chat room that comes up in the results is the site that we'll use."

"I do not think it is wise to send a message so soon."

Bunching the blanket and pillow in her arms, Leisha shook her head. "No, I'm not saying we contact each other. I want us to look it up on the same day so we're sure that we are using the same site."

Together, they strode into the hallway. "What will your username be?" Tafari asked.

"Rosepetals." She answered. "If it's already taken, I'll add a number at the end. What about you?"

Smirking, Tafari said, "Something like vintagewines."

Leisha gave a small chuckle. "You really do love your wine, don't you?"

"Yes." He was completely unabashed about it. "I must say I am not surprised your favorite flower is a rose." He frowned. "It is sad I did not know that until now, though."

Samantha and Nikita looked up as she entered the front room. Leisha told them the plan and both agreed it was the only course of action.

"We still haven't figured out what to do about Nik," Samantha complained, worry etching her features as she looked over at him.

Nikita waved a hand. "I already told you, I'll be fine. I still have my hoodie packed."

"You'll still burn," The girl protested.

"Maybe, but even if I do, it won't be anything I can't recover from. It will be fine."

When Samantha looked unconvinced, Leisha put her fears to rest. "You forget how fast we can run, Samantha, even in a forest." She took Liam from her friend and smiled at his alert eyes. "We'll be able to cover quite a distance in no time. Then we can lie low until the sun sets. That's when we'll really be able to travel."

Samantha's features relaxed as she contemplated it. She gave a strained smile and stood. "I'd better check out the kitchen and see if I can find some snacks. "

Nodding, Leisha called after her retreating form. "Hurry, we don't have much time."

Rinwa entered at that moment. The immortal studied each figure before commenting. "Looks like you heard my little conversation out there."

"Only tidbits, but we got the gist of it," answered Leisha.

Tafari then informed their daughter of the plan.

"Works for me. Better hurry, though. Willem is talking to the assault team right now. They'll be here soon." The blonde brushed her hair off her shoulder. "It will be nice to go back to my regular lifestyle."

Hearing her comment upon reentering the room, Samantha jibed, "Oh, come on, Rinwa. I know you're going to miss us. Haven't you loved all the adventure we toss your way?"

Rinwa rolled her eyes as she placed her sunglasses over her nose, but the immortal had warmth in her expression. "I get plenty of adventure on my own, but you go on thinking that the sun rises and sets just for you, Samantha." Looking at her watch, she turned her attention on Leisha. "Better get moving."

Leisha nodded and found Nikita's bag on the floor next to the couch and dug around until she found his hoodie. She tossed it to him before she handed the baby to Tafari so she could work on making a sling out of the blanket she'd grabbed. Once she'd finished, she looked over to see father and son gazing into each other's eyes.

"Who's winning the staring contest?" Leisha asked as she reached for Liam.

Smiling softly, Tafari tore his gaze away from the babe. "Definitely him." He stroked Liam's cheek with the back of a finger. "Take care of our child, Leisha."

Leisha nestled the boy in the makeshift sling and tightened it to be sure he was secure and comfortable in it. Then she glanced at her husband. "I will." Placing her hand over the side of his face, she leaned in. "Take care of yourself, too."

He nodded as he reached over to squeeze her hand. "Until Alexandre, then."

Forcing a soft smile, she nodded.

Samantha was saying goodbye to Rinwa and turned to Tafari to bid farewell to him, too. Leisha met her daughter's gaze. The immortal didn't step closer, but her expression softened and she nodded in her mother's direction. It wasn't a touching parting, but it was definitely an improvement compared to the last time Rinwa had said goodbye to her. Smiling, Leisha returned the nod.

Tafari turned to Rinwa. "We should begin to spar now. The rest of the team will be here soon and we need to look like we have been fighting."

"Yeah, and we should get some good punches before Willem tries to come to the rescue." Rinwa pulled her hair back, using a strand to hold it in a ponytail. She crouched in a fighter's stance, Tafari matching it before he swung at his daughter.

The group didn't stay to watch. With Nikita in the lead, they headed to the back bedroom to climb out the window.

Leisha could feel the fatigue seeping through her body and hoped that she would be able to keep a fast pace as they ran.

Nikita kicked out the window and shards of glass sprayed everywhere. Using his foot to clear the frame of sharp ends, Nikita jumped out and turned to help Samantha down.

Knowing she wouldn't be able to jump down the five feet with her injuries, Leisha kept her hold on Liam as she started to straddle the pane. She had been too distracted by her wounds and their desperate situation to realize that immortals were creeping around both sides of the house.

Glancing over, Leisha saw Nikita watching Samantha intently as the girl stepped away from him, looking miles away. Before she could open her mouth to warn Nikita, a shot cracked from the far corner of the house. Nikita's shoulder jerked back, the momentum forcing the hood from his head.

Samantha screamed as his flesh instantly began charring with a sickening sizzling sound. Leisha pulled the girl back through the window and to the side. The injured vampire immediately jumped back into the room, bringing the strong smell of burnt flesh with him. Once out of the sun, his neck and face stopped searing until just a little puff of smoke rose from his head.

Samantha tried to run to him, but Leisha grabbed her hand and propelled her toward the bedroom door. "He'll be fine. We have to get out now."

But immortals were already standing in the hallway, machine guns raised and swords sheathed at their sides. Cursing, Leisha jumped forward and slammed the door closed. A bullet went through the door and struck her shoulder, only inches from Liam's head. The baby appeared unaffected by the clamor and slumbered on.

Gasping, Leisha ran to a corner between the window and the door, trying to keep her baby out of the crossfire.

Meanwhile, Nikita pushed the bed against the door and dragged a heavy dresser behind it. "Looks like we'll be fighting after all," he quipped through scorched lips.

Two immortals climbed through the window then. One grabbed Samantha from behind and brought a large blade to her throat. "Give us the baby," he demanded. Leisha and Nikita held still. The only sound was the loud banging of the other immortals trying to break through the door.

The other, a woman, took a step toward Leisha and held her arms out. "We'll let the girl live if you hand over the child right now."

Springing forward, Nikita grabbed the woman from behind and held her arms down with one hand while grabbing her hair with the other. He glared at the man holding Samantha. "You kill mine, I'll kill yours." His voice was savage, and his expression matched.

The immortal holding Samantha hesitated. Leisha watched with a mixture of surprise and hope as Samantha used that moment to yank the man's hand away from her neck while simultaneously kicking back into his knee. The man loosened enough that Samantha was able to pull out of his grip, but was sliced in her forearm as she disentangled herself from him and fled to Leisha.

"Get out," Nikita said. "Or I'll snap her neck."

The immortal glanced between his comrade and Leisha, slowly walking backward until he was at the window. "Let her go now."

"Not until you're outside."

The man jumped. Nikita used his hold on the woman's hair to push her out the window as well.

The top of the door snapped, chunks of wood scattering through the air. Three immortals pointed their guns, more behind them.

Pulling his hood back on, Nikita gestured for Leisha and Samantha to climb through the window.

Leisha barely stayed on her feet when she landed, the jarring impact exacerbating the bullet wound and her delivery injuries. But there was no time to think about pain. Liam was still in his sling, though her blood had soaked a good portion of his legs.

Leisha crouched over him as an immortal swung at her. The blow resonated through her shoulder, but the baby was unharmed.

Spinning as she stood up, Leisha kicked at the immortal, snapping his head to the side. Again, she kicked out, hitting him squarely in the stomach. Breath gushed out of his lungs as the man doubled over. As his head came down, Leisha smashed her knee up into his face. Bones cracked and she could hear the soft cartilage grind. Blood spurted onto her shoes.

Just as her opponent dropped to the dirt, the pommel of a sword hit Leisha in her left temple. Her body reacted before her mind, kicking out at the new attacker to hit her in the arm. The

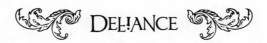

immortal didn't drop her weapon, and lunged to stab Leisha in her neck.

The vampire bent back, barely missing the strike. Her injured shoulder and the added weight of Liam caused Leisha to fall onto her bottom instead of springing back up. On the ground, she leaned back and hastily swipe-kicked the woman's feet. The immortal fell. Leisha instantly wrested the sword from her grasp, then impaled the woman through the chest.

Looking up, she saw that Nikita and Samantha were close by. Nikita kept the girl behind him as he fought off his opponents, careful to keep his hood over his face.

Six more immortals were running toward Leisha. She knew she couldn't fight them while protecting Liam.

Ignoring her protesting body, she rushed over to Samantha. "Take him," she said as she pulled off the sling and handed the baby to her. "Nikita and I will fight to protect you two. As soon as you can get away, run. We'll find you."

Leisha turned to the oncoming assailants and twirled the sword in her hand.

CHAPTER 34

Samantha clutched Liam to her chest as she watched the two people she loved most fight a crowd that only seemed to get larger and larger. She felt like there would never be an opportunity to run and find a safe place. Leisha was pulling on their bond, making Samantha weaker by the moment. Samantha couldn't begrudge her though—Leisha had already killed four more immortals.

Glancing on her other side, Samantha saw Nik fighting brutally. One of his attackers knocked off Nik's hood, but the vampire was quick to replace it while counterattacking.

Even with the vampires flanking her and fighting so valiantly, one black immortal got through and approached Samantha. His brown arms were reaching for the bundle she held. Samantha stepped back, uncertain of what she should do.

The man lunged suddenly, pushing Samantha to the ground. She cried out as her back hit the ground. The immortal stood over her and reached down for Liam.

"No!" Samantha screamed as she jerked to the side, the baby still clutched to her chest.

The man stretched out his hands and grabbed Liam's right foot. He started to tug. Samantha didn't want the immortal to pull the baby's leg out of joint, but couldn't bear the thought of relinquishing him either.

Suddenly, the immortal was pulled upright. Leisha appeared behind him and twisted his head. There were two sharp snaps, and then his body fell right next to Samantha.

Leisha held out her hand to Samantha, but before the girl could take it, four immortals grabbed her friend. Each had their swords ready at Leisha's neck, stomach, and two at her chest. The vampire froze.

Helplessness threatened to overwhelm Samantha. She forced herself to stand while keeping Liam secure in her arms.

Strong hands grabbed her around the waist and pressed her against a large body. An ice cold blade was at her neck before she could blink.

"Samantha!"

Moving only her eyes, Samantha saw Nik charging toward them. Immortals tackled him from every direction. Among the crash of bodies, Samantha couldn't see what was happening. It lasted only moments before three immortals were holding Nik. It looked like they were getting ready to remove his hood.

"Don't!" the girl shouted. No one paid any attention to her.

Samantha couldn't see Nik come to his end now. Not in this way.

"Stop!" a deep voice, boomed. All heads turned in its direction.

Tafari and Rinwa were at the edge of the house, standing with Willem.

Liam's father was impassive, standing proudly, radiating a sense of regality. "We must have the baby before we continue with the executions."

Gasping at the implication of those few words, Samantha

tried to search the immortal's face, but he wasn't close enough. One immortal standing by Leisha came forward and took the baby from Samantha. Tears flooded her eyes, and she was drowning hatred and despair. Leisha screamed, and Liam suddenly let out an earsplitting wail. The immortal didn't try to coddle the baby as he walked over to Tafari. The man was only twenty yards away.

Just when Samantha accepted their defeat, Nik bolted from the hands holding him down. The immortals tried to contain him, but they only succeeded in pulling off his hoodie. The vampire's raw skin began to char once again, smoky tendrils rising from every ounce of exposed flesh, but it didn't stop him.

Samantha couldn't tell what happened. All she saw was a blur toward the immortal holding Liam. The immortal was suddenly prone on the ground, the baby gone. The blur changed directions and disappeared into the woods.

Another blur caught her eye, Samantha saw Leisha taking her opponents down. The vampire was cut in the neck and stomach, but was moving quickly.

Swallowing down her fear, Samantha raised her knee and stomped on the foot of the man holding her and tried pushing the blade away from her neck. Her aim was off, and her left hand landed directly on the blade. Crying out at the sharp pain, the girl continued to push while kicking back blindly.

She couldn't be sure if her tactic would have worked, because Leisha was there in a flash, snapping the man's neck and grabbing Samantha's hand.

Loud reports from the immortals' guns suddenly filled the air. Nearby branches burst when bullets hit them. Covering her head, Samantha started to crouch down when Leisha stopped her.

"Get on my back," the vampire instructed.

Without a word, Samantha squeezed her eyes closed and buried her face in Leisha's back as more bullets struck all around them. Leisha jerked when one hit her in the side. She knew Leisha was hurting, but she ran faster than any car. Wind and what felt like tree limbs brushed over her head at record speed. Shouts and sounds of pursuit began to fade.

Samantha wasn't sure how long they'd been going like that. It felt like just a few minutes, but it could have been much longer.

Without breaking pace, her friend spoke up. "You need to get underground before you burn to death."

Whipping her gaze up, Samantha could see that they were now running alongside Nik. She almost wished she'd kept her head down. Nik's face was completely black with small rivulets of blood pouring down. It looked like his cheeks would sink in at any moment.

Keeping his sight ahead, Nik answered. "I know my limits. We can go for at least another fifty miles before I'll collapse."

"Hand me Liam," Leisha said briskly. "I don't think you should hold him in your condition."

Samantha kept her legs and arms tight around the vampire as Leisha shifted and took the baby from Nik. The extreme speed was making Samantha sick, so she closed her eyes again and put her head back down . . .

SHE WAS IN A HOUSE she didn't recognize, standing in the large kitchen. She could see through a magnificent archway into the front room.

Leisha was there, looking vibrant in a red tank top with her long hair flowing down her back. She was on the floor, giggling as she helped a boy with his homework. He appeared to be around nine or ten years old. His hair was black, his skin tone a light coffee color, and his emerald green eyes were a perfect match to Leisha's.

"You're such a good mother," an unfamiliar voice spoke. Samantha couldn't see the woman from her vantage point and moved to the doorway for a better look.

The stranger sat on a microfiber couch, holding a coffee mug. She had light brown hair with large waves, and a long, pointed nose.

"That's sweet of you to say," Leisha responded, her attention still on her son. "But I think I'm being a terrible hostess to you."

The woman waved her hand. "It's pure entertainment, I assure you."

Leisha stood and went to the couch opposite of her guest. "So you said you wanted to tell me something. What was it?"

She set her mug on a side table and leaned forward. "Yes, I did." The lady cast a meaningful glance at the boy. "I think you may want to send him out of the room for it."

Brows drawing together, Leisha spoke to her son. "Honey, could you give me a few minutes? Why don't you grab a snack from the fridge?"

Looking between the two women, Liam nodded and walked toward Samantha into the kitchen. Samantha wanted to stay and hear the conversation, but felt compelled to follow the boy instead.

Liam went to the fridge and opened the door. He was standing there for a moment, staring into space, when he suddenly growled. The sound made Samantha jump. His face was contorted in fury and fangs were growing low over his lips. Slamming the door closed, he turned back toward the front room. As he stood, glaring in that direction, sharp claws slowly emerged from under his fingernails.

Liam blinked, then looked directly at Samantha. She felt rooted to the floor. No person in a vision had acknowledged her presence before.

Giving a predatory grin around his fangs, he sprang forward. It was faster than Samantha could track. He had jumped past her and back into the room with Leisha and the woman.

Hearing Leisha's outraged shout gave her mobility to rush into the room. Samantha wished she hadn't. Liam was standing over the stranger, who was slumped to the floor. Her neck had been completely ripped open, her mouth frozen in a scream that she never uttered.

"SAMANTHA." LEISHA'S HAND WAS ON her shoulder.

Gasping, Samantha brushed the vampire's hand off. The aroma of earth and plants filled her nostrils. She was lying in a bed of leaves. "What happened?"

"You fell asleep while we traveled." Leisha smirked. "I'm surprised you could do that."

Samantha sat up slowly and noticed a hole in the ground to her left. "Is Nik alright? How badly did he burn?"

Lips compressing, Leisha glanced at his resting spot. "He's in a bad way. He'll probably have to feed every night for a week to fully recover." The vampire placed a hand over the sleeping bundle next to Samantha.

The girl jerked when she realized Liam had been right next to her the entire time.

"But I'm grateful to him," Leisha was saying. "I don't know what would have happened to Liam, or any of us, if Nikita hadn't sacrificed himself like that."

A feeling of warmth for Nik warred with a new foreboding of Liam. Shivering, Samantha wrapped her arms around herself. "I think I'll sit with Nik. He might need my blood before we can move on."

Leisha grabbed her arm and brought Samantha's hand closer for inspection. "In a way, I'm glad you're a human servant now. At least you're not bleeding anymore. But I think it's best if you don't donate."

Glancing at the deep cut in her hand, Samantha knew Leisha was right. Even though she recovered faster than normal humans, it would be a while before this wound healed properly.

Nodding, she stood and walked over to Nik's hole. "I'll just sit with him."

"We'll be leaving in an hour or so. We have to get to the city and feed so we can get out of the country as soon as possible."

Samantha turned back to her friend. "What about the immortals? They could find us while we sit here."

Shifting in clothes now stiff with dried blood, Leisha shook her head. "Nikita and I knew what we were doing. They won't be able to track us."

I wish I could feel as confident. Samantha went on her knees to ease herself into the hole, mindful to not step on Nik.

He appeared to be sleeping. Samantha glanced over his flesh. It looked like charred paper. She didn't want to touch him, thinking his skin would flake off at the lightest contact. Instead, she crouched into a sitting position by his feet.

"Are you okay?" Nik mumbled. "Did you have another vision?"

"You're awake." Leaning forward, she asked, "Can I do anything for you?"

"I'll heal." It sounded like he was having trouble talking. "Did you have a vision?" he repeated.

"It was just a nightmare. Don't worry about me." She gingerly touched the top of his shoe. "You rest as much as you can. We'll be going into the city in an hour." The atmosphere between them seemed more like it used to be before Samantha's birthday.

When Nik didn't respond, Samantha assumed he'd taken her advice.

The baby was gurgling happily from above. Leisha cooed at him in response. It sounded so adorable. Resting her head against the side of Nik's hole, Samantha closed her eyes. Unfortunately, the image of Liam as a boy with blood dripping down his chin flooded her vision.

What is he? The thought echoed through her mind over and over. *What could he possibly be?*

ACKNOWLEDGMENTS

First, I must thank my fabulous critique group and the amazing BETA readers who helped with this novel—Ashleigh Miller, Karyn Patterson, Rebecca Rode, Roxy Hanie, RJ Craddock, and Mary King. I'd also love to thank my editor, Reece Hanzon, all my author friends who encourage me, and my wonderful fans who've reached out to me—you keep me going.

ADRIENNE MONSON IS THE AWARD-WINNING author of the *Blood Inheritance Trilogy* and a paranormal Regency novella, *Eyes of Persuasion*. She resides in Utah with her husband and two children where she works on more stories to share with the world. She also enjoys reading, kickboxing, and cooking.